Toby and the Secrets of the Tree

Toby and the Secrets of the Tree

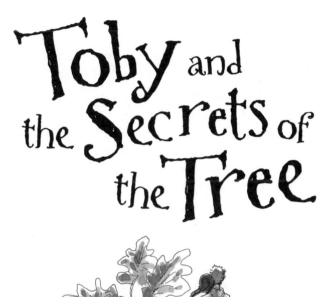

Timothée de Fombelle

translated by Sarah Ardizzone

illustrated by François Place

CANDLEWICK PRESS

Text and illustrations © 2009 by Gallimard Jeunesse
English translation © 2009 by Sarah Ardizzone

First U.S. edition 2010

Library of Congress Cataloging-in-Publication Data
De Fombelle, Timothée
Toby and the secrets of the tree / Timothée de Fombelle ;
illustrated by François Place. — 1st ed.
p. cm.
Summary: Thirteen-year-old Toby's tiny world is under greater threat than ever as Leo Blue holds Elisha prisoner while hunting the Grass People and anyone who stands in the way of his devastating plans for the oak Tree in which they all live, but this time Toby is not alone.
ISBN 978-0-7636-4655-4
[1. Adventure and adventurers — Fiction.   2. Fugitives — Fiction.
3. Ecology — Fiction. 4. Oak — Fiction. 5. Trees — Fiction. 6. Allegories.]
I. Place, François ill. II. Title.
PZ7.D3615Toc 2010
[Fic] — dc22   2009014833

10 11 12 13 14 15 MVP 10 9 8 7 6 5 4 3 2 1

Printed in York, PA, U.S.A.

This book was typeset in Adobe Caslon.
The illustrations were done in pen and ink.

Candlewick Press
99 Dover Street
Somerville, Massachusetts 02144

visit us at www.candlewick.com

For the Forest where I grew up

Contents

Through the indecisive branches
went a girl
who was life

Federico García Lorca

PART ONE

1
Broken Wings

The Major was as light as a grain of pollen, but the weight of his stupidity should have snapped the branch he was sitting on, feet dangling in midair, firing arrows at a black shape writhing around below.

Major Krolo put a lot of effort into being this stupid. He wasn't just an expert in stupidity; he was a stupidity genius.

It was nighttime in the Tree, a night of thick mist and freezing wind. But it had been dark all day long: a black apocalyptic sky had shrouded the Treetop since the previous day, and the damp was causing a heavy smell like spiced bread to rise from the branches.

"Two hundred and forty-five, two hundred and forty-six . . ."

How many arrows would the Major have to fire to finish off the huge creature stuck in the sap? Wrapped in a stiff fur coat, he kept on counting.

Krolo slipped his thumbs under his coat and made his suspenders go *ping*.

"Two hundred and fifty-eight . . ."

He felt a satisfied tingle and buttoned up his coat again.

The Major had a long-standing reputation as a bully. Following a few "personal issues," he had changed his name and made a new life for himself. He even tried to disguise himself by wearing suspenders instead of a belt. He had also awarded himself the rank of major, and to be on the safe side, these days he tortured only animals. He did this on the sly, at night and out of sight, like a grown man smoking in secret from his mother.

Below him, the poor creature lifted its head toward its executioner for the last time. It was a butterfly. A butterfly with broken wings . . . The job had been botched, thanks to a poorly sharpened ax. All the butterfly had left on its back were two ridiculous stumps that flapped emptily. This was the work of a thug.

"Two hundred and fifty-nine," counted Krolo, hitting the butterfly on the right flank.

A shadow suddenly passed by, in the thick fog behind the Major.

A silent apparition. The nimble shadow had come from above, brushing against the bark before disappearing into the night. Yes, somebody was watching this scene. But the Major hadn't noticed a thing, because being stupid was his full-time job.

Krolo's last arrow sank deep into the flesh of the butterfly. The wounded animal reared up but didn't groan.

The shadow passed by again, twirling with extraordinary agility. Half-dancer, half-acrobat, it was surveying the scene. This time, there was a reflection in the butterfly's eye.

Krolo turned around, suddenly uneasy.

"Soldier? Is that you?"

He scratched his head nervously, through his hat. He had a low-set forehead and wore a woollen cap with a few greasy curls peeking out from under it.

Now, Major Krolo may have had a small head with limited neurons, but he still knew that the shadow hadn't been cast by any of his soldiers. Everybody was talking about it: a mysterious shadow that moved around the Treetop in the evenings. Nobody knew who this furtive person was, but it was as if he or she was on guard duty.

In public, Krolo refused to believe this story. Instead, he made himself look even sillier than usual with pathetic remarks such as, "What? A shadow? At night? Ha-ha!"

But, given his problems in the past, the Major was scared of everything. One morning in bed, he had tried to squash one of his own toes, mistaking it for an insect sticking out from under the sheets.

"Soldier!" he shouted, trying to convince himself. "I know it's you! If you move again, I'll impale you to the branch!"

A cloud of fog rolled over the Major, and in the freezing dark, he felt a hand on his shoulder.

"Eeeeeeeeek!"

Krolo turned his head sharply and bit into flesh.

The Major prided himself on his exceptional reflexes. And it was certainly true that he hadn't wasted a second in attacking his aggressor's hand. His speed was impressive. But he *had* made a simple mistake about which way to turn, and he felt his incisors sinking deep into his own shoulder and hitting the bone.

Stupidity on that scale really *is* a form of genius.

Krolo let out a raucous cry and jumped in agony. He landed at the feet of an odd character in a bathrobe.

"It's me, only obliging with your respectyness, it's me. Am I scaringly you?"

The newcomer bowed, lifting the hem of his bathrobe.

"It's me, Clotty," he added.

Krolo bared his teeth.

"Soldier Clot!" he exploded.

"Don't be afraid, Major."

"Afraid? Who's afraid? Not me!"

"Please to forgive the meddling of my curiosityness, Major, but why did you eat your own shoulder?"

Krolo pointed threateningly at Clot.

"If you mention to anybody that I was afraid . . ."

The Major was still down, and the blood from his wound had painted a red epaulet on his coat. Clot bent over and held out his hand to help Krolo get up again.

"May I have the hon-hah of helping you?"

Clot tried to comfort the Major by patting him on the shoulder, but he clumsily slapped the wound and Krolo turned white with pain.

The Major's strength was running out, so he spat at the soldier to keep him at bay.

Clot leaped sideways. He was saddened by his superior's lack of education. The soldiers figured that Krolo was an overgrown bully, but Clot saw him as more of an overgrown baby.

What Clot really wanted to do was stick a pacifier into Krolo's mouth, make "goo-goo-ga-ga" noises, and pat his cheeks.

The Major contemplated the soldier's outfit.

"What kind of a getup is that?"

"A bathrobe, Major."

"And that?" He pointed at the pair of slug slippers the soldier was wearing on his feet.

Clot suddenly became coy.

"Slipperties, Major."

"You what?"

"It's the middle of the night, if I'm not abusing you, so I put on my slipperties. It's just that I was asleeping when you called."

"I didn't call, you idiot. Go back home."

Clot heard the butterfly flapping in despair and leaned over to take a look. The Major blocked the way with his arms.

"What d'you want?"

"I can see something moving over there. . . ."

"Mind your own business."

"There's an animal stuck in the sap, or am I mistaking me?"

"What are you doing here, Clot? Are you looking for trouble?"

"Well, as it happens. . . ."

"Speak!"

Clot whispered, "It's because of *her*."

"Her! Her again!" roared the Major.

"Allow me to be sharply spearing you the details: the prisoner is asking for the Great Candle Bearer."

"What for?"

"For her hot-water bottle."

"The Great Candle Bearer is asleep!" barked Krolo. "I'm not going to wake the Great Candle Bearer up for a hot-water bottle!"

"I know the prisoner is making your high-brows frown, Major," said Clot. "But if she can have the Great Candle Bearer to heat up her hot-water bottle . . ."

Krolo wasn't listening. He was staring at Clot's feet.

He was jealous.

Slippers. He wanted a pair just like that.

Krolo couldn't resist the temptation. He stood on the pointy ends of Clot's slippers. Then, using the arm that still functioned, Krolo gave a great whack that sent the rest of Clot flying thirty paces.

A few minutes later, Major Krolo knocked on the Great Candle Bearer's door. The wind was howling.

"She wants the candle," he explained through the wood.

Someone opened a shutter. A small face appeared in the gap. It was the Great Candle Bearer himself. Even on a night as dark as this, it was clear that he wasn't someone to mess with. He had a long face that looked like a bone, and two red, sickly eyes. He closed the shutter again and reappeared on the doorstep, grumbling.

The Great Candle Bearer was short and hunch-backed. He carried a candle protected by a lantern, and he hid his hump under a dark cloak with a hood that shaded his face.

He stopped for a moment to look at Krolo's feet. Major Krolo blushed and bounced on his toes several times while looking at the ground.

"They're slipperties," he explained.

Without saying a word, the Great Candle Bearer followed the Major.

The whole region was a confusion of twigs. You had to know the route to avoid getting lost in this enormous ball of branches so different from the rest of the Tree. On a clear moonlit night, it was possible to see what this huge bundle of sticks stuck on the Treetop was.

A nest.

An oversize nest. Not one of those wagtails' nests that a hundred men can easily dismantle in a night. No.

It was a nest that seemed to go on forever. A nest once inhabited by a giant bird in the highest branches.

The use of fire was forbidden in this parched landscape. The privilege was granted to the Great Candle Bearer alone, who was called upon in cases of absolute necessity. Or, as was the case on this night, to heat a hot-water bottle.

The fog was getting thicker. The Major walked in front. With each step, he nearly came out of the slippers he had stolen from Clot.

"A hot-water bottle! Far be it for me to criticize," he muttered, "but I really don't think the boss should give in to the girl's every wish. . . ."

The Great Candle Bearer didn't say anything, which is a good strategy for looking smart. Not that he had anything to fear from being compared to Krolo. Next to the Major, a toilet would have looked like an intellectual.

The Great Candle Bearer came to an abrupt halt. There was a noise behind him. He turned and lifted his lantern. A damp breeze made his black hood flap. He had the strange feeling that he was being followed. He peered into the darkness but didn't see the shadow that had slid all the way along a branch and landed on another and was now crouching just above them.

"Are you coming, Great Candle Bearer?" the Major called out.

The Great Candle Bearer hesitated, and then started walking again.

The shadow was still following them, three paces away, undetected.

Despite the first impression of chaos, it soon became clear that the labyrinthine Nest was actually quite organized. Lanterns glimmered at specific junctures, lighting the way on moonless nights and acting as beacons in the fog.

They were cold lamps; each one was made up of a pyramid-shaped cage with a glowworm inside it. These lamp-worms were raised specifically for this purpose. Two or three Master Worm Rearers were renowned for the quality of their worms. They formed a thriving corporation that was the envy of the rest of the inhabitants of the Tree, who had been living in poverty and fear for a long time.

The Treetop Nest was clean; the twigs had been planed down, and the intersections were reinforced with rope. Stairs had been sculpted out of the steepest passageways. Mixed in with the wood and dry moss, hollow straw provided an impressive network of tunnels leading to the heart of the Nest.

There was obviously a superior intelligence behind this citadel of dead wood. It was a frozen world, austere even, but one that had been perfectly designed. So who was the architect behind the Treetop Nest? Clearly, it wasn't just the creation of a bird's brain.

When the two men reached the top of the Nest, a gust of wind unveiled something even more fascinating from behind the mist.

Pointing toward the sky, pink and smooth as a baby's cheek, three hundred cubits high, and perfect in form and majesty, three eggs rose up.

They looked like tall towers whose tops snagged the shreds of mist.

"The Eggs!" the Major shouted, as if his companion hadn't noticed.

They climbed one last slope of dead wood and stopped to breathe in the night air. A storm had left a smell of powder in the air. They had only to cross the White Forest—a forest of down and feathers that covered the heart of the Nest and protected the Eggs—before reaching their destination. Three paths had been cleared through the undergrowth. The rest of the jungle was as spotless and pure as a snowy landscape.

ᘓ

One hour later, the sentries of the South Egg saw two men approaching. They let the Great Candle Bearer climb onto the footbridge that penetrated the Egg. He disappeared inside the shell.

Outside, one of the guards appeared to be hypnotized by Krolo's feet.

"They're slipperties," the Major explained with false modesty.

The other guards drew near. "You what?"

"Slipperties," a fat soldier repeated.

"They're what?"

"Slipperties!" Krolo roared.

Not one of them had noticed, on top of the Egg, at a dizzying height, the shadow that was climbing the wall and spying down on them.

Soon the Great Candle Bearer reappeared on the footbridge. He was walking quickly and looked furious. Krolo wanted to interrogate him about the prisoner, but the Great Candle Bearer pushed him aside dismissively. He was heading for the White Forest.

"The Great Candle Bearer isn't happy," one of the guards remarked to the others.

"What could she have done?" asked the Major.

They couldn't see the Great Candle Bearer's expression. He was hidden under his cloak. Krolo caught up with him.

"I'll accompany you, Great Candle Bearer."

The Great Candle Bearer said nothing, just continued walking.

They ran into Soldier Clot almost immediately, as he was climbing barefoot up through the White Forest.

Clot's bathrobe was in tatters and some of his teeth were missing, but he was mostly in shock from what he had discovered on Krolo's departure. The butterfly . . . the poor animal lay dying before his eyes, banished from the sky forever. Was the Major capable of this horror?

"Ith not pothible," he had whispered.

In that whack from Krolo, Clot had lost seven teeth and a great deal of innocence. Krolo wasn't a big baby: he was a murderer. Nothing less. Anger welled up inside Clot.

"Nathty beathtie . . ."

Clot watched the two men pass by. They didn't even notice him. Soldier Clot was on the lookout for the slippers that Krolo had stolen from him. But his gaze came to rest on another pair of feet.

The Great Candle Bearer's.

"Cwikey . . . cwumbth . . ."

Clot froze. He couldn't believe his eyes.

Two small feet.

Two small white feet.

Two small white feet that peeked from the hem of the cloak with every step. Two feet that shone like stars against the cloth of the cape.

Two feet so delicate, so light, so supple . . . Two feet

so soft you wanted to be a branch, just to feel them walking over you. Two angel's feet.

Clot nearly swallowed his remaining teeth.

"Cwikey Cwot, an old Gwate Candle Beawah with feet like that . . ."

The rest of the figure was dark. The hood hid his face. Clot couldn't help smiling. He turned and walked away as though he hadn't seen anything.

When the two travelers reached the entrance to the White Forest, the Great Candle Bearer with the angel's feet put down the lamp and lifted a great log of a feather shaft that was blocking the way. Surprised, Krolo went up to him.

"Is there a problem?"

In the minute that followed, the forest rang out with the sound of Major Krolo roaring eight times in succession.

The first roar was when the heavy feather struck him on the feet.

The second roar was when the Great Candle Bearer leaped on the feather, crushing Krolo's toes still more.

The third was roar when the Great Candle Bearer, fast as lightning, landed on Krolo's shoulders, right on his wound.

The fourth roar was when, hands diving under the poor Major's coat, the Great Candle Bearer pulled his elastic suspenders and, in a flash, looped them over a log above him.

And finally, Krolo let out four long shrieks of horror when he realized, as fast as his poor brain could register, that he was trapped.

His feet were stuck on the ground beneath the feather and his suspenders, stretched toward the sky like archery bows, threatening to send him flying into space if he pulled them free of the log.

He was catapult and cannonball at the same time. Especially the cannonball.

A second later, Angel Feet landed softly on the ground. He picked up his lamp. A breeze gently drew his hood back from his forehead, and his face appeared in the lamplight.

It wasn't exactly the Great Candle Bearer's bony head.

They were the eyes, the nose, the mouth, the perfect oval face of a sixteen-year-old girl. You could say she was pretty, but in the Tree there are twenty-five pretty girls for every branch.

No, she was more than pretty.

"The prisoner . . ." breathed Krolo.

It had only taken one minute for this nuisance to overpower the Great Candle Bearer in her Egg. She had stolen his clothes and left the prison in his place.

The Major tried to raise the alarm, but the girl set her foot on the feather, the message clear: In one movement, she could roll away the weight that was keeping Krolo in contact with the ground and send him flying up into the air. The Major chose to keep quiet.

The prisoner pulled the hood back over her face and turned her back on him.

After taking a few steps into the White Forest, she stopped. She could feel fine water droplets left on her cheeks by the mist, the wind blowing across her feet. A few fronds of white feather were stuck to her cloak. She felt good.

Freedom wasn't far now. She closed her eyes for a moment.

Ten times she had tried to escape. Maybe ten was her lucky number. She clenched her fists, her body filled with wild hope.

A quiet rustling sounded in front of her. Then another, to her left.

No, she thought, as all hope drained away. *No . . .*

At first she didn't dare open her eyes.

Behind each of those feathers that disappeared into the mist, a soldier rose up. Dozens of armed men aimed their crossbows at her.

In the candlelight, they saw her smile. A joyful, insolent smile that made those surrounding her tremble.

Not one of them could see how, in the shadow of her hood, Elisha's eyes, when she opened them, were glistening with tears.

She was caught.

2
Beauty and the Shadow

"The boss says it's too cold to go for a walk."

"I don't have a boss," said Elisha.

The man talking to her was out in front. His hands were tucked inside his jacket pockets. He had blue eyes and looked quite old, with worn-out clothes that must have been colorful in their time. Tinges of red and orange were all that remained, and the cloth had grown so shiny from use, it looked almost like leather.

"Follow us," he said gently.

This kindness was at odds with the thirty crossbows and wild glares that gleamed behind him in the night.

"Where is he? Your boss, I mean," asked Elisha.

"Come along, miss."

"If I were to drop a handkerchief, I'd pick it up myself. So why can't he come to find his runaway fiancée himself? Gentlemen, you have a sad boss."

Their answer was silence. She might have been small, but this girl was a force to be reckoned with. In that silence, a small flutey voice could be heard whimpering, "What about me? Can you do something about me?"

It was Major Krolo, hanging by his suspenders in such a way that his pants were hitched painfully up into his bottom while his slippers were still trapped on the ground.

The man with blue eyes continued as if he hadn't heard anything.

"Where have you put the Great Candle Bearer, miss?"

"You'll find him. I think he's made a new friend. . . ."

She had locked the hunchback in the glowworm's cage that lit her Egg. And sure enough, they would find the Great Candle Bearer later on, unconscious, in his underwear, being embraced by the worm, which must have taken a liking to him.

"Can someone help me?" Krolo screeched.

Responding to a sign from their chief, two soldiers went over to the Major. They were about to remove the feather that held him to the ground.

"No!" he roared. "Don't do that!"

So they got out their long knives and prepared to slice his suspenders.

"Noooooo! Not that either . . ."

What was going on in Krolo's head set a new record in stupidity. He was afraid that without his suspenders his previous identity would be revealed: W. C. Rolok, the horrible Chief Weevil Rearer, formerly known as Pinhead.

Rolok had met with a bad end. He had become an object of derision—"Thing" to his fellow men—and had only escaped by a miracle. By slipping the last letter of his name to the beginning, he figured he could start again from scratch. Good-bye, Rolok; hello, Krolo.

If all it took to have more brains or more heart was moving a letter in your name, there'd be a lot more people doing just that. But Krolo was just the same as W. C. Rolok. Just as stupid, just as nasty.

The soldiers looked questioningly at their chief. He shrugged, annoyed. He couldn't care less about the Major.

Elisha started walking, and everybody followed. The first glimmer of light was rising over the three Eggs.

For Major Krolo, abandoned there and hanging from his suspenders, the day was getting off to a bad start.

What would I do? I'd tip my head back in the rain, with my mouth and eyes open wide. What would I do? I'd stick my hands into honeypots. . . .

Several hours had gone by. Elisha was lying on her yellow mattress in the middle of the Egg. Her body felt empty; her mind was hovering above her. It was siesta time. She was lying on her back, wearing a green dress. A sheet covered the top of her head. She was looking up at the great curve of the Egg. The stormy weather had calmed at dawn. Now it was like a summer's day that had strayed into the beginning of winter. The sunlight made the wall of the Egg radiant. This was a golden prison, a windowless palace.

Elisha was thinking about what she would do if she found freedom again.

I'd rub my back against the buds. I'd run on the first leaves of spring. I'd swim in my lake. I'd hang hammocks from the top branches to watch the clouds go by. . . .

They had offered to furnish her Egg, to make it an abode fit for a princess, but she had sent the furniture men away and just put a yellow mattress at the bottom of the shell. It was enough for her. The rest of the South Egg was empty. She had been living there, in captivity, for a long time.

I'd climb through the moss forests. . . .

Elisha stopped daydreaming and thought back to her escape attempt the night before. She couldn't understand how it had gone wrong. Who had tipped off the soldiers? Who had known how to read the plan written only in her mind?

Elisha was still staring at the high dome of the Egg. The air was warm; the shell smelled like a bread oven with a leaf cake waiting inside it for dessert.

The Shadow. Again.

The Shadow of the Treetop.

Elisha had been secretly waiting for it, and it appeared just at that moment.

Thanks to the sunlight, Elisha could see it from inside as it made its way along the grainy wall. It stood out against the dome of the Egg. She felt her heart quicken.

These last few days, the fog had deprived her of this appa-rition, but for several weeks now the Shadow had assumed an important place in Elisha's life.

Where did it come from, this being that braved the dizzying heights and came to visit her every day without revealing itself?

In this high-security fortress, a bit of mystery had managed to slip in. Courage, the element of surprise, and dreams: the Shadow summed up everything Elisha was missing. And her one wish, above all, was that this Shadow might be able to help her.

The Shadow stopped at the top of the Egg, where a hole had been cut out. The Egg had been emptied through the hole at the time of the Great Works. When it rained, Elisha would watch the cool water fall through the gap.

That was where the Shadow positioned itself.

It was the same game each time. Elisha knew she was being watched. She opened her eyes wide and stayed lying down. The Shadow didn't move. It was unsettling. Neither of them said anything.

There was a noise at the door. The Shadow glided across the length of the shell and disappeared.

A man walked into the Egg—it was the old, blue-eyed chief. He had taken off his long coat. He wore a vest made from moss felt, and a hornet stinger in a scab-bard hung from his belt. She liked his quirky elegance, his flared pants, and his old blue scarves, but the man himself scared her.

His name was Arbayan. He was likable and merciless in equal measure.

"I entered without asking. I'm sorry, miss. But you do the same thing when you leave."

"What else is there to do in prison, apart from escape?"

"You're not in prison."

"Ah, yes," Elisha answered. "That's what your boss says. . . . He should try finding better jokes."

She was still lying down, and when she finally sat up, the sheet slipped from her head.

Arbayan couldn't get used to the sight of Elisha's painfully short hair.

For a while, her head had been completely shaved. It was enough to bring tears to one's eyes. Elisha's features were so strong and so strange that her face evoked fear and amazement.

Some months before, Arbayan had seen her arriving in the Nest with her long hair tied back. One morning, he had discovered her with a shaved head. She had committed the crime alone in the night. She had flung her braid in the boss's face. She was counting on him not marrying her while she looked like a convict. He would wait a bit, to save face.

And sure enough, he waited.

Arbayan took a step toward the girl.

"The boss is going to leave. He would like to speak with you."

"I don't have a boss."

"Your fiancé."

Elisha started laughing.

"My boss, my fiancé . . . what else does he want to be? My cook, my pet, my brother, my butler, my gardener?"

Arbayan answered with a whisper, "Perhaps, miss, he would like to be all of those things to you."

Elisha stopped laughing. Arbayan was highly intelligent. She made a weary gesture with her hand.

"Well, tell all of them—the cook, the pet, and all the others—that I'm not receiving guests today. Tell them to come back next year."

It was a clever answer, but Elisha knew she wasn't up to his level. Arbayan was talking about love. He spoke eloquently on the subject. His boss was in love with Elisha. His boss would have turned himself into a flea or a gnat in order to get close to her. He would have turned himself into the flask of water next to her mattress.

"He will come to speak with you," said Arbayan. "You don't have to listen, but he *will* come."

Elisha didn't say anything. She took the water and brought it close to her lips. It was a soft flask made from a ladybug's egg.

"Don't they give you a bowl?"

"A bowl has a sharp edge," said Elisha between sips. "Your soldiers are wary of my talents as a hairdresser."

Her hair was growing again at last. She mustn't be allowed to try again.

"Good-bye," said Arbayan.

As a farewell, he kept his head lowered for a long time, in a pleasantly old-fashioned way.

He withdrew toward the door.

Elisha called him back.

"Who alerted you to my escape?"

Arbayan smiled.

"I was just told to position myself in the White Forest with thirty soldiers."

"By whom?"

"I have only one boss. He's the one who gives the orders. He knows everything."

Arbayan left. Silence settled again in the Egg. All that could be heard was the wind brushing against the shell. Elisha was thinking about the dead leaves that travel and fly through the air. She envied their freedom.

Elisha stood up.

Having made sure that she was all alone, she suddenly started running. She was heading for the wall of the Egg. She should have been able to smash it, but its curved incline made her run up its side instead. Elisha ran as fast as she could until she was almost upside down. Then she did a backward flip and landed on her feet. Right away, she ran in another direction, starting all over again.

This was her training. Freedom lies in movement. As long as her body and her spirit could move, Elisha was still a tiny bit free.

Someone who was decidedly less free was Rolok. His mind had never been very lively, and this time his body wasn't responding either. He didn't dare make the slightest movement in his suspenders. The afternoon was getting on. He was still stretched between two feathers.

When he saw Clot pass by, a few paces away, he finally had an idea worthy of a Krolo or a Rolok. He was going to ask Clot to cut his suspenders. If the soldier recognized him as Rolok the Chief Weevil Rearer, as soon as he was freed, Rolok would wring his neck and throw him down a hole.

"Hey, soldier!"

Clot looked up to find out where the voice was coming from. With exaggerated movements, he looked in the wrong direction, his hand shielding his eyes, as if peering into the distance. Then, as if he hadn't seen anything, he went on his way, whistling.

It was like a piece of bad theater.

"Soldier!" Rolok roared again.

If a bunch of toddlers had been asked to mime surprise, they would have acted it out better than Clot.

He turned his head toward Rolok, his neck jutting

out and his eyes bulging, and made "Oh!" and "Ah!" noises. Then he held his face in both hands in dismay, raised his arms to the sky, put them on his heart, knelt down, got up again, and did all this several times over, with the gestures of a clown or a hammy actor.

Any old idiot would have realized that Clot was plotting something. But Rolok wasn't any old idiot. He was a champion, an artist, an ace when it came to being a nitwit. He didn't suspect a thing.

"Goodneth gwaciouth!" Clot exclaimed. "Cwikey! Who could pothibly be hanging like that?"

"It's me," Rolok answered miserably.

Clot stuck out his right foot out and kept waving his hand as he exclaimed each time.

"What! Leth thee! O my goodneth! The Major — can it be? What Wath hath thtwuck to detherve thith bad luck?"

He had heard the word *wrath* somewhere and thought it was a kind of monster with hairy legs and a big club.

"Come and help me, Clot!" shouted Rolok.

"I'm coming, I'm flying, I'm wunning! I will thave the Major."

Clot was still performing all the flourishes that go with such lines while he leaped like a cricket in love and landed at Rolok's feet. There he pulled up short.

Time for the big emotional scene. Clot wiped his eyes, made his lips tremble, and, looking at the place where the Major's feet were trapped, said, "What do I notithe here? May the Wath pwetherve me. Yet again, the emothionth are more than detherve me. They had gone away, but now you found my thlippertieth. At latht! I am theeing them, here on your feethieth . . ."

"No," whimpered Rolok, "don't touch . . . Not on that end! Cut the suspenders for me!"

Clot stayed bent over Rolok's feet, his hands slowly drawing near, as if discovering treasure.

"Stop it! Clot! For pity's sake!"

"Where had you gone? Now I can thay 'phew!' Coth you're on the Major, looking so beauteeefew . . . !"

In one movement, Clot rolled the feather away and grabbed his slippers. Rolok's feet skidded. The catapult effect worked perfectly. Rolok went flying into the air with giddy speed.

Clot stared at the blue sky for a long time.

He felt relieved.

For years, Clot had been this "different" character: nobody took him seriously, and everybody teased him a little. He had tolerated this semi-comfortable, slightly weak role. Now, for the first time, he had been able to change the world by ridding it of someone harmful. He thought about the birds and the insects that would see this strange projectile passing by.

Well, at least he'll make the butterflies laugh, he thought.

Clot put his slippers back on with relish and set off.

The guards at the South Egg were waiting.

Arbayan had told them to be ready for the boss's visit. Four of them were standing at attention, lined up next to each other. The fifth was having a little fun, marching up and down like an army inspector.

"Look how scared you are. He's terrorizing you. You've been waiting for him for the last two hours, and you're still behaving like teacher's pets!"

The fifth guard was eating grub cheese with a thick crust. Now and then he drank from a small gourd.

"You're hilarious, the four of you. Want to know what I've got to say to the boss?"

He thrust his head down to the ground, displaying his bottom. Except that, his head between his legs, he suddenly discovered someone standing behind him. He stopped dead.

"I'm all ears," said the man. "What would you say to him?"

"I'd say . . . Hello, Boss."

With his head upside down and his mouth full of cheese, the guard was having a hard time expressing himself clearly.

The boss drew near. He had a handsome, disturbing face, and he stood tall. His firm lips didn't concede the slightest smile and made you forget that this was a young man. He grabbed the guard's gourd and looked at him questioningly.

"It's . . . water," said the guard, standing up again.

The boss chucked the liquid in his eyes. The man cried out in pain. It was strong alcohol. The boss kneed him in the stomach and he collapsed in a puddle that stank of alcohol and grub cheese.

The other guards held their breath.

The boss stepped lightly onto the footbridge.

Elisha didn't turn around when he entered the Egg.

The young boss scanned the semi-darkness of the room.

"I'm leaving," he said. "I'll be back in a few weeks."

He could now make out Elisha's neck and one shoulder in the gloom. She didn't answer.

"I'm leaving, Elisha. If you like, you can come with me."

Elisha was thinking about the word *leaving*. Just the word was enough to make her want to throw herself into the young man's arms. But she didn't move.

"I'm going far away, very low down," he continued. "Toward the Low Branches and the Great Border."

Did the boss see the blood surging beneath Elisha's skin? She had turned as pink as the Egg wall at sunset at the mention of the Low Branches.

"All you have to do is say 'yes' once. And you can come with me."

Yes, she thought, *Yes! Far away! Let's go. That's what I want. I want my Low Branches, my mother, my snowy mornings, my scorching hot pancakes, the water in my lake, my life!*

Elisha stopped herself from answering and closed her eyes. She knew what a "yes" meant for him.

The young man's arms were at his sides. Leather straps crossed behind his back, holding two sharp boomerangs in place, at waist level.

There was still something childish about his hands. He looked about seventeen. He must have been a talented boy once, full of life. But year after year, he had directed all his intelligence toward his darker, dangerous side. He had chosen to play on the knife edge of madness.

"No," came Elisha's answer at last. "No! Never!"

So Leo Blue set off alone.

Night came, and he left the Nest for the long journey toward the Low Branches.

3
Someone Returns

At the bottom of the Tree, before it comes into contact with the earth, the wood from the Trunk rises up to form high mountain ridges.

Needle-like rocks, bottomless precipices . . . The surface of the bark is crumpled, like rippling curtain folds. Moss forests cling to the peaks, trapping snowflakes in winter. The valley passes are blocked by ivy creepers. It makes for a dangerous, nearly impassable terrain.

Excavating the bark at the bottom of the canyons can turn up the remains of unlucky adventurers who risked their lives in these mountains. The wood digests them over time, leaving a compass, a pair of crampons, or a skull that's a quarter of a millimeter across—all that is left of their heroic dreams.

But in the middle of these inhospitable mountains is a small protected valley where a chalet would fit snugly, where you could spend Christmas under the bedcovers, listening to the fireplace snoring—a green valley that gathers rainwater in a small lake surrounded by soft bark.

The only inhabitant of this region is a wood louse who comes every morning to graze on some of the greenery.

There are plenty of havens like this in the Tree, which would be far better left to harmless wood lice.

On this particular morning, a wood louse was leaning over to drink from the transparent lake when the surface of the water began to tremble.

The wood louse heard shouting.

What kind of animal lets out cries like that? The wood louse had never encountered anything like it.

The predators were still a ways off by the sound of it, calling out across the hills. Some blew their horns; others clapped their hands and let out terrifying "Yaaah!" noises. The wood louse reared up on his hind legs.

Just then, a figure appeared at the other end of the

valley, striding toward the pond. From its silent movements and shortness of breath, the wood louse could
tell this wasn't a predator: this was the prey. Its panting
was audible, but not the sound of its feet, which barely
touched the bark.

The bellowing of the horn resonated from across
the valley. The animal on the run leaped to one side,
but the sound rose up from another direction, and then
another. . . . The shouting encircled the valley now. The
poor prey slowed its pace, jumped into the pond, and
stopped moving.

It was wearing a pair of pants cut off at the knee. The
rest of its body was covered in mud. A long peashooter,
taller than itself, was strapped to its back. The wood louse
couldn't decide what family of insects it belonged to.

The predators' cries were even closer now. Without
pausing to catch its breath, the fugitive waded farther
into the pond. Its head disappeared underwater. There
was a brief moment of calm.

Suddenly, a dozen creatures of the same species as
the prey rose up on all sides. The wood louse flattened
himself against the bark and froze. The color of his shell
made him look like a bump in the bark. But it was an
unnecessary camouflage, since the hunters weren't after
him.

"Where is he?"

"No idea."

"He hasn't left any tracks."

The predators were wearing hats made from the

heads of bumblebees. The bedraggled state of their thick coats betrayed their long journey.

"We can't go any farther. We have to head back up before the snow comes."

A tall predator with a double-pointed harpoon stepped forward.

"I'm staying. I'm not letting him get away. I know he's here somewhere."

In his anger, the predator sent the harpoon crashing against the wood louse's shell.

The poor animal didn't flinch. Another predator, which had crouched down to drink from the lake, said calmly, "You'll do what you're told, Tiger. And that's the end of the matter."

It stood up, wiped its mouth, and pointed to a new group approaching them.

"We've got nine, including two young ones. Joe Mitch will be satisfied."

The predators were pulling a sled mounted on runners made from feather shafts. A second sled followed. They were carrying crates with a hole on each side.

"It'll take us ten days to get to the Great Border. We can't lose any time."

The predator with the harpoon, Tiger, went to retrieve its weapon from the wood louse's shell.

"We'll be sorry," the predator whispered. "He wasn't like the others, that one. . . ."

They all started walking. The sleds glided over the bark.

The predators looked tired. One of them was limping. They kept their heads bowed to avoid looking at the great mountain ridges they still had to cross.

The sad convoy was about to disappear on the other side of the valley. Already, they were far enough away for the rubbing sound of the feather runners to be barely audible.

But from the last box, something could be seen coming out of the hole and gripping the wooden slats, trembling.

It was a child's hand.

Several minutes went by. The wood louse stood up. The predators had gone.

All he had felt was a burning sensation on his back, where the harpoon had jabbed him. Nothing's more solidly built than a wood louse.

He shuffled off, and the valley fell quiet again.

ᘓ

A head finally rose out of the pond. The fugitive pulled his lips away from the peashooter, which had enabled him to breathe underwater. He scanned the landscape.

Nobody.

He stood up, his hair, face, and body dripping water.

It was Toby Lolness.

Toby. His body was stronger and more supple than ever, but there was a worried look in his eyes. Once again, Toby had taken on the life of the fugitive.

He left the pond and rapidly slipped the peashooter away into the long quiver on his back.

Toby had left the Grass people two months earlier. Moon Boy, his friend, had set out with him, along with an old guide named Jalam. Both had intended on accompanying Toby all the way to the foot of the Tree.

In the beginning, Toby had refused to drag them into his adventure. But old Jalam had explained that this expedition would be his last, and that afterward he would retire to his ear of wheat to live out his old age. For this final voyage, he would be happy to accompany Toby.

"What about you?" Toby had asked Moon Boy.

"It's my first voyage. I want to come with you, Little Tree."

Toby had allowed himself to be won over.

Jalam didn't approve of the young boy tagging along.

"He's a ten-year-old Strand of Linen. He'd be better off in his mother's ear of wheat."

"I don't have a mother," Moon Boy had replied.

Jalam felt embarrassed and hadn't persisted. So all three of them had set out.

Toby knew that his companions would also take the opportunity to search for the tracks of the friends who had gone missing most recently.

Each year, dozens of Grass people disappeared because they ventured toward the Tree. Heedless of the danger, others tirelessly continued to set out. The Trunk provided them with material they couldn't get in the Prairie: hard wood, wood that doesn't burn in an instant like straw. But what attracted them most of all to the Tree was the mystery of the disappearances and the hope of finding their loved ones again.

The three travelers had spent the first week walking in regions familiar to them. Toby had wanted to let old Jalam take the lead. But Jalam had refused.

"I'll bring up the rear. If I get left behind, I'll be that much closer to taking my retirement. . . . So I can't lose, either way."

What Jalam really wanted to do was to keep an eye on young Moon Boy. He still thought they shouldn't have brought him along, and he let Moon Boy know this at every opportunity.

Toby, on the other hand, impressed the old guide with his knowledge of the Prairie. His sense of direction was perfect, thanks to his study of the shadows cast by the stems. He could forecast wind and rain by listening

to the music of the grass. He could always find something for dinner: he knew how to dive into marshy areas
and reappear, his arms laden with damselfly eggs. Toby
knew the sweet taste of grass juice and the spices of certain creepers. By pounding a cereal grain with water, he
knew how to make small loaves to bake in the embers.

Ever since they'd set off, Moon Boy had been silent.

Jalam scolded him from time to time when he walked
too fast.

"Will you look at that Strand of Linen! It flies with the
wind, but it has no idea whether it's coming or going!"

Moon Boy would slow his pace. Neither these
reproaches nor Toby's imminent departure was the cause
of his dark mood. The Grass people only cry for the dead,
never for those departing on a journey.

"Leaving means living *more*," Jalam would say, sound-
ing nostalgic for those great expeditions.

So? Why did Moon Boy have such a closed expression? Only Toby could guess the secret behind his silence.

It was the fifth night. They were spending it in a leaf
rolled into a tube, near a wild carrot arboretum. At the
end of the meal every evening, Jalam took out a grass
cylinder pinched at either end and, from this vial, poured
three drops of purple liquid onto his tongue. Then he
rolled up one end of his long clothing into a makeshift
pillow and drifted off to sleep.

The love song of a frog could be heard far off. Fireflies
were crossing the night like lazy shooting stars.

Toby and Moon Boy were trying to bring the fire back to life. They were turning the embers over.

"I know what you saw," said Toby.

"I saw because I have eyes," said Moon Boy in the riddle language of the Grass people.

"Forget what you saw."

Moon Boy blew on the embers. A flame lit up their faces. Moon Boy was barely ten years old; Toby was older by five or six springs. Moon Boy passed his hand over the fire, as if he was spinning a top, calming the hay fire to make the flames last longer. A shadow fell over the two boys again.

After a long silence, Moon Boy said, "You have to tell me what my sister Ilaya did."

"Forget about it," said Toby. "It was nothing."

𝒞𝒬

The day before their departure, Moon Boy had discovered Toby pinning Ilaya to the floor of his ear of wheat. She was resisting. Toby was holding her firmly by both wrists. Moon Boy rushed in. He was about to intervene when he stopped in his tracks.

The young girl's right hand was gripping the pointed end of an arrow.

Recognizing her little brother, Ilaya had dropped the weapon and fled.

"You have to tell me, Little Tree. You have to tell me what she wanted to do with that arrow."

Moon Boy was speaking bravely. His emotions rose to the surface with every word. "Something broken cuts deeper than something whole. Something broken can kill like a shard of ice," he said. "I know there's been something broken inside my sister for years now. If she's dangerous, you have to tell me, Little Tree."

Moon Boy was convinced that Ilaya had tried to kill Toby. Just the idea of it pierced his heart. Ilaya and Toby were the two people he loved more than anyone else.

But Moon Boy would have given anything to be mistaken. His eyes searched Toby's.

"Tell me the truth, Little Tree. Tell me that Ilaya wanted to kill you with that arrow."

"Don't talk like that."

"I have to know. I'm begging you."

Toby was silent. He stirred the fire, avoiding Moon Boy's pain-filled gaze.

But his companion wasn't giving up. "Say it!"

Far off, the frog in love stopped singing. Toby held his breath and let out, "Ilaya . . ."

He stopped.

"Say it!" whispered the young boy.

Even the fire kept quiet to let him speak.

"Ilaya wanted to die," Toby explained. "Ilaya was trying to kill herself."

He looked down.

There could be few words more dreadful. Few words that provoke such a strong desire to cry out. And yet Toby knew these words would bring great comfort to Moon Boy. His sister was no criminal; she was just sad.

Desperately sad. Sad enough to die.

Moon Boy lay down on his back and murmured, "Thank you, Little Tree."

Toby let out a long sigh. He lay back, next to his friend. They could hear the humming of the fire again. Toby looked up at the huge parasols of carrot flowers above them, adding more stars to the autumn sky.

Toby had problems sleeping that night. Perhaps he already knew that one day, much later, Moon Boy would learn the cruel truth.

But on this particular night, in order to console his friend, Toby had lied.

The next day, they entered the Bramble Thicket of the Great West.

Toby hadn't been this close to the Tree since he'd left his former life.

For a long time now, Jalam had refused to cross the Bramble Thicket at ground level. He had lost too many men on that route. The bramble bushes were infested with large predators, such as field mice and voles. Even if you're an old and experienced guide, you're better off not crossing paths with big game like a young shrew.

The only sensible route was to take the high path. Jalam showed Toby the long spiky bramble stems that rose into the air, making figure eights, loops, and narrow suspension bridges. He looked at Moon Boy.

"I find it hard to believe that a Strand of Linen could cross the Bramble Thicket of the Great West."

"I'm not a Strand of Linen. I'm called Moon Boy," the youngest traveler reminded him sharply.

Jalam didn't push the point, and they went through the Bramble Thicket by the high path. It took them ten days.

The coils of brambles formed impressive aerial walkways, but the journey was often less acrobatic than it looked. The thorns doubled as ladder rungs, and the velvety leaves prevented them from slipping.

Jalam knew of a few refuges hidden inside hollow thorns. All three of them huddled into those tiny recesses suspended in thin air.

The food didn't vary much. A few abandoned spiders'

webs offered them the occasional crunchy dried midge. Sometimes there were even a few shriveled berries that had survived the end of summer. Not enough to make a summer pie, but it was something at least.

They had made it without incident to what should have been their last night in the brambles before rejoining the Prairie.

That evening at midnight, they were woken by a violent shaking.

"Watch out!" shouted Jalam.

Toby rolled on top of the old guide. Suddenly, they were hurled toward the roof of their shelter and crashing down together on top of Moon Boy. They felt like marbles inside a rattle.

"I'm going to see what's happening," said Moon Boy, sticking his nose outside.

"Noooo!" roared Jalam, an instant too late.

The boy had already disappeared, thrown into the air by a whiplash effect.

Toby and Jalam huddled in a corner of the thorn.

"I told him," whispered Jalam between clenched teeth.

The tumult continued.

"It's a bird caught in the brush," Jalam went on. "We might have to stay put for several days."

"What about Moon Boy?"

The old guide didn't answer right away.

"Do you think he fell right down to ground level?" Toby asked.

"If that's the kind of fall he's had, he'll be a sorry sight. . . ." Jalam looked at Toby before continuing: "You won't escape a field mouse or a snake for long when you're only ten and the chances are you've got two broken legs."

Toby didn't say anything. He knew that even at the age of ten, when you're scraped and grazed and tested by life, you can escape the clutches of all kinds of things.

Jalam and Toby stayed in their thorn for the rest of the night, the whole of the next day, and another night too. They tried talking to make the time pass more quickly and to forget about how hungry they were.

Jalam talked about when he was a young man. Toby listened. Lulls sometimes followed the violent thrashing of the brambles, but they never lasted.

At dawn on the second day, helped by being so tired, Jalam began to broach more intimate subjects — his childhood, his loves, his first courtship with the girl who went on to become his wife. . . .

"A nettle!" he explained, laughing. "I made a date with her on a nettle! Young fool that I was! We were too young to wear much linen in those days. . . . People saw us coming back, both of us with our arms and legs on fire from the nettle's stingers. Our love didn't stay a secret for long. . . ."

Toby laughed with him. But no sooner had they done so than both of them thought of Moon Boy's shiny eyes and the mood turned serious again.

Jalam admitted to having been too harsh.

"I'm a little afraid of children," he said.

"Didn't you have any of your own?" Toby asked.

"No," said Jalam.

"Didn't you want any?"

Jalam didn't answer. It was more a matter of the children not wanting him. He and his wife had dreamed of having children for a long time. Perhaps, deep down, Jalam held that against children.

Toby took his hand. Danger exposes hearts and brings them closer. They stayed like that for a long time, almost peaceful in the small hours of the morning.

Later, Toby talked about Isha Lee.

Ever since he had found out that Elisha's mother was born among the Grass people, he was burning to find out more. Toby dived into the old man's silence.

"What about Isha? Did you know Isha when she was in the Grass?"

Jalam's eyes glimmered, and there was another long silence.

"Little Tree, I've told you, my wife was the most wonderful thing that happened to me in my life; she brought me great happiness. I hold to her like the soles of my feet. But for a long time, I thought I would never be able to forget Isha."

"You . . . ?"

"I asked for Isha's hand in marriage thirty-seven times."

He looked down.

"And I wasn't the only one. Some asked her a hundred

times. Nouk threw himself out of his ear of wheat for her. For beautiful Isha . . . If you knew, Little Tree, what she represented for us. . . ."

Jalam's face clouded over, and he added, "There isn't anybody among the Grass people who doesn't regret what we all did."

"What did you do?"

"Our hearts are gentle, Little Tree. I don't know how the story of Isha could have happened."

"What story?"

"We're all responsible, because she made all of our hearts leap."

"Jalam, tell me what happened."

Suddenly, the Bramble Thicket was shaken convulsively, and then everything stopped. Jalam gestured at Toby. The old guide was waiting. The silence lasted several minutes, then Jalam said, "It's over. That's unbelievable. I've never seen a bird free itself on its own after two nights. Usually, he frees himself the first day or you have to wait a week for him to die of exhaustion."

"A week?"

"Yes. And I can tell you that my old body wouldn't have lasted a whole week. You had your youth to count on, Little Tree. But I thought I'd be ending my days here."

Toby held both of Jalam's hands.

"But you laughed when you were telling me your stories. . . ."

A shout echoed in the distance.

"That's the little one!" said Jalam. "He's survived!"

The old guide rushed toward the entrance.

"Moon Boy!" he called.

The boy's voice answered him.

Jalam called out the child's name again. He was glowing with happiness.

"I'm coming, Moon Boy! I'm coming!"

Day was breaking. The Prairie was rippling beyond the last brambles. Jalam slipped outside.

Despite his relief, Toby was still haunted by the mystery of Isha Lee.

4
Between Two Worlds

It took several days for Toby and Jalam to realize that Moon Boy was responsible for their freedom.

"I was lucky," he said. "I was in the right place at the right time."

But his adventure was much more than a good-luck story.

After being thrown from the bramble when it first started shaking, Moon Boy had lost consciousness. He had woken up on the stem that was holding a blackbird prisoner. He could feel the bird's warmth just below him, as well as the panic-stricken beating of its heart while its wings whipped the brambles.

To withstand the storm of feathers, Moon Boy had tied himself to the stem using the end of his linen cloth. He'd waited for night to end.

At dawn, he had spotted a place just next to the bird's

head where the bramble was weak; it was half worn through by the bird's thrashings. The bird would be free if not for this tiny stem.

Moon Boy had dragged himself in that direction as quietly as possible, not daring to let the starving bird see him.

He had tried tearing away at the thorny stem for hours, until nightfall, using both teeth and nails, but it was a hopeless battle.

"That was when I had my little idea," he explained. "Who could help me? Who would save me? Who, in the Bramble Thicket, was strong enough and close enough to rescue me?"

Jalam and Toby looked at each other. An understanding smile spread across their faces, and their chests got all puffed up.

"Us!" they said in unison.

"No . . . not you," answered Moon Boy, almost apologetically. "But the bird! The bird, with his beak right there next to me! I was hiding from him when he was the only one who could help me."

Toby's and Jalam's feathers were a bit ruffled. Their friend continued, "On the second morning, I took my cloth in my hand like a long train. I climbed the stem and started dancing."

As he was telling the story, Moon Boy began to dance close to the fire.

"In ten seconds," said Moon Boy, "I saw the blackbird's eyes rolling my way. I saw his beak open and get

close. At the last moment, I threw myself to the side, flat on my belly. He had snapped the bramble stem instead of me."

Astounded, Jalam acknowledged for the first time how these few milligrams of a slip of a boy were packed with courage and imagination. So that's what a child was.

Moon Boy acted out the scene by firelight. When he was playing the role of the bird, he got closer to the flames and his giant shadow was projected onto the grass.

"He retreated a bit. I got up and started dancing again on the same spot. The bird attacked for a second time; I jumped back. His beak tore off a strip of the bramble. . . . And that's what my little idea was."

Toby and Jalam were starting to get the picture. With a mixture of fondness and fascination, they watched their young companion dance. A little idea? He called that a little idea? Jalam looked away. He was overcome. Moon Boy had saved their lives.

"With the final snap of the bird's beak, the bramble broke. The blackbird was able to spread its wings, disentangling itself at the cost of a few feathers. He flew off. I was flung upward again, but my linen cloth was caught on a thorn and kept me hanging in midair."

Moon Boy got even closer to the fire.

They had set up camp on a dry clod of earth, having already put the bramble far behind them. But this was the first time that Moon Boy had told them about his feat.

"I was in the right place at the right time," he said again.

Jalam corrected him, "The worst place, young man, at the worst time. But you were the right person."

The downpour began the next day. Tepid rain, with drops as big as houses.

"That's just as well," said Jalam. "I've been waiting for this day."

He took his peashooter and started tapping the tall grass spindles around him. With each tap, he strained his ears to listen to the acoustic of the stem. Finally, he pointed to one and got out a small knife made of hard wood, which he wore on his belt.

"Let's lay this one down."

Toby and Moon Boy took their knives and followed

orders. The grass fell with a hissing noise. Felling a green blade of grass was a rare and solemn moment. In the Prairie people talked about "laying down" a blade of grass. Dried grass was sufficient for everyday use, but on a few occasions the laying down of green blade of grass was necessary.

The main reason was building boats.

They worked for two days in the rain to build a handsome green boat. It was a good centimeter long. The greenness of the grass weighed it down and made it float well. At the back, two long poles enabled the sailors to push their boat forward.

The water was starting to rise.

It was autumn, and as with every autumn, the Prairie was being transformed into a flooded forest.

The voyage over the waters lasted several weeks. Time seemed to slide by in slow motion as the boat drifted between the blades of grass. They had devised a small shelter at the prow. One of the sailors would sleep there while the other two pushed their poles behind them, in the rain.

Toby savored the gentleness of this boat journey.

He liked the way time had slowed down, the easy tedium of life on board, one day blurring into another. His hair was always wet, the rain clinked over the marsh, and water bugs skated between the droplets.

Jalam would bathe before dawn, while the youngsters were still asleep. With one eye half open, Toby would

watch him climb back into the boat, naked in the cold November air, wrapping his long old man's clothing around him. He would throw off the moorings and start pushing with his pole, then signal to Toby to drink a bowl of hot water with him.

Jalam was relishing every moment of his last voyage.

In the evenings, Toby would light the fire on a floater next to the boat and cook standing in water up to his shoulders.

The rest of the time, nothing happened. . . . Just the boat being pushed forward, the way it swayed, a concert of toads in the distance, the rippling water, the Grass Forest unfurling — all this was enough to fill their days.

In the course of these long stretched-out weeks, the water began to have an effect on Toby's memories, as if the autumn rain was dripping onto the dust that covered his past.

For the first few days, terrible memories were exposed, so that it was like black mud in Toby's heart. The nightmare he had lived through in the Tree was still there, intact: flight and fear. He could see himself running through the branches, pursued by his own people. He rediscovered the horrors of the prison at Tumble, along with everything he had left behind when he went to live in the Grass.

But, slowly, the pure rainwater washed away these black memories. And all he was left with was the dazzling beauty of what he was setting out to win back.

First there were his parents, Sim and Maya Lolness. Their faces floated above the boat, in the shadows of the marsh. And their voices . . . Voices Toby was frightened of forgetting, but that came back to him, whispering in snatches.

He could even feel their lips brushing against his ears. He closed his eyes and gently drew in his hands, hoping to grab his mother's silk scarf, to climb up it like a rope ladder, until at last he could touch her skin, her hair.

He only ever found air, the damp air of those rainy days. But he wasn't sorry to have believed, even if only for a moment.

Toby tried to picture his parents. They were in Joe Mitch's hands. Would they be able to hold out until their son's return? Would Sim deliver Balina's Secret, the invention that threatened the vital energy of their Tree, to the enemy?

Another ghost haunted the young adventurer.

When he was resting at the front of the boat, he could feel a hand touching his own and playing with his cheeks.

"Wait," he whispered sleepily. "Wait for me. I'm asleep; I have to get strong again."

It was as if this hand was trying to take him some-where, tugging at his hand insistently.

"Not just yet. I have to finish this journey," Toby repeated.

But he didn't put up much of a fight. He was enjoy-ing the invitation, and his gentle refusal encouraged the other person to linger.

"I'm coming—I promise. Just give me the time to get up there."

He woke up when he uttered his ghost's name.

"Elisha."

That was when he realized that his hand was sticking out of the shelter and being rained on. The invitation had come from those big raindrops on his hand. He sighed but left it outside to find Elisha's rain fingers again as quickly as possible.

Toby kept trying to encourage old Jalam to continue with Isha's story.

"I've told you what I know," answered Jalam. "She was there with us in the Grass, and then one day she left. I don't know anything else."

"But you were starting to tell me . . ."

"I don't know anything else."

Toby couldn't quite understand.

"But . . ."

Jalam's face was inscrutable.

"That's all, Little Tree."

In the Bramble Thicket, Jalam had started talking about everything because he thought he was going to die. But he'd been given back life, with all its locks and barricades. Perhaps it would be better if your whole life had that same transparency as in its final moments.

Today, Jalam was back in the world, and he had slammed the door on his memories.

A door.

During all his years in the Grass, Toby had never seen a single door. The ears of wheat were left wide open. He had forgotten that down there, like everywhere else, there are still doors inside people's heads, and one jab of the elbow is enough to close them again forever.

Jalam fell quiet. Toby lifted the long pole and pushed it behind him. He was reflecting on all this. Even Grass people have secrets and things they're frightened of.

Deep in the eyes of Ilaya, Moon Boy's big sister, there had always been several locked doors. Toby had never tried to open them, preferring to stay outside her secrets.

But it would have taken so little for those barriers to crumble to dust at his feet.

Ilaya was in love with Toby.

He had felt the heat of her passion for him. An all-consuming passion into which she threw the loss of her parents, the death of a fiancé, and all the unhappiness that had built up since she was small.

Ilaya was a bundle of despair, ready to set herself on fire for the first man that came along.

When Toby announced that he was leaving, she could think of only one thing: holding on to him. Even if it meant killing him in order to keep him all to herself.

"The line's heavy."

Toby surfaced from his thoughts.

"What?"

"The line's heavy," old Jalam repeated.

Toby let go of his pole and grabbed hold of a fishing

line that was attached just behind him. He tugged it deftly out of the water.

"A pupa," said Jalam, who was helping Toby remove a small gray insect. "A mosquito pupa. My wife makes a stew from these."

Toby looked at his older companion. Clearly, he wasn't going to find out any more about Isha Lee's story.

The water level started to drop at the end of November. On the first day of December, the boat ran aground. Moon Boy was the first to set foot on dry land. He disappeared, running off.

Toby and Jalam turned the boat over on a mud beach and tied it to a grass trunk.

"You never know," said Jalam. "I might be able to use it on the home journey with the little one, if the snows don't come."

"But what if it *does* snow?"

"If it snows, then we'll use boards."

Toby had discovered boards for the first time when he arrived in the Grass. They were slats of wood strapped lengthways under the feet, used to glide over the snow. The front of the boards rose up and curled like a snail shell.

Toby and Jalam heard shouting and saw Moon Boy running toward them.

"Come and see! Quick!"

The boy led them a few centimeters away. They clambered over grass crushed by the rain and emerged on a leaf that formed a sort of terrace. They followed Moon Boy right to the edge.

As far as the eye could see, bark-covered hills rose up in the middle of the Grass, like a giant wooden snake that went underground and came out again.

"What is it?" asked Moon Boy.

"We're closer to our goal than I'd thought," said the old guide.

"Is it the Tree?"

"Yes."

Toby was startled. No, his Tree didn't look like this.

"It's the Underground Tree. These hills are in the open air, but all the rest of the branches are underground. The Underground Tree . . . It shares the same Trunk as your Tree."

Toby's face lit up. He was thinking of his father and his big research files. He could picture the little image that he had carved at Onessa, on the door of their house in the Low Branches. The same sign that he carved every-where. The emblem of the Lolness family.

During the long voyage by boat, Toby had sculpted the sign on a wooden medallion that he had given to Moon Boy.

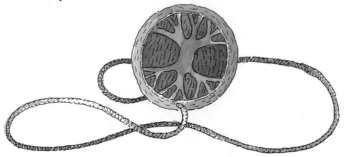

"These are roots," Toby had explained. "The roots of my Tree. They come out at this spot, but most of them are underground. My father knew they existed."

Moon Boy was looking at the emblem around his neck.

Jalam smiled grimly when he heard Toby talking. Roots . . . Why that word? Couldn't we just as well say that the Branches in the air that Toby knew were actually the roots of the Underground Tree? Who was to say which way was up for the Tree? And which were its Roots?

But the old guide remained quiet; he didn't want to stir up a debate that was too old and too painful for the Grass people.

An hour later, the travelers arrived at the foot of the first bark hill. Slowly, Toby walked over and put his hand on the wood.

"The days are shorter," said Jalam. "I hadn't even noticed. We're in the shadow of the Tree."

Moon Boy touched the bark for the first time.

"It trembles," he said.

Toby put his forehead against it. He could already feel the flow of sap that was fighting for survival in the depths of the Tree.

One evening, the trio stopped underneath a root that formed an arch. There, hidden in the grass, another boat was moored. They walked around it. The rain hadn't risen to this level since the fat springtime droplets. Jalam touched the side of the boat, whose grass hull had dried out and was starting to crack in places.

"This boat was made among our people," said the guide.

"Who by?" asked Moon Boy.

"I don't know. Its passengers must have abandoned it. I hope nothing happened to them."

Just then, Toby saw a blue linen rope tied to a blade of grass. He undid it and showed it to the other two.

"It's as I feared," said Jalam.

"Mika and Liev . . ." whispered Moon Boy.

Toby wound the linen around his wrist.

Mika and Liev were two close friends, about the same age as Toby. They had set out in search of wood at the start of spring. The Grass people had tried to discourage them, but Mika had already made up his mind.

He would look after Liev; he was used to it.

You might wonder why a strapping young man like

Liev needed looking after. But it only took a short time to realize that there was something different about him.

Liev had suffered from oats disease, which targets the five senses, one after the other. At ten, he had gone deaf. A year later, he had lost his sight. By a strange twist, the disease had stopped there, leaving him his three other senses: touch, smell, and taste.

"Without the blue rope," said Toby, "I don't know how they would have been able to manage."

This rope linked the two friends. It allowed Mika to direct Liev as well as to communicate with him by tugging on the rope.

"They must be dead," said Jalam.

Luckily, even wise old guides with a great deal of experience are sometimes wrong.

Somewhere in the Tree, Mika and Liev were still alive.

5
Alone

In the hollow of the valley, in the middle of the highest mountain range, Toby caught his breath. He had escaped those on his trail, but he needed to stay on his guard.

He was alone now and had been since the previous day. Toby had separated from his two traveling companions because the season was too far advanced. Jalam and Moon Boy needed to head for home before they got caught by the winter. Toby promised to find out what had happened to Liev, Mika, and all the others.

The three companions had said their good-byes in the manner of the Grass people. Which is to say, without much show of emotion.

"Good-bye."

"Be brave."

"See you soon, Little Tree."

They hadn't even shaken hands or touched foreheads. Then Jalam and Moon Boy had rushed down the slope.

Toby had to stop himself from running after them and giving Moon Boy a fierce hug. He would have liked to kiss Jalam's hand, to have called out to them to think of him, not to forget him. He longed to tell them what an impression life in the Grass had made on him.

Later, Toby frequently regretted not having done this.

In his two months of traveling, despite all the trials, Toby hadn't really felt as if he'd left the Prairie. The challenge remained the same: to live or survive in spite of nature, or rather, *with* nature.

But since the previous night, the rules of the game had changed.

Hunters had appeared on the scene.

Toby quickly realized that these hunters weren't after him. They wanted to capture the Grass people. They had chased Toby as if he was just another Grass person risking the Trunk. And it would be fair to say that, in just a few years, Toby had started to look a lot like the men of the Grass.

Toby surveyed the countryside around him: the lake, the green valley, the mountains rising up behind, and the outline of the gigantic Trunk above them, in the light of the gray morning.

It was a long journey ahead. But something up there was drawing him to it, sucking him in like a black hole:

the great shadow of the Tree and the labyrinth of branches where he was needed. Toby set out at a trot, leaving the valley behind him.

All day long, without stopping for a moment, he climbed walls, jumped over streams, crossed mountain passes, skirted around bark craters as chiseled as lace, ran on high plateaus, dropped into valleys, and climbed up the other side.

He didn't feel tired. He decided to keep on running the following night, sprinting over patches of low-lying moss, ducking under waterfalls that sparkled in the clear night. He felt invincible. Nothing could stop him.

By dawn, indestructible Toby had used up all his reserves and found himself in a small green valley.

A small valley where a wood louse had come to drink, just as he did every morning. The wood louse noticed Toby and was thoroughly taken aback.

Well, really! Hadn't he already witnessed this scene the day before?

Panting, Toby looked at the lake, then the wood louse, then the valley. His eyes started rolling in their sockets. He looked at the lake again, then the wood louse, then the valley. He collapsed to the ground.

High mountains are not to be undertaken lightly. Toby had set out impulsively, his blood whipped up by his boundless energy.

He hadn't stopped to think.

He had worn himself out for twenty-four hours, only to find himself back at exactly the same spot. Mountains are traps. You can't treat them like parks, crossing them with your nose in the air.

If he kept going like this, archaeologists excavating the ridges of a small bark valley in a hundred years' time might find a peashooter and a few bones, in memory of Toby.

So he went back to the beginning. Sleep.

When he woke up that evening, Toby's head was back on his shoulders and he had put aside his thirst for revenge and the drunken attitude of a hero. At last he could think.

That was when he saw an object left behind on the shores of the lake.

Toby bent down to pick it up. It was a black fur hat lined with worn silk, which a hunter must have forgotten, and it provided an answer.

The hunters. He just had to follow them. Winter was setting in, and they would certainly be heading home.

Toby's job was to hunt the men who were hunting him.

He threw the hat into the air. It landed on his back, catching the top of the peashooter, and stayed there. Toby walked around the lake, finding the tracks of the convoy right away, and began following them.

The next day, in the valley, the wood louse waited for Toby to come, but he didn't see anything. The wood louse was almost disappointed. It's funny how quickly you can feel attached to something.

"Hey, it's snowing."

"Yes, it's snowing. Winter's starting now."

"You don't have your hat?"

"My hat?"

"Your hat! You don't have your hat."

"No, I don't have my hat."

Two hunters were guarding one of the feather sleds loaded with crates. The troops had finished crossing the mountain range. Tomorrow they would begin the assault on the vertical Trunk. They were going to take the Ring Road, a route that spiraled up the Trunk.

A third man stepped out of the shadow. It was a hunter with a harpoon.

"It's me, Tiger."

"Can't you sleep?"

"No. I've been thinking about that one we let get away."

"Don't worry. The boss'll still be happy."

"It's not that. . . ."

"What is it, then, Tiger?"

"I don't like leaving leftovers. It's messy!"

The two others started laughing loudly, but they were half terrified of Tiger. The snow was starting to fall heavily. Tiger knocked on one of the guard's heads.

"Rat-a-tat-tat! No hat?"

"No, I don't have my hat."

"Where is it?"

"I lost it."

Tiger stood up. He went over to the crates and started whacking them with his harpoon handle.

"No sleeping, you inside!" he roared. "No sleeping. You should be thinking long and hard about your uncle Mitch, who'll be taking care of you in a few days."

The three hunters laughed together. The one who'd lost his hat added, "Things might be calm for you in your crates at the moment . . . but the good life will be over soon enough!"

At the same time as a fine film of snow was covering his body, Toby felt his heart being covered with frost. He was stretched out in the dark, just three paces from the hunters. He hadn't missed a single word of their murky conversation.

An hour earlier, Toby had moved in closer to steal a few warm clothes. He had found a thick jacket and a pair of boots that one of the men had taken off in order to sleep. He was heading off furtively when he heard the guards talking.

He closed in. Good news. The convoy was transporting Grass people, and there were nine in total. Everybody who'd disappeared since last spring, no doubt. When he heard Joe Mitch's name and how aggressive Tiger was, Toby pushed his face against the bark to keep himself from shouting out.

What was going on in the heads of these peaceful people when they heard the hunters banging on their wooden cages and shouting? And even if they did escape, how could they contend with the winter, the snow, the hugeness of the Tree?

Poor oppressed people!

"We're going to crush you," Tiger continued, standing on the crates. "We're going to crush you, one by one."

Then Tiger stopped. He felt something on his left foot. A small hand had poked out of a hole in the crate and grabbed hold of his ankle. Tiger struggled to break free. Another hand escaped from another crate and grabbed his right foot. He roared like an animal and went sprawling on top of the crates.

It was a nightmare. There were hands gripping Tiger's arms, hair, and belt. He kept crying out in horror, seeing himself stuck like a suction cup to the pile of crates. The other hunters had woken up and were coming over to try and wrench him free. They pulled him; they shook him; they banged on the Grass people's crates.

When all the hands let go at the same time, the hunters who were tugging on Tiger's clothes went flying, and, along with Tiger, they all ended up crashing into a bark wall. A block of snow became dislodged and covered them.

Toby grinned, wide-eyed. How could he have forgotten how brave and strong his friends were? A poor defenseless people? Poor powerless victims? No! They didn't need Toby's pity. They were noble fighters who had confronted far worse opponents than Tiger and his sidekicks.

They were going to put up a fight.

Toby retreated and disappeared into the night.

An ambush. That's what he needed to set up: an ambush to free the prisoners. It didn't matter that it was snowy and cold. If they got away, they'd manage to get home alive. At least winter is a predictable enemy.

Toby ran through the snow. The Ring Road was narrow but well worn. There was no risk of getting lost. He wanted to get ahead to put his plan in place. In the leather jacket and boots, pants cut off at the knees, and his bumblebee fur hat, with the peashooter slung across his back, he was quite a sight. He braved the wind and snow on this highway carved around the Trunk.

The Ring Road had been a major undertaking in recent years. It coiled snail shell-like around the Trunk, all the way to the uppermost branches, ensuring that the captured Grass people could be driven swiftly to the top. As a matter of fact, they were the people who had been used to dig it in the first place. The building site lingered in common memory as being particularly lethal. Every day, a few Grass people, suspended parallel to the Trunk to dig the Ring Road, fell off.

As he walked along the cliff road, it looked to Toby as if the snow was giving off a soft light. It was a clear, crisp night, and his feet weren't yet sinking into the white carpet.

After climbing for two hours, Toby stopped at an awkward bend in the road. A block of bark had become dislodged and was jammed between two branches five millimeters above the road. The snow was getting heavier now. It might only take one kick for the chunk of bark to fall and block the road.

Toby climbed the wall to look down on the Ring Road. His goal was to split the convoy in two. He'd release the block just in front of the feather sleds carrying his imprisoned friends. He'd have enough time to free them.

With one foot, he brushed against the chunk of bark hanging in the balance. It moved a little. Perfect. He simply needed his trap to hold out until morning and not melt or topple over before then.

As if the snow had heard his wish, it started falling less heavily.

Toby settled himself just above the action spot. Huddled in a ball, his arms around his knees, he waited.

His first thoughts were of Moon Boy and Jalam. It was reassuring to know they were in the Prairie. Now that the snow had come, they would make themselves boards and the return journey would be quick. One long slide back home.

The Prairie was perfect terrain for snowboarding.

Last winter, Toby had set out with Moon Boy and Ilaya for eight days in the snow. They'd gone to fish for damselfly eggs in the frozen marshes.

It was a happy memory. The sun had shone strongly on the snow-covered grass. Boards strapped to their feet, they had glided through a white world. After spending a large part of the winter shut up in their ears of wheat, they suddenly found themselves in a landscape of infinite purity.

Moon Boy hooted as he sped down the slopes with his arms in the air. They left board marks in the powdery snow. Ilaya smiled at Toby, who waited for her when the climb back up was too steep.

Winter fishing involves building big fires on the ice. A hole forms and the larvae rise to the surface of the warmed water. Damselflies are small dragonflies with green and black bodies; their larvae remain underwater for years. The aim is to catch the youngest larvae, which are succulent and sweet.

Toby could remember moments together with Ilaya, as they crouched on the ice. They had stuck their boards into the snow, a little way off. Moon Boy was keeping an eye on the fire, on the other side of the marsh. Ilaya would say to her brother, "Leave us."

If Toby had looked Ilaya in the eye, he would have

understood what she meant. Ilaya was in love, and Toby should have realized this. Why had he closed his eyes to it?

Thinking about it now, Toby was forced to admit that perhaps he had led her on to try and recall that forgotten feeling. To find with Ilaya what he had tried to sweep away forever: Elisha's beautiful eyes and her fierce bravery.

Moon Boy would sneak up on them, grab Ilaya's foot, and laugh as he made her slip on the ice. She would shout angrily.

From a distance, they would have looked like three specks of dust and a tiny fire.

Toby was woken by muffled voices. He stood up abruptly, feeling a bit lost. Where was he? His nose was cold and his hair icy. Suddenly, he remembered his plan to ambush the convoy.

"Here they are. . . ."

The troops were still a few centimeters from the bend. Toby eased himself into the spot from which he could set his trap.

The first hunters passed by. They walked in silence. The rest followed, dragging their feet. The Ring Road was narrow. They were hugging the Trunk. At last, Toby saw the sleds being pulled by the men. The crates were there. Toby waited for the right moment before giving the block of bark a hefty kick.

Nothing.

Nothing happened.

The bark hadn't budged.

He gave a second kick. Again, nothing. He only had a moment to play with. He started jumping frantically, to no avail.

Toby climbed onto the block of bark to watch the convoy pass by. He had failed. He fell to his knees, unaware of the danger that threatened his perch.

Enormous snowflakes were starting to fall again.

The crates were about to disappear around the corner, when Toby realized the airholes had been blocked. A traumatized Tiger had given the order to prevent the previous night's fiasco from happening again. The nine prisoners were having trouble breathing.

Toby noticed a finger that had managed to slip between the slats of the smallest crate. It pained him to see. But he didn't know the worst.

That hand, a tiny, frozen hand sticking out of the wooden crate, belonged to Moon Boy. He wasn't down below in the Prairie, snowboarding, slicing through the air on snowy slopes. He was directly below, huddled in a crate, worrying about the health of old Jalam in the crate next to his.

"How are you holding up?"

The reply took a while.

"I'm up."

Just then, Moon Boy heard the dull sound of an avalanche reverberating in the distance. The sled stopped. Feet pounded over the snow as someone ran to see what had happened.

The man reappeared, breathless.

"It's on that bend we just came around. We were lucky. A big chunk of bark has collapsed under the snow."

"Is the road blocked?"

"No. It rolled over the precipice."

6

The Garrison at Seldor

⌒⌒ In the old days, when Seldor Farm woke up under a blanket of snow, the girls of the household would go out at dawn, each carried by one of their brothers. Lola and Lila would put up a fight, but the boys were too strong and they couldn't escape. With the girls in their arms, the boys waded into the snow until it reached their thighs, their bodies steaming in the cold light of morning.

A bit farther out, they would toss the girls in their night-gowns into the thick whiteness. The sisters disappeared almost completely, shrieking and refusing to laugh.

In the old days, when Seldor Farm woke up under a blanket of snow, their mother would come out of the house, extremely upset to see such barbaric customs still being enacted. She would bring hot towels and try to rub her daughters dry while scolding her sons.

Snow baths make young girls grow into wise women. So claimed three generations of Asseldors.

This generation had fun with a tradition invented by an eccentric grandfather, but Mrs. Asseldor didn't join in the laughter.

In the old days, when Seldor Farm woke up under a blanket of snow, the family didn't work for several days. They would get out cicada drumsticks and grill them on a spit in the fireplace; they drank warm beer and ate honey cakes.

In the old days, when Seldor Farm woke up under a blanket of snow, they would play music at the windows and listen. . . . The acoustics off a field of snow are pure and mysterious. Best of all is playing there at night.

In the old days, when Seldor Farm woke up under

a blanket of snow, everyone wanted their whole lives to be like this first morning of winter.

But Seldor Farm had changed.

A farmyard muddied by soldiers' boots; barns converted into dormitories and canteens; raised voices; and, farther off, the old aphid aviaries were now converted into cages for people. The Grass people were detained in this garrison before being driven down to the Lower Colonies.

Leo Blue had arrived in the Low Branches the night before, after his great journey down the Tree. He listened to his men's explanations.

"The cages are empty. We're waiting for the next convoy."

"They're late. It's December 20, but—"

"Quiet," interrupted Leo Blue.

He was looking at the front of the great house at Seldor, carved out of the bark. Leo stood completely still. Everybody was watching to see what he'd do next. He inspired fear. His story was well known. First, that his father had been killed by the Grass people on the Great Border, when Leo was small. And then his own story, in which revenge had little by little become an obsession.

Seeing that he was interested in the farm, Garric, the Garrison Commander, ventured some explanations. "It's the home of the Asseldor family."

"Quiet," Leo ordered again. "I didn't ask you anything."

Leo knew all about it. A family had been living there when the barracks were set up. And he had made his own journey to this house to find Elisha.

He felt he was registering how handsome this building was for the first time: the thick scars in the wood revealed its age.

A figure passed by—a young woman carrying a bucket around the perimeter of the house, before quickly disappearing inside.

"That's the Asseldors' daughter—"

"I know!" Leo lashed out.

He stroked the boomerangs hanging on his back, and nobody made a sound.

The Asseldor family had chosen to stay within their own walls despite all their land being confiscated. They had been offered other farms, higher up in the Tree, but they had refused. The soldiers tolerated their presence in these old walls. The family scraped by from hunting and gathering.

"I don't like them staying here," said Leo. "They mustn't disturb the work."

"They don't disturb us," said a soldier. "They used to play music, but Joe Mitch banned it a year ago."

"Was it nice?"

The man didn't answer. How could he say that the music had made him weep?

"The risk is that they help the Grass people," said Leo Blue. "Keep an eye on them."

"We search the house every evening, and we do surprise daytime searches three times a week."

Leo Blue looked unconvinced. When it came to fear, he was a perfectionist. He knew that one of the Asseldor sons, Mano, was on the run. Mano's name was on the Green List of most wanted people.

"What about at night? Search them at night! That's an order."

Leo Blue set out the same day.

The young woman with the bucket who had just gone inside the house closed the door behind her and leaned against it. It was Lila, the older Asseldor daughter.

"I can't take it anymore," she said under her breath.

She wiped her face with her sleeve, picked up her bucket, and carried it over to the fireplace. Then she started talking in an upbeat voice.

"I'm here. Everything's fine. It's been snowing. It's very white out there. There's a bit of sunshine. The boys have found a maggot over by Onessa. They've saved some of it to preserve in honey, and we'll have the rest for dinner. Our parents are on their way. They'll be here in an hour."

The room was empty. So who was she talking to in such a reassuring voice? She emptied her bucket into a big pot that was heating on the fire.

"I'm melting the snow," said Lila. "I'm going to take a bath. I feel cold."

There was something extraordinary about hearing this young woman describe her every movement.

When the Asseldor parents arrived a little later on, they played exactly the same game.

"We're back," said the father. "I'm taking off my socks. Your mother has got some snow on her scarf."

If there hadn't been so much tenderness in their voices, it would have been laughable.

"Mo and Milo are just behind," Father Asseldor continued. "Here they are. They're coming in. Mo is wearing that hat I don't like."

"It took a long time," Milo, the older brother, said. Sure enough, he was wearing a torn old hat. "But we're back. We won't go off like that again. I've got the maggot in the bag and a mushroom. Mo has put the mushroom on the table. Lila is getting out a knife to help him."

Mo and his sister did exactly as Milo narrated. Lila started chopping the mushroom into huge chunks, big as fists.

Father Asseldor went into the room next door, followed after a moment's discreet hesitation by Mo, the younger brother.

He found his father in the girls' bedroom.

What they called the girls' bedroom was in fact a larder. The room hadn't been used to sleep in since Lola, the youngest sister, had left. Lila slept alone in the living room now, in front of the fireplace.

Father Asseldor was busy moving a large grasshopper ham that was hanging from the ceiling. Mo came in, closed the door, and went over to him.

"What's wrong, my son?"

"We've got to leave, Father. We're suffocating here. We have to leave Seldor."

"All of us?"

"Yes," said Mo.

"We can't all leave Seldor — you know that."

"I know it's hard when this was your father's house, Dad."

"It doesn't matter about it being my father's house; I'm not the one who can't leave. You know who I'm talking about. If I could, I would already have taken you far away from here."

"We can take him with us," Mo said. "I've got an idea."

Milo burst in.

"Come and see!" he said.

His father and brother stared at him.

"Come right away!" Milo insisted.

They dropped everything and followed him.

Lila was standing in front of the window, with a folded piece of paper in her hand.

"It was just pushed under the door. Look."

"Again . . ." said Mo.

He took the letter and held it out to his brother.

Written in big letters was: FOR THE YOUNG LADY.

Milo unfolded the piece of paper and read out loud.

"'Meet me behind the aviary at midnight. . . .' I'll go myself and I'll slit his throat," Milo remarked to his sister.

"Stop it, Milo. Read the rest."

"'I want to help you. I know.'"

Father Asseldor tore the letter from Milo's hand and read it again.

"'I know.'"

In any other family, someone would have asked, "What does he know?" but this didn't even cross their minds. Here, they knew full well what nobody, absolutely nobody, was allowed to know.

Father Asseldor folded the message again. As usual, there was no signature.

For several months now, Lila had been receiving letters addressed to "the young lady." Her father had intercepted the first few before she'd seen them. But Lila Asseldor had found the little bundle of mail under the boxes of herbal tea.

"What's this, Dad?"

"They're . . . letters."

"Who for?" asked Lila.

"They're addressed to 'the young lady.'"

Mrs. Asseldor, who knew all about it, looked as embarrassed as her husband.

"Are you the young lady?" Lila had asked her father.

"I . . . I thought they were for your mother. . . ."

Gallantry can sometimes come in handy. Mrs. Asseldor wasn't exactly a young lady. She still looked young and was very beautiful, but she didn't try to hide her sixty-five years.

Lila read all the letters. They were very ardent and very clumsy. They talked about her eyes being as blue as flies, and her hair like fine noodles. A real poet . . . Some of them suggested a meeting. Others were columns of numbers. The author was doing his finances and ended with a final sum, which he underlined in red.

As you can see, miss, I am quite rich, which never hurts.

The letters kept on coming. Lila never replied.

Of course, Lila was less indifferent than she let on. When you're twenty and you live with your brothers and parents, when you've seen your little sister carried off by a brave young man, you're bound to feel something when someone invites you on a date—even if he's a big fat bug.

Lola, the youngest Asseldor daughter, had left several

years ago. A neighbor in the Low Branches, Lex Olmech, had come for her. It had all happened one night. Now they lived in secret somewhere very far away, with Lex's parents.

Mr. and Mrs. Asseldor had no regrets about this relationship, even if they missed their daughter. Lola had proved her love for Lex over a long period of time, and Lex had proved his affection and courage. The whole family knew that Lola was better off in Lex's arms than between the walls at Seldor.

But Lila's mystery suitor didn't inspire the same confidence. Grandfather Asseldor used to say to his daughters, "The ridiculous won't kill you, but watch out: it'll try to marry you. . . ." The author of the letters belonged in this category.

"I'm going to the aviary at midnight," said Lila.

She had a hard time convincing her family. Milo paced up and down the room. Mo sharpened his hunting dagger. Their parents were forced to admit there was a menacing tone in the most recent message and they needed to find out more.

Night fell early. They waited for the sounds of footsteps to die down in the farmyard.

"All clear," said Father Asseldor, spying out the window.

He fitted a wooden board over the windowpane. Mo removed the pot from the fireplace and doused the fire.

"We're putting out the fire. Mo has removed the soup

pot. We're coming." (Again this odd habit of describing every action out loud.)

Lila blew out the lamps. She left just one candle lit on the table. The two brothers were crouched in the fireplace, where they pulled out a board from the back.

"Come on, it's nighttime—you can come out now, Mano."

Mano Asseldor had been living, hidden behind the fireplace, for the last three years. For three years, he hadn't seen daylight. For three years, he had come out only at night, walking around the house a little, washing and eating, but before dawn he always had to go back inside that recess full of soot.

The family had hidden him there when he had escaped from Joe Mitch's Enclosure with Toby Lolness. He was only supposed to stay in the cubbyhole for a few weeks, but he had been trapped by the arrival of the soldiers stationed around the farm. Every exit from the garrison was guarded, the house was searched, and Mano was on the Green List.

The boy who emerged from the fireplace looked like a moth, with black powder on his cheeks. He stretched and uncurled his arms and legs, as if emerging from a long hibernation.

"At one point, I couldn't hear you anymore," he said.

"We warned you, Mano," his mother reassured him, taking him in her arms. "We had to go out for a few hours in search of food. We would never desert you."

"I couldn't hear you anymore," Mano repeated.

Milo put his arm around his little brother's neck.

"We'll get you out of here," he promised.

"I thought you'd left. . . ."

"No, Mano. We always come back. And we always talk to you as soon as we get in."

As they watched Mano eating, they told him about their day again. Then silence.

Mano never had anything to tell them about his day. Never.

Lila was skirting the wall. She wished the snow was still crisp and crunchy so she could hear any approaching footsteps, but she was walking through black sludge. She crossed the path, walked along the hedge, and came out near the old moss garden.

In the old days, there were thirty kinds of creeping moss in this garden. One that flowered only on New

Year's Day, another that produced delicious little beans, another that smelled like caramel. But now the bark had been scraped away and lichen was taking over.

At last Lila reached the aviary, where she followed the wire caging for a few paces.

"Turn around!"

Lila turned to where the order had come from. A lamp was being shone in her direction; it dazzled her.

"What are you doing here?"

Lila's eyes were gradually getting used to the light. She could now make out a face. It was Garric, the Garrison Commander.

"You're not allowed to come out at night," he stated.

By now, Lila was sure it was him.

Garric was the author of those letters. She recalled a few intense looks when she'd been walking through the farmyard. Now, alone in front of Garric, she wanted to run away, but she had to find out if he really did know . . .

"Good evening."

She chose her gentlest and most caressing voice, her musician's voice.

Garric lowered the lamp.

"I'm going for a little walk," she said.

Garric still didn't say anything. Few men would have been capable of saying anything faced with Lila's beauty. She stood there in her pale fur collar, her back against the aviary, her mittened hands gripping the caging. She studied the ground like a runaway who'd been caught, but every so often she stared Garric in the eye. Each

time she looked up, it made him step back. He was crazy about her.

"Aren't you going to say anything?" she asked.

He chewed on a few inaudible words and then said, "Will you come back?"

"Possibly, if you tell me what you want to say to me."

"Ah . . ."

Garric knew that he was running a risk. He had discovered that Mano was hiding out in the Asseldor house. He should have told Leo Blue about this. By keeping quiet, he was risking his own life. But the sound of Lila's breath was all it took to convince him.

"Come and see me tomorrow," he said.

At that moment, horns rang out in the night air. A voice shouted, "Here they are! They're coming. The last convoy's coming!"

Garric took a step toward all the noise. Lila followed him.

"Tell me what you wanted to say."

Flares were lighting up all around. Garric could feel Lila's hands on his coat. He wanted to disentangle himself. But she held tight. The garrison was waking up.

"Tell me," Lila begged.

"Go back home."

"Please . . ."

Garric stopped. He whispered, "Your house . . . From now on, we're going to search it at night too."

Lila let go of his greasy fur coat. The Garrison Commander repeated, "Come back tomorrow."

Lila ran toward the house. She hunched over, not wanting to be seen by the men now marching toward the aviaries.

"They've caught nine of them," they were saying. "It's the last convoy. The Grass people will stay for three days."

Lila walked into the living room and looked at everybody in turn, her parents, Mo, and Milo, and then she turned toward Mano. She didn't dare speak. Her breath caused the fur on her collar to flutter. She managed to blurt out, "They're going to search at nighttime too. You won't be able to come out at night, Mano."

Mano stood there in silence for ten seconds, then he let out a long cry that pierced the night.

The soldiers guarding the convoy of Grass people rushed toward the house when they heard the cry. They forced the door and entered the main room.

They stumbled upon a strange sight. The oldest

Asseldor son, Milo, was lying in the middle of the room, and his sister was sponging his forehead. His parents were kneeling at his side, and Mo, his brother, was blowing on the fire.

"He fell," explained his father apologetically.

"He fell," repeated his mother, red-eyed.

They searched the whole house. Garric stayed by the door, his hands behind his back.

That night, the soldiers didn't find anything.

Mano was curled up behind the fireplace.

7
The Low Branches

Leo Blue always traveled alone. He ate alone; he slept alone; he lived alone. The only company he would tolerate was his trustworthy adviser, Minos Arbayan.

Arbayan had joined forces with Leo at the start of his battle against the Grass people. He had introduced himself as a friend of Leo's father, El Blue. Arbayan hated the Grass people, who had killed El Blue. He wanted to help Leo protect the Tree from the Great Grass Threat.

But there was another reason for Arbayan's hatred of the Grass people. He felt guilty. He was the one who had urged El Blue to set out on his final adventure. Without him, El would never have traveled down the Trunk and crossed the Border on that fateful day when he was killed. Arbayan hadn't mentioned this to Leo Blue.

Leo admired Arbayan's pride. He knew about his peaceful reputation as a butterfly hunter. One day, eaten up by remorse, Arbayan had decided that he would take up arms after all; provided they helped the cause, he would no longer reject cruelty and violence. He had kept his colorful clothing and was recognized everywhere as the great butterfly hunter he had once been.

He had simply changed his silk nets for combat weapons.

Leo started running, chased by a disgusting smell. He had just passed alongside a weevil cemetery. The poor animals had died in an epidemic. There were only a few left now, and Joe Mitch looked after them better than the closest of his fellow beings.

Leo Blue had left the mud of Seldor and the gray atmosphere of the garrison behind him, setting off in search of something he had wanted to learn about for a long time. His desire was so strong that it woke him at night when he was sleeping in the Treetop Nest.

The Low Branches. The region haunted him.

He had only set foot there when rushing through on his way to the Great Border. And yet so many of the strands of his life passed through there.

Deep down, Leo Blue didn't believe that Toby was dead. The enemy doesn't die. He sleeps. He might wake up at any moment. Leo knew it was in the Low Branches that Toby would wake up one day. Perhaps he was still fast asleep there.

Leo arrived at Onessa in the middle of the day. He stopped a short distance from the Lolness family home, on the lookout for the slightest movement. So this was where Toby's family had spent their years of exile and where they had prepared their act of treachery.

He waited.

Strips of bark had been ripped from the roof, and a clump of black mushrooms blocked the door and front steps. Just as it had done everywhere else, the lichen forests had invaded the garden.

Leo didn't trust appearances. He grabbed a boomerang from his back and sent it spinning in the direction of the house. The weapon sliced through a window and disappeared inside the room for a second, before shattering the shutters and reemerging from another window. The boomerang came back toward Leo. He lowered his shoulder, and it slid back into its sheath without his having touched it.

Nothing had moved. The house was empty.

Leo went in.

There was a smell of old sheets washed in black soap. Leo touched the few objects that remained and lifted the curtain by the small bed near the fireplace. He spent a while in Sim's office. The drawers had been pillaged long ago, but a small piece of notepaper had fallen between the wooden floor slats. Leo managed to read the faded ink.

To do Monday
Play with Toby
Dance with Maya
A little more ❤
A little less brain

Leo recognized the handwriting. It belonged to Sim Lolness, Toby's father. He read and reread the words several times. He could hear the deserted house creaking.

Leo Blue crumpled the piece of paper in his hand. He mustn't show any signs of emotion. He got up and hurled Sim's chair against a small picture, which fell off the wall.

The round painting shattered on the floor. It was a portrait of Maya Lolness, drawn by Toby.

Leo left the house. His fear of betraying any weakness made him even more violent. He ran in the snow between dead branches and lichen thickets. He banished Sim's words from his mind. That crazy old professor was dangerous, as was his entire family.

Leo sped up.

An even stronger desire was driving him now: Leo wanted to see the branches where Elisha had grown up. By an extraordinary coincidence, his greatest enemy and his greatest love had lived in the same humid jungle region, a few hours apart.

Leo wondered if they had ever met.

The whereabouts of the Lee household in the Low Branches had been explained to him. But it took him two days to find it because the vegetation was dense and tortuous. Leo was able to move around with astounding agility. He could make it through certain passages by his arms alone, swinging from twig to twig for several minutes without ever touching the ground.

Leo's heart was pounding as he approached Elisha's house. Throwing caution to the wind, Leo walked straight in through the round door. Thoughts of his beloved Elisha swirled with thoughts of Sim Lolness's note, and of his former best friend, Toby. He surveyed the colorful drapes and eventually thrust his head into one of the faded mattresses, but he couldn't manage to cry. For a long time now, he had been a stranger to tears.

Leo lay on his stomach, listening to the sounds of the wilderness.

He didn't know that a long time ago Toby had spent his first night in the Low Branches in the home of Elisha and her mother, on that very same mattress. Nor did he know that Elisha had sobbed into it for weeks on end after Toby's mysterious disappearance.

Leo stood up. Why didn't Elisha want him? He would give her everything.

He left the colorful home.

If his heart hadn't been so full of anger and turmoil, he might have noticed a bluish haze rising from the hearth and that the embers in the fireplace were hot.

Someone was still living in the house.

Leo lost his way again before finding a path in a moss wood that snaked along a wide branch.

When he reached the top, he discovered the kind of landscape he had least expected to find at the heart of the Tree. It was extraordinary: a huge frozen lake surrounded by smooth bark beaches, overlooked by a snow-covered cliff.

A waterfall hadn't yet been caught by the ice and cascaded into a little pool of clear water. The rest of the lake was covered by a fine white carpet.

Leo made his way down. He wondered how the sun penetrated this far. He walked on the frozen lake, turning around to admire the beauty of his surroundings. One day, when it was all over, he would bring Elisha here. And that was a promise.

One day, when this is all over, I will come back here with Elisha.

Hidden two paces away, Toby Lolness was promising himself the same thing, when, all of a sudden, he saw Leo Blue standing on the frozen lake.

Toby recognized him right away, and a shudder ran through his body. He hid in the snow.

Leo Blue. There. Walking on Elisha's lake. How had he gotten there?

Elisha had fallen for him. She must be with him. Leo had won. These were Toby's immediate thoughts.

Toby was crouching on the cliff overhanging the lake. For several hours, he had been digging to force his way into the secret cave. There must only be a few fistfuls of snow left to clear now. It was the beginning of winter, and the sunny weather had softened the fine layer of snow that had formed. Toby knew that the answer lay in this cave. For the next few minutes, his life would hang in the balance.

Following an attack of vertigo, he had turned around to breathe deeply, and that was when he'd noticed the figure on the lake.

Now, half buried in the snow, he was watching.

Leo Blue was on his own and looked as if he was taking in the landscape for the first time.

Toby started to get his hopes up again. . . .

Leo didn't have the face of somebody who lived with Elisha. He didn't look like somebody who saw Elisha every morning, who watched her drink her milk from a bowl and saw the tip of her nose get covered in cream, or who saw her braiding her hair with one hand, faster than a spider spinning its web. He didn't look like somebody who could touch the butterfly powder that her green skirt left on his knees or who listened to Elisha's slightly husky voice, her tinkling laughter, her rustling footsteps, and everything else.

Leo didn't look like somebody who enjoyed all that, each day and for always.

If he was really that lucky, he would jump, he would dance, he would fly. He would make the ice melt, thought Toby.

For fun, Leo threw his boomerang. It brushed against the snow on the lake before heading toward the cliff, spinning very close to Toby. It followed the shore all the way around. Leo started to head back to the path again. The boomerang slid into the sheath on his back.

For a moment, Toby thought about throwing himself on top of Leo before he disappeared. He wanted to fight. But he realized he didn't know anything. "Forewarned is forearmed," his horrible grandmother, Radegonde Alnorell, used to say. Toby knew nothing, or very little, about the recent history of the Tree, so he needed to bide his time before acting.

Leo Blue vanished.

Toby let a few minutes go by before starting to excavate the snow again. Very quickly, the final layer gave way.

Toby entered the cave, covered in sweat.

All those months he had spent in this cave suddenly came back to him as a cruel memory. Fear, loneliness, silence. He stopped in the darkness, unable to go any farther. He closed his eyes and waited for his rising panic to subside.

Once he was sitting down, he grabbed his peashooter and put the tip on some wood shavings that he had scrabbled around for. He held the peashooter between his palms and feet, rolling it very quickly in the style of the Grass people. Flames appeared and he threw on other bits of wood gathered from around the cave.

When his eyes were warmed by the firelight, he looked up at the cave walls. The drawings were still there, as red as ever, just as he had painted them years before. Toby went over to the place on the wall where he had depicted Elisha, all that time ago. He was about to find out . . .

There she was, drawn in red ink, sitting on her heels. During his years in the Grass, whenever his memory failed him, Toby pictured this portrait in order to recall his friend's features.

He ran his hand over the painted face, then rested it on her eye.

The Tree Stone was there. It hadn't moved. Toby felt as if a ray of sunlight had entered the cave: Elisha hadn't betrayed him. He took a long deep breath.

Since the first days of snow, he had known that he would head straight for the lake. Miraculously, he had had a narrow escape from his collapsing trap on the Ring Road. The avalanche had carried him off, but the snow wasn't too deep at the start of the season. It was thick enough to soften his fall, but not enough to suffocate him.

Toby had groggily gotten to his feet. He had followed the convoy of hunters all the way to the gates of the Low Branches. He had dodged the terrifying Border Guards and found his country overrun by lichen forests.

The world had changed. The wood of the Tree was crumbling under moss, ferns, and snaking snow-covered ivy. The Tree was tired, and its lack of summer leaves meant that an abundance of weeds was able to spring up in full daylight. A hanging garden had sprung up in the branches.

Toby traveled through the landscape with his eyes wide open.

He hadn't gone by his house at Onessa, or by Elisha's, but had come straight to the cave before the snow blocked its entrance.

The Tree Stone was Elisha and Toby's secret. If it was still there, it meant there was still a chance that Elisha . . .

Toby's hand went instinctively toward the other eye in the painting. There was a small object pressed into the wood, just as the Stone had been on the other side. He removed it with his nail and walked over to the fire.

It was a translucent red shell. This time, Toby started crying. Three words echoed in his memory: *I'm coming back.*

Toby had given the tiny shell to Elisha when they were separated for the first time. He had let it drift to the surface of the lake, and she had bent down to scoop it up before drying it on her dress.

Elisha had given it back to Toby on his return, weeks later.

"I kept it with me all the time," she had said, blushing a bit. "I even called it 'I'm coming back.'"

She had shown Toby how she liked to look at the sun through the translucent red shell.

"I'd hold it in front of my eyes and say to myself, over and over again, 'I'm coming back.'"

Toby clutched the shell.

When Elisha had had to leave her home, long after Toby had disappeared, she had come up to the cave one last time and had pressed the shell into the painted eye. For all these years, her portrait above the lake had never stopped saying, "I'm coming back."

This hope continued to sparkle in Elisha's eyes.

Toby took the Stone and put it with the shell at the bottom of his peashooter quiver. He looked at the picture on the cave wall for the last time. It had just made him a promise.

Toby clambered down the cliff below the cave and skirted the lake to avoid leaving any tracks. He knew he shouldn't linger in the Low Branches. He needed to be quick, especially with Leo Blue in the region. Toby needed to find out where Elisha, Sim, and Maya were, and what fate awaited the captive Grass people.

He knew of only one free man who might be able to help him. Still free? He hoped so. Three years earlier, this boy had saved his life, as Toby had learned from Elisha's lips during his last winter in the Tree.

He was a woodcutter's son.

His name was Nils Amen.

Toby pushed his fur hat down on his head and set out.

What he hadn't noticed, not even for a moment, were two wild eyes staring at him from under the waterfall. Two eyes surrounded by long eyelashes and a strange face.

A woman was bathing in the cold water. Her loose hair floated around her. Her shoulders appeared and disappeared again under the surface. Her cheeks were slightly flat.

After Toby disappeared, she had quickly gotten out of the water and run toward her clothes, which were laid out on a twig. She'd only seen Toby from behind and hadn't recognized him in his hunter's hat. Those kind of men often roamed the region. She had to hide. Once her daughter had left, she had gone back to live in her old house and had stayed there in secret, without a single person knowing about it.

Her name was Isha Lee.

8
Night School

"Parasites! Don't talk to me about parasites!"

"I just wanted to say—"

Sim Lolness stood up solemnly and said, "There's no such thing as a parasite."

The professor was addressing about thirty students sitting solemnly in front of him. Most of them were over eighty. They were all dressed in brown pajamas and didn't exactly look like school children.

Some of the most influential characters from the Tree Council were gathered there: scholars and thinkers, in short, all the brains still alive between the Treetop and the Low Branches. They were prisoners of Joe Mitch, and they worked in the Crater.

In the back row, Zef Clarac and Vigo Tornett rubbed shoulders with Councillor Rolden, who was close to one hundred and three years old.

For several months now, at nightfall, after infernal days spent digging in the Crater, this brilliant group attended night school.

Joe Mitch had accepted Sim's proposal, despite having no idea what a school was. Of late, Mitch had been trying to go easy on his prisoner, because Sim had made him a promise. Namely, that Sim would surrender the keys to his famous discovery before winter was out. He knew that Mitch would take it out on Maya if he didn't keep his word.

Just the thought of knowing Balina's Secret at last was enough to make the Friendly Neighbor squeal with pleasure every evening.

As for the night school, Mitch had only imposed two conditions: no writing and no Grass people. The first condition didn't surprise Sim. Writing had been forbidden in the Tree for some time. Luckily, the spoken word and drawing can convey even the most complicated ideas.

But Mitch's second condition had given the professor a few sleepless nights. Dozens of Grass people were digging in another part of the Crater, which was separated by fencing and stakes. Sim was deeply interested in their fate. To his mind, the night school should include them too.

The professor ended up giving in to these two demands. It would have been as difficult to change Joe Mitch's mind as it would to swap the cigarette butt in his mouth for a piece of straw to chew on.

Sim found the building where he wanted to set up

the school. It was the former Weevil Keepers' hut. The
Crater had expanded so much that this hut was now
right above the precipice. High up and deserted, it towered over the depths of the mine.

It took only a few days for the school to open. There
were twenty subjects. Sim taught seventeen of them, and
the rest were divided between a few aging specialists.

On this particular evening, Sim Lolness was giving a
lecture entitled "Ladybugs Don't Have Trash Cans."

He was standing behind a large upturned wooden
crate that served as his desk. Next to him, brave Plok
Tornett, the grubber from the Low Branches, was
improvising as the professor's assistant. He took his tasks
seriously, wiping the big blackboard that Sim was drawing on, helping Sim with his experiments. Plok, who was
mute, was the youngest member of the group. He hadn't
spoken a word for at least sixteen years.

"Ladybugs Don't Have Trash Cans." Sim Lolness wanted to prove to his public that nature doesn't produce garbage. His presentation was brilliantly clear. Zef Clarac, who had forgotten how much of a dunce he'd been in his youth, was listening attentively. He thought it would be a good idea to raise his hand and offer a summary: "So basically, if I've understood this right, the parasites act as trash cans."

Hearing the word "parasite" threw Sim Lolness into a rage.

"Parasites! Vermin! I don't want to hear those words here, Mr. Clarac! Everybody is useful, and everybody depends on others."

He had concluded with his famous phrase "There's no such thing as a parasite."

Everybody was familiar with Sim Lolness's theory. He had revealed it for the first time when defending Nino and Tess Alamala in one of the greatest trials of the century.

The elderly night school audience had recognized Sim's allusion to the moving story of the Alamalas, who had frequently been accused of living like parasites. Nino was a painter. His wife was a dancer and a tightrope walker. So how could they be useful to society?

Theirs had been a tragic end. Deep down, the professor was convinced that they had died of these accusations.

For personal reasons, the Alamala story had affected Sim deeply. He cast a watery eye to his right.

Maya.

Sitting on a stool in a corner of the classroom, Maya Lolness was knitting. She had a scarf on her head and was wearing the same brown pajamas as everyone else. She sat bolt upright, her sleeves, which were too wide for her, falling like wings. The convicts' uniform looked more like haute couture on her.

For most of the time, Maya listened distractedly.

She knew all of these subjects by heart and mainly looked forward to old Rolden's history lessons. Sometimes she stopped knitting to watch these impressive characters reduced to slavery by a few imbeciles. The worst part was seeing them digging from dawn till dusk in order to destroy the Tree, which they had always served.

The night school had, however, given them back a little hope and dignity.

During those long days, Maya inevitably thought about Toby. She remembered him as a two-year-old, running around in their first house in the Treetop. The muffled sound of his feet in the hallway had never left her, and part of her still expected to see him push the door open and walk in.

At the time, she used to say, "The world belongs to toddlers." Now she knew that the world belonged to other people. Her son had been cast aside and devoured by this world. But Maya Lolness had decided to survive.

She and Sim always said, "We're living for three." Their existence had become all the more precious. They had to hold on.

Sim had secured a less exhausting job for Maya than

breaking wood with a pickax. She knitted socks for the guards. From the outside, these socks looked very comfy, but Maya had developed the "breeze stitch" especially for the occasion, which lets the cold and damp in but doesn't let the sweat out. Thanks to her, the guards always had frozen feet that stank of cheese.

Among themselves, the prisoners referred to this kind of indirect action as sabotage. It had started when one aged detainee, Lou Tann, an ex-shoemaker, produced clogs that were hobnailed on the inside and gave them to Joe Mitch's men.

Sim passed between the rows of students and stopped in front of Zef.

"Perhaps what I should say is that we're all parasites, Mr. Clarac. . . ."

Zef smiled. He was still as famously ugly as ever, but his humor and charm had grown with the years.

"When we understand the state our Tree is in," Sim continued. "The way the lichen is taking over, the layer of leaves that diminishes from spring to spring, bees becoming increasingly rare . . . all the signs are alarming. Perhaps, Zef, *we* are the parasites you've been talking about. In the old days, I used to say to my son —"

He stopped. His chin trembled a little. Maya's knitting needles had slowed down.

"One day . . . I said to my son," he went on in a fragile voice, "that the greatest discovery I ever made in my life was that dead leaves don't fall by themselves. They fall when they're pushed by the bud of the future leaf. It is life itself that pushes them. Life! But today, dear colleagues, the leaves that fall are not replaced."

The professor's voice broke. He knew that he was also speaking about his own life and about Toby. He and his wife would die one day, and the bud that should have been behind them, full of life and hope, the bud that would have pushed them aside, well, that bud was no longer there. Their son had disappeared.

In the passageway outside the room, two guards were doing their rounds. They came and went, passing in front of the windows.

"Will you excuse me for a moment, please?" asked the professor, and he took the glass of water that Plok was holding out to him.

In the silent classroom, two small taps were heard on the crate that functioned as the professor's desk. Instantly, Zef Clarac glanced over at the window, slid from his chair to the floor, and started walking on all fours under the tables, between his colleagues' legs.

It made for a very bizarre sight.

The others pretended they hadn't seen anything.

"Any questions?" Sim asked loudly.

Zef Clarac, still down on all fours, had reached the crate in front of the professor. A guard passed by the window without noticing anything.

Zef knocked twice on the crate. A trapdoor opened. A little old man emerged, covered in sawdust and wood shavings, and Zef went inside in his place. The trapdoor closed behind him. The little old man shook his clothes and crawled over to Zef's chair. He heaved himself up onto it. The old man answered the few glances that were cast in his direction with a smile that made his white mustache rise up.

The night school was no old men's folly. Since it had been set up, two months earlier, it had served as a cover for an enormous escape plan: Operation Liberty. Under the professor's desk every evening, the old men took turns digging. They had already triumphed over five centimeters of hard wood.

The hut had been chosen because it was above the Crater, a few dozen paces from the Enclosure. According to Tornett, who knew all about escaping, and by Sim's calculations, there were no more than two centimeters left to dig. In a few days, the tunnel would be finished.

Since Pol Colleen's escape a year ago, they knew this dream was possible.

Suddenly, Sim froze. All the students strained their ears.

A procession in the distance was making the floor vibrate. Guards ran past the windows. The floor was creaking. Sim glanced at his assistant. Plok Tornett's face had turned white. The great door opened, and a figure that was immediately recognizable appeared.

This figure nearly got stuck in the doorway. A wobble of his backside tore the door from its hinges and allowed him to enter.

Joe Mitch's dull stare covered the room. He was exhausted from having climbed all the way, and his jacket was stained with greasy sweat that looked like meat broth. From the smell that hung around him, he must have been wearing the "breeze stitch" socks knitted by Maya. His cigarette butt rolled around his lips.

He took three steps as wearily as if he were on a high-altitude hike.

Joe Mitch hadn't changed much over the past three years. His clothes were still the same, although he'd easily gained a gram. His rolls of fat were fully exposed around his belt. His chunky calves made his trousers ride up.

The skeletons in striped suits that followed behind him were none other than Razor and Torn, his two right-hand men. Neither of them had gained any wrinkles, since they barely had any skin left on their bones.

Joe Mitch went straight to the professor's desk. He put down a knee-size elbow, pushed aside two glass beakers on the crate, and looked at the dignified assembly before him. These gray heads, honest gazes, and intelligent minds represented everything he hated. He continued to face them for some time, using his finger to try to fish out the cigarette butt that had apparently gotten stuck in his gums.

Sim Lolness had stepped to the side to hide his assistant, Plok Tornett. Plok was trembling in his corner. Joe Mitch noticed him and pushed Sim out of the way.

"Plook," he said.

From the moment he'd first arrived at the Crater, Plok had been terrified of Joe Mitch. This clearly wasn't the same fear felt by the others: just the tiniest glimpse of the Friendly Neighbor, and he was beside himself. Even his uncle Vigo Tornett couldn't understand why Plok was quite so scared stiff. What dreadful memory did the sight of Mitch trigger?

Joe Mitch was thrilled to discover the effect he had on Plok. He had a great deal of fun making nasty faces and baring his teeth. He called him Plook. Occasionally he took him for a walk, on a leash. When Plok came back from these sessions, his teeth wouldn't stop chattering. He would lie limp in his uncle's arms. Plok, who was mute, would wake up shouting in the middle of the night.

Mitch took a step toward his toy. He brought his face close to Plok's. The boy wasn't far from fainting. His eyes rolled upward in terror.

"P-Pl-Plook!" Mitch exploded, grabbing him by the ear.

But Joe Mitch had no time to lose. He stood up, making his quadruple chin flap in the direction of one of his sidekicks.

Razor began translating: "The Friendly Neighbor is very interested in your school. He can see that you like to work."

"How kind of him," said Sim mischievously. "For us, work is a way of escaping from . . ."

Sim was half smiling. Razor coughed and added, "Professor, if you don't mind, I believe Mr. Mitch is asking you to follow us."

Maya looked at Sim, who reassured her with a wrinkle of his nose. Sim Lolness was often summoned in this way, and he always returned safe and sound.

He grabbed his beret and headed for the door. He didn't want these brutes hanging around here. They must not find out that Zef Clarac was missing. The professor wrinkled his nose once more at his wife, who returned the sign.

Mitch was starting to stir into motion, but he stopped in front of the desk. The floor felt slippery under his feet.

Joe Mitch bent down painfully. He collected a bit of

sawdust from the floor. His head was virtually touching the trapdoor to the tunnel.

Between his fingers was the fine dust that had come off the clothes of the old digger with the white mustache. Mitch raised his head to see if the sawdust could have come from the ceiling, then he sniffed.

A terrible silence hovered over the rows of students. Mitch was pressing the sawdust to his nostrils and frowning.

The only sound was the Friendly Neighbor's sniffing.

"It's fresh," Sim Lolness called out from across the room. "It's fresh sawdust."

Mitch was still sniffing his hand. When he was suspicious, his animal reflexes took over and his eyes rolled in their sockets.

Maya no longer dared to breathe. She sent her husband an imploring look.

Sim's face lit up. "Wood powder," he said, cleaning his glasses. "I . . . I grated some sawdust just now, to demonstrate to my colleagues the decomposition of dead wood caused by molds. A simple experiment. Are you interested in the subject, Mr. Mitch?"

Sim put his glasses back on his nose. He added, "A mold that eats wood. Does that remind you of anyone?"

A big smile passed from student to student. A smile of relief and pride. In a few words, Sim had just saved Operation Liberty and managed to find a subtle way of insulting the Friendly Neighbor.

Two guards pushed him outside. Mitch followed, gasping for breath.

Razor and his men led the professor to the Grass people's prison.

Each time a new convoy arrived, it was the same story. The most recent captives would be presented to Sim Lolness. Supposedly, the Grass person who declared that he recognized Sim would be set free immediately.

The aim was to prove that Sim was in league with the enemies from the Grass. Joe Mitch had long claimed that Sim had sold the secret of his invention to them. If a Grass person recognized him, this would provide official proof of the professor's guilt.

To Sim's great surprise, not one of the Grass people had ever succumbed to this blackmail. This fascinated him. It would have been so easy for them to pretend they recognized him. Who were these people who preferred to be prisoners than to lie? He himself might not have been capable of such integrity.

Sim felt friendly toward these intriguing people who kept saving his life.

On this particular evening, nine Grass people had arrived at the Crater. Among them was a ten-year-old boy.

Moon Boy was staring at the man who sat in front of him. He didn't look like the other hunters he'd come across since his arrival in the Tree, with that funny flat object on top of his head and see-through disks in front of his eyes. Behind those windows were handsome eyes with a bit of a dreamy, far-off look about them.

Each of the eight other Grass prisoners passed in front of the man with the disks on his eyes. One of the guards would say again, "Look harder, look harder! Just one word and you'll be able to go back home!"

Jalam, like the others, declared that he didn't know the man.

Then it was Moon Boy's turn.

Pretending to be nice, the guard stroked his neck and said, "It's your last chance, little one. I'm going to step back. I'll leave you for a minute to have a good look. Tell us if you recognize him. Otherwise we'll put you in a hole and you'll come out in fifty years, walking on your white beard."

But the young Grass boy didn't know the man in front of him, who was looking at him curiously. Moon Boy could feel how much goodness there was in his gaze. Despite being dreamy, it was clear and bursting with intelligence.

All of a sudden, the transparent disks steamed up. The man took off his windows, and his cheeks were shiny with tears. He checked that the guard wasn't listening before whispering, "Where did you find that, little one?"

Moon Boy didn't understand. The man repeated himself as quietly as possible.

"Tell me where you found what you're wearing around your neck."

The boy put his hand on the bit of wood carved by Little Tree. Was this a trap? Should he answer this question? He instinctively trusted the man.

The guard didn't leave him enough time. He headed back over and asked, "Well?"

"No," Moon Boy said quickly.

He was shoved roughly toward the others.

Sim Lolness didn't really believe in chance; he believed in life. But how had the emblem of the Lolness family ended up around the neck of this young Grass boy?

He rejoined his companions in the dormitory.

"Piece of cake!" he said as he walked in.

He always said this after he'd exerted himself. He could dig for three hours in the mine and still come out saying, "Piece of cake!"

Sim didn't tell Maya what he'd seen hanging around the young Grass boy's neck, but over the next few days, he felt a hope brewing. A tiny hope, almost invisible, that lit him up from inside.

"Are you all right, dear Sim?"

"Yes, Maya."

"Are you thinking about something?"

She always smiled when she asked that, because in more than thirty years, she'd never once seen him think about nothing.

"Possibly, Maya. Possibly."

"What are you thinking about?"

They were half starved, exhausted, frozen stiff, their hands were injured, and they were trying to sleep on the plank of wood they'd been given as a bed. And yet when they talked at night, they sometimes sounded as if they were still on their honeymoon.

Lou Tann, the old shoemaker who slept on the plank above them, was amazed by the Lolness couple.

Listening to them, Lou Tann sometimes thought of his own family.

When things had turned nasty for the Tree Council, Lou had tried to hide Councillor Rolden in his workshop. He had made this his job for a few days. Rolden lived in the shoemaker's leather storeroom.

The soldiers had turned up after a week.

"Smells like old clogs in here," the Patrol Chief had said.

Lou Tann had looked at his wife, who averted her eyes. In a flash, he understood.

"You?" he said to his wife.

The men dragged Rolden out from the lean-to, removed his shoes, and put them on his hands to make fun of him.

Lou Tann had been denounced by his own wife and by his three children. The two men were imprisoned in the Crater that same day.

"What are you thinking about?" Maya asked again in the dark.

"I can see some light, Maya."

She thought Sim was talking about a glimmer of moonlight on the dormitory ceiling. But there was only one light in Sim Lolness's mind.

The possibility that Toby was alive somewhere.

9

Woodcutter 505

Nils Amen was settled comfortably in his hut perched high above a clump of old lichen, looking at the huge map spread out before him.

Each day, the green gained more ground. Each evening, he had to add new lichen forests to his map. His one thousand woodcutters were no longer enough; he just kept on recruiting more.

Nils looked out of the window at the snow-covered cluster of lichen and remembered it was Christmas. He wiped his hand across his face.

Nils had succeeded in life. He'd made his fortune in just a few years, winning his father's confidence, his woodcutters' loyalty, and his territory's independence.

Fortune was on his side. The lichen had started to invade the branches, taking over the heart of the Tree. So the whole Tree relied on Amen Woods, which now brought together all the woodcutters.

Nils paid his men well. He had set them up, with their wives and children, in the kinds of remote villages that no longer existed anywhere else. People said, "Happy as a woodcutter," "A smile bright enough to chop wood," and "Plump as a woodcutter's baby."

It was widely recognized that the young Nils Amen looked after his own and resisted pressures from the Treetop Nest or Joe Mitch's Crater. Nils Amen didn't depend on anybody, but many depended on him.

Nils had succeeded in life. And like many others who have succeeded, he was all alone on Christmas morning.

"Can I go home now?"

"Of course," said Nils.

He had forgotten about this last man, who had come specially to sharpen Nils's ax.

"That boy came to see you again—woodcutter 505."

"Doesn't he have a name?"

Nils didn't like his woodcutters being called by their number.

"I told him you weren't here."

"Thanks. That's the third time he's stopped by," said Nils. "I don't have time. You can go now—close the door tightly. Merry Christmas. Give your wife a kiss from me."

"You too," said the man, heading out.

Nils smiled. He didn't have a wife to kiss.

He could have given his dad a kiss, but for the last few weeks, Norz had been working at the other end of the Tree, in a logging yard.

Norz Amen was a great support to his only son. It hadn't always been this way, but all he'd had to do was change the way he looked at Nils for his son to blossom and reach his full potential. Norz advised Nils and tried to pass on to him his obsession that Amen Woods remain independent.

Nils was the last in a long line of woodcutters. Some time ago, his father had betrayed the independence of Amen Woods in order to work for the great estate owners. At the time, he had worked for Mrs. Alnorell, Toby Lolness's rich grandmother. But now, like all those who have once made a mistake, Norz was ready to do anything to defend his newfound freedom.

His refrain had become almost tiresome. "Remember, Nils: you're either free or you're dead."

Norz adopted a stern expression when he said these words, but Nils acted like a saint and knelt down in front of his father, whispering, "Amen!"

The two men had learned to love each other.

Nils felt a draft. He pushed his hands into his pockets and looked at the big map of the Tree again. His father would be in a region at the top, celebrating Christmas with his friends.

Norz knew how to live.

Nils picked up a bowl and a paintbrush.

"There's work to be done."

"Yes," he said, "but I like working."

It took Nils a few seconds to realize that someone had just spoken behind him. If he had turned around, he would have seen a young woodcutter his own age, who had entered his office as if by magic. But he kept on looking at his map, drawing his green paintbrush over a vast region.

"I'm woodcutter 505," said the boy.

"I know," replied Nils. "Aren't you celebrating Christmas with your family?"

"No," said woodcutter 505. "You neither?"

"No. What do you want?"

"I wanted to say thank you and to ask for your help."

"Ask for the help first; you can thank me afterward."

"You already helped me, a long time ago."

"Maybe."

"You risked your life for me."

Nils Amen stopped painting. That . . . well, that had only happened once. Was it possible that—"Toby?"

"Yes, Nils."

Now, at last, he turned around.

Nils took in Toby's outfit, then burst into tears and fell into his friend's arms. They hugged, looking at each other every once in a while before immediately giving each other another hug. They couldn't stop laughing and shedding silent tears. So many months had gone by, so many years. . . . Each of them knew what he owed to the other.

Finally Toby said, "Now I understand why your wood-cutters like you so much, if this is how you greet them all."

Nils smiled and pushed Toby away. "Be quiet, 505."

He made his friend sit in front of him.

"You're wearing my men's uniform."

"They were looking for woodcutters. I wanted to see you. I got hired."

"How long ago?"

"Two days, if that."

"Tell me," Nils went on. "They think you're dead here. You must have something to say."

"Yes. I'm hungry."

Nils pulled on a rope that was hanging from the window. A basket filled with cold meats and sweet pastries appeared. Toby dived in with his hands and bit into a syrupy waffle.

Years earlier in a woodcutter's hut not far from here, while he was being chased by hundreds of men, Toby had enjoyed another meal thanks to Nils Amen. The menu had improved since then. . . .

"Who prepares this for you?" asked Toby, his mouth full.

"Friends."

"This tastes like the homemade food I grew up with."

Toby was thinking of the delicacies from Seldor Farm.

"Where's your home now?" Nils asked seriously.

Toby stopped chewing. He hadn't been able to answer that question for a long time.

"Tell me about the Tree," said Toby, changing the subject.

"What do you want to know?"

"Everything. Pretend I've come from somewhere else."

Nils looked at his friend. He certainly did come from somewhere else, that much was clear.

Toby's appearance had changed a bit. His hair was

longer and wilder. His shoulders didn't yet fill his new woodcutter's jacket, but his actions were powerful.

Nils started to tell the story of being reconciled with his father, the advance of the lichen forests, his small business taking off. . . . He said all this modestly, taking little credit and insisting a lot of it was luck. He explained the organization of his huge forests, how they were divided into different sections, about the woodcutters' villages and the calm prosperity of his line of work.

Toby listened carefully and watched Nils moving his hand like a butterfly over the map of the Tree, explaining the names of the main regions, the types of lichen, the difficulty of cutting wood in areas of bearded lichen, with its long trailing strands.

"So there you go," Nils finished. "It's not so bad. Life takes care of me."

Toby was silent for a while. He wiped the crumbs from his hands and fixed his eyes on Nils. "And what about the rest?"

"The rest?"

"Yes, the rest. The rest of the Tree. When you stick your nose outside your own woods . . ."

"Ah, yes. The rest of the tree. I don't think it's very good."

"You don't *think* . . . ?"

"I've . . . I've got a lot of work, Toby. I can't take care of everything."

Nils stood up. He went over to a small cupboard and took out a bottle.

"So you don't know anything?" asked Toby.

"I know *some* things."

"Tell me what you know."

"I know that the Tree isn't well. I know that your parents are in the fat lunatic's Crater. I know that the other dangerous madman controls the Treetop. I know that people everywhere are suffering because the world belongs to the reckless. I know all this, Toby, but I'm not the guardian of the Tree. I take care of those around me, and that's already a lot."

He served a gray-colored brandy in two little wooden goblets.

"It's *eau de Tree* from Usnay. It lifts the spirits."

Toby gently picked up the conversation again. "I know about your courage, Nils. It's thanks to you that I'm alive. But what I don't understand is how you can talk to me for so long about the Tree without mentioning the Grass people, or saying the names of Joe Mitch and Leo Blue. . . . "

"I take care of those around me," repeated Nils. "What about you? Where have you been? What have you done for the Tree?"

The hut was bathed in silence. All they could hear was the sound of small clumps of snow occasionally sliding off a lichen bough and falling to the ground. The two friends looked at the floor.

"Sorry," said Toby after a while. "I'm criticizing you for something I criticize in myself."

Nils looked like he was on the verge of saying something, but he checked himself and silence fell again. Eventually, he explained, "Everything you've just told me is what I think about every night. I don't sleep. I think about all that's wrong in this world. I think about your parents. I only saw your mother once, in the Treetop when we were little. For three years now, I've thought about her every evening. Every evening! But I lack the strength, Toby. . . . Where do we start?"

"That's the only question that matters," Toby told Nils. "Where do we start?"

"You look exhausted."

"The hotels haven't been up to snuff these past few months," said Toby, stretching.

"I may have something better to offer you."

Nils showed Toby the way. They climbed down a rope ladder and walked for an hour through the dark woods, snaking their way between moss creepers.

Toby noticed Nils's tricks to avoid leaving any trace. There was a secret path in the ivy with hidden routes and creeping hallways under the bark.

Later, they went into an area of sticky lichen that grew its leaves as high as a man.

"Are you taking me to the end of the world?" asked Toby, bending over.

"Yes. We're nearly there."

The forest was a tangle. Nobody seemed to have explored these branches for at least a century, and the bushes closed up again behind them.

They crossed a suspension bridge over a bark abyss, and then headed back once more into the woods. Suddenly, a white ball fell from the lichen arch overhead. Toby jumped backward, but Nils didn't have time to move out of the way. The ball covered his head and shoulders, and he shook himself to get rid of it. Toby thought it was a lump of snow.

Sure enough, his friend exclaimed, "Snow!"

But hands and feet had just poked out of this white bundle, as well as a head with two eyes.

"Snow, let go!" Nils Amen called out again.

He caught the living ball by its feet and threw it into the real snow.

It was a little girl, three years old, who was microscopically tiny and wearing a cape of thick white silk. Hopping mad, she made a cloud of snow fly up behind her and disappeared.

When the cloud of white dust settled again, Toby wondered if he hadn't been dreaming. But Nils confirmed what he'd seen. "That's Snow. The terror of Amen Woods."

A few moments later, they saw her at the door to a house covered entirely by lichen bushes. Snow was sitting on the back of a young woman. Both of them watched the approaching visitors.

"The little one told me you were on your way with company."

The woman didn't recognize Toby at first, but he exclaimed, "Lola!"

He hadn't forgotten Lola Asseldor's beautiful face.

"Toby?" she asked, as if talking to a ghost.

She touched his head to make sure he was really there, in the flesh, in front of her. Snow couldn't take her eyes off the new arrival.

Just then, Lex Olmech appeared at the door. Little Snow went from her mother's back to her father's shoulders. Toby embraced the whole family.

Lola, the beauty from the Ladies' Pond! And Lex, the miller's son from the Low Branches! Memories of Seldor Farm, of the Olmechs' Mill, and of the prison at Tumble jangled inside Toby's head. He looked at tall Lex, his wife, their little Snow, and then at Nils Amen.

"He's the one who lets us stay here," said Lex, pointing to Nils. "Nobody knows this house even exists. My parents live with us. And this is our daughter. . . ."

Toby noticed two shadows inside the house. He went in and greeted Mr. and Mrs. Olmech.

A long time ago, this couple had betrayed him. One

look at their faces was enough to see they weren't the same people today. Mrs. Olmech knelt at Toby's feet.

"My little one. My little one . . ."

Toby tried to make her get up, but it took the combined strength of the three other men to get her on her feet. She kept on saying, "My dear little one . . ."

Everybody was laughing tenderly to see her so emotional.

"Mom, don't let the Christmas pudding burn!" said Lex, knowing this was the best way of getting his mother to disappear into the kitchen.

Toby surveyed the table in all its finery. It was that magic Asseldor touch, capable of putting on a feast at the end of the world. And in the great tradition of Seldor, places had been set for the two visitors, even though they hadn't been expected.

Toby glanced at Nils. Earlier on, to counter Toby's accusations, his friend could have defended himself by explaining about this family he was hiding in the depths of his woods. . . . He hadn't said anything.

"I take care of those around me," Nils had simply repeated. His heart must be as big as a banquet table to hold all those people.

It's hard to say what makes a party unforgettable. An unforgettable party is a mystery that can't be manufactured.

But among this small group of people hidden deep in Amen Woods, there were a thousand ingredients to turn

a meal into something magical: parents, grandparents, a little girl, a friend whom everyone had given up for lost, good bread, absent friends and family in their hearts, a reconciliation, a fire in the hearth, somebody who'd been expecting to spend Christmas all on his own, snow outside the window, the fragile emotion of happiness, Lola's beauty, wine that slipped down with ease, shared memories, and black pudding.

It's amazing what you can fit inside a small room that's not even big enough for a ladybug to stand up in.

Toby now understood where the basket of provisions which Nils had shared with him came from. During the meal, they told him how the rest of the Asseldor family had stayed on at the farm to protect Mano. So Toby found out what Seldor had turned into and what had become of the whole Tree.

The people from the Heights and the Branches were living in dread and poverty. They were grouped together in the former Welcome Estates, which were protected by ditches and walls against dangers that didn't exist. Close to Joe Mitch's Crater, long lines of wretched people came to beg for a scrap of sawdust to make into revolting soup.

Pol Colleen hadn't been lying. The branches were in an alarming state. The timer was going backward, and the countdown had begun.

After putting a stethoscope to the Tree, any reasonable doctor would have said, "This is looking serious. You have to stop everything. Rest for fifty years; watch the clouds go by. And then come back and see me after that."

When Toby found himself alone in front of Lola—the others had gone out to watch Snow ice-skating on a frozen stream—he dared to say, "I wanted to ask you . . ."

Lola smiled. She knew what he wanted to find out about. She didn't even wait for the end of the question.

"He came to get her. . . ." she said, looking sadly at Toby. "We were all at Seldor. Leo Blue came to get her. . . ."

Outside, they could hear little Snow laughing.

"Elisha and her mother were living with us," Lola continued. "Mitch's men had destroyed their worm beetles. So they came to seek refuge at Seldor. One day . . . One day, Leo Blue turned up with three soldiers to take her. He had only met Elisha once on the slope of the Grim Branch, an hour from the farm. There was nothing we could do. The next day, her mother, Isha, left too, unaccompanied. We don't know where she went to hide. . . ."

"But what about Elisha? Where is she now?" asked Toby.

"Lex says she's in the Treetop. There's a lot of talk about the Nest. . . ."

"The Nest?"

"Leo Blue lives in the Nest. She's almost certainly up there with him."

Toby glanced over at the door. Nils was standing there. He had heard everything. He knew Elisha by name, as the girl who Blue had found in the Low Branches. But until now he hadn't known that anything linked her to Toby. . . .

Lola and Nils exchanged a faint smile when they saw their friend's shiny eyes. Toby was the only one in the room who didn't realize he was in love with Elisha.

At the end of this special day, Nils headed off alone. He arrived at the foot of his hut during the night. When he opened the door, he saw traces of snow on the floor. Someone had been here while he was away.

Nils lit a lamp. There was a man in his armchair, sitting in front of the big map of the lichen forests, with his back to Nils.

"Where have you been?" asked the man.

"It's Christmas," answered Nils.

"Today?"

"Yes, today."

"Ah . . ."

"I was with some friends," Nils went on.

"My aunt never liked Christmas. I used to live with her when I was little, so I didn't often celebrate it. But I know that woodcutters like to keep traditions alive. . . ."

The man turned toward Nils. It was Leo Blue.

"I was passing by," he said. "So I climbed up."

Nils looked at him without moving. Leo's winter outfit had been specially commissioned by him and was made from the black fur of a hornet's belly. The window was battered by snow, and the wind let out high-pitched shrieks around the hut. It was as if whining children were throwing snowballs against the windowpane.

"I told you not to come here," whispered Nils Amen. "We mustn't be seen together."

They shook hands.

Toby soon settled into the house with Lola and Lex. For the time being, even if he'd wanted to leave, he'd have had to take Snow with him, because the little girl clung to his neck and wouldn't let go under any circumstances.

Toby was happy in this refuge, lost in the woods. He liked the warmth of this family around him and knew that he could sleep here when he wasn't at work.

His job as woodcutter 505 remained key to his plans. He didn't want to disappear into the woods forever. He knew that it was only by spending time with the people in the Tree that he would be able to build on his plan.

10
The Visitor

Elisha was breathing in the sweet smell of pancakes. She could see the colorful drapes and mattresses, the curves of her home in the Low Branches. She was alone, except for a shaft of light that was being cast through the open door to form a pool on the floor.

Suddenly, fine particles of golden dust flew and spun around the beam of light, as a scorching whirlwind from outside spiraled around the walls. *It's Toby,* she thought, trying to walk over to the door, but the wind was too strong for her.

Then she felt a hand touching her arm.

Elisha woke up in a flash. Without opening her eyes, she rolled up into a ball, fast as a spider under attack. She balanced on her heels and suddenly uncoiled, springing half a millimeter off the ground and crashing down on her assailant, forcing his arm behind his back.

"Not teeth, miss. Don't smash my teeth."

Elisha finally opened her eyes.

"It's me; it's Clot. Don't smash my teeth—they're new."

"Clot?"

"I was bringing you pancakes."

The smell of pancakes . . . that's what had inspired her dream.

"Sorry, Clot. And thank you for the pancakes."

"My pleasure, miss, but it is I who is greasily yours."

Good old Clot. His flowery language wasn't always as accurate as it could be.

"I thought . . . What time is it?" stammered Elisha.

"Midnight."

"It's cold."

"Might you be in a position to let go of my arm, if I'm not abusing you?"

Elisha laughed and let go. She hadn't even noticed that Clot had spent the first part of their conversation with his forehead touching the ground. She took a pancake and folded it in four. They were chunky pancakes, as thick and dry as a bad book, but Elisha wanted to pay homage to her guard's culinary skills.

Elisha had a soft spot for this soldier, having been reunited with him on her arrival in the Nest. Clot had immediately recognized the girl who had caused him so many problems in Tumble prison. But he was also grateful to her for introducing him to the joys of language and refinement. So he didn't let on to anybody that he already knew her.

Elisha insisted that it be Clot, and nobody else, who brought her meals and looked after her. This funny character's fantastical speech made her laugh out loud.

Unfortunately, she had explained to him that you shouldn't turn your back on a lady. Since that day he always walked backward while in the Egg, stumbling over every obstacle. He would try to find the exit by groping the wall behind him. Elisha would say, "To your right! Left!" to guide him. And when he banged his head on the shell, she had to stifle her laughter.

She had fun taking expressions such as "Putting your foot in it" and "So easy you could do it with your eyes closed" or "Head in the clouds," and deliberately mixing them up in front of him.

And, seeing as he repeated everything she said, this

led to him making confessions such as "You know me, miss, I'm a bit of a dreamer, always putting my feet up my nose and my fingers in the clouds. . . ."

He would say this fluttering his eyelashes, head tipped back. It was rather touching.

Elisha continued eating her cardboard pancakes.

"Would you like some?"

"No, thanks," said Clot.

"Still on your diet?" Elisha smiled.

For some time now, Clot had considered himself to be a bit chubby in the knee area. He had admitted to Elisha that he went on diets.

"No. This time it's my teeth."

"Your teeth?"

"I got new teeth."

"What are they made of?"

"Bread crumbs."

"I noticed your elocution. Bravo."

Humble Clot started blushing. "You smatter me too much about my speechiness," he said gratefully. "I also wanted to warn you: He's back."

Elisha finished off her third pancake as if she hadn't heard anything. But Clot didn't give up. "The boss is back. He's with the young stranger who came this summer. Without meaning to speak out of brine, I think there's something going on. . . ."

"Whatever," she said. "I don't care about the boss."

"I get the impersonation that you don't like him."

"You've very observant, dear Clot," Elisha remarked.

Clot made a humble face.

"I'm going to sleep," said Elisha.

She lay back down. Clot didn't move. In the end, Elisha had to get up again.

"Anything else?" she asked.

Clot clearly felt uncomfortable. He was tapping his bread-crumb teeth with his fingernails. "I . . . Perhaps I can collect your plate?"

Elisha shot him a dark look as she took out the plate, which she had hidden in her nightshirt.

"You've got eyes in the back of your head, Soldier Clot."

"I like to be fernickety," he said, squirming with satisfaction.

He took back the plate she'd been counting on converting into sharp pieces to give herself a winter haircut or for her next escape. Elisha lay down again on her mattress.

Clot drew a little closer.

"Don't move," he said. "I'm taking my key that you've slipped under the mattress."

Elisha was having fun in her corner. Every evening it was the same charade.

"And what else?" she grumbled. "Do you want your laces too?"

"Exactly so. Gladly. They must have led me astray yesterday."

Elisha removed two black shoelaces, which she'd hidden beneath her clothing. Behind his comical manner,
this guard was scrupulous to the last degree.

"You'd be better off wearing your slipperties," she
said, lying down again. "Then you wouldn't have to worry
about laces."

It was Elisha who had introduced Clot to the delights
of slippers, by giving him a pair that she had made herself. He called them slipperties, and he adored them.
Recently, he hadn't worn them so much because he was
wary of robbers.

"They make people jealous. . . ." he announced with
satisfaction.

Clot tidied his laces away into his pockets.

"Perfect. I've got it all now. Tip-top. Good night,
miss."

He walked backward as far as the door, banged his
head, lost his balance, and exited, tottering.

A few steps away, on the other side of the footbridge, the East Egg was lit up. White steam emerged from the bath and spread over the ground. A delicate smell of bud oil filled the room. Old Arbayan was standing at a distance, with the steam licking the soles of his feet and a serious expression on his face.

"You know how much I trust your intuition."

"I know, Arbayan," said Leo, with the water up to his chin.

"I'm just asking you to be careful. This boy came to see you six months ago, offering his help. That's what I call a 'lucky coincidence.' I'm wary of him. For years, he ignored you, and now all of a sudden here he is!"

"He's got a thousand woodcutters taking orders from him."

"Exactly."

"We need him."

"But does he need us?"

"Yes," said Leo. "Who doesn't need us?"

Minos Arbayan frowned. He looked at his boss in the pigeon-claw bathtub. The adviser took a step toward the lamp. He let a corner of cloth fall on the glowworm's cage. The light dimmed softly.

Sometimes Arbayan wanted to leave, to set out in search of his butterflies, to drop this horrible battle. He didn't like the mediocrity of those around him.

At least Leo Blue wasn't mediocre. He was crazy but

gifted, and Arbayan had signed up because of him. The others were all cowardly, stupid, and rough.

"I'm voicing my concern, because I'm always honest with you," he told Leo sharply. "When I say to one of my men: 'Uncover that glowworm, because it's dark,' I know perfectly well that it isn't actually a worm. But I want to keep things simple; I want to be understood. I know as well as you do that what everybody calls a 'glowworm' isn't a worm at all. It is, in fact, a 'coleopteran,' or beetle. But I degrade myself and say 'glowworm,' like an ignorant person, in order to be understood by ignorant people. With you, Leo Blue, I use real words, just as I did with your father, long ago. With you, I don't lie. And the truth of the matter is, I don't trust the way this Nils Amen has become your friend."

Leo had been completely still while he was listening. Now he dunked his head in the water and disappeared for nearly a minute. When he reappeared, his face showed no sign of breathlessness.

"You keep on telling me what you think fit to tell me, Arbayan. And I'll do what I think fit to do. Leave. Go and get me Nils Amen from his room."

Arbayan bowed before his boss and left. Leo kept on thinking for several minutes, in the warmth of his bath.

He had taken this pigeon-claw bath from one of the ruined houses pillaged by his men. The claw had been filed down, and its horn shape was so white, it was almost luminous. Eventually, Leo stood up. He could

sense someone waiting outside. He took a thick towel and wrapped himself in it.

"Enter," he said.

Nils Amen appeared.

"I was just thinking about you," Leo said. "You sought me out this summer. You suggested a secret alliance between Amen Woods and the Nest. . . ."

"Yes, I think we'll be stronger that way."

"You weren't always of this opinion."

"A child listens to his father. Previously, my father, Norz Amen, rejected the idea of an alliance. But today . . ."

"Yes?"

"Today I've learned to think for myself."

"Your father remains an obstacle."

"Don't worry about my father. We just have to make sure he doesn't know anything about our agreement."

"Normally," warned Leo, "I destroy any obstacles."

Nils shuddered. "Like I said, I'll take care of my father," he repeated coldly.

Leo went over to a table where his two boomerangs had been placed on a square of cloth. He took one in each hand and began sharpening them against each other. They resembled two dangerous knives, twenty thumbs long, in the shape of an upside-down V. Leo made the blades vibrate as he ran his finger along them. He put them back down on the table.

"And now you're offering me this new kind of assistance."

"If you need me."

"Why would I have brought you here if I didn't think you could help me? This time it's about what matters most to me and is most secret."

"I know."

"How do you think you can change her mind about me?"

Nils didn't answer the question. He took Leo by the shoulder and said, "We aren't always as others think we are. That's what I'll say to her."

The next day at noon, Elisha noticed the return of the Shadow on the top of the Egg.

The Shadow . . . The young girl prisoner couldn't remember the last time she'd seen it—a month ago, perhaps? She was happy to be reunited with its reassuring presence.

Elisha knew she wasn't the only one to have come

across it. Clot had said that everybody was afraid of this mysterious shape that roamed about in the Treetop. Recently, to explain the Shadow's lengthy absence, a guard had boasted about having killed it and claimed it was a black bloodsucking spider. But today the Shadow was back. The guard had lied.

When Arbayan entered Elisha's room, the Shadow remained flattened against the shell. The old butterfly hunter stood stiffly in his handsome uniform. He didn't look happy.

"Somebody has been given permission to speak with you, miss."

A young man entered behind him. He had a gentle face with fine and delicate features. He looked pointedly at Arbayan, who understood that he should leave them alone. Elisha was crouched at the bottom of the Egg, against the wall.

Arbayan exited, teeth clenched.

The visitor ran his eyes over the large room. He didn't appear to be paying Elisha any particular attention.

"My name is Nils Amen."

Nils. Elisha recognized this name. A long time ago, someone named Nils had saved Toby's life. What could a friend of Toby's be doing here? Elisha felt her breath quickening. She glanced to check if the Shadow was still there.

For his part, Nils Amen felt as if he was losing his balance.

So this was her. Elisha.

He thought of Toby, hidden in his moss forests far below. Toby's two friends were face-to-face today. Nils and Elisha.

But how had Nils Amen managed to become close enough to Leo Blue to approach the boss's fiancée all alone?

It had all started one summer's morning, six months earlier.

Nils was about to leave the Lower Regions where thirty of his woodcutters had just chopped down a colony of lichen that was threatening Joe Mitch's Crater.

The woodcutters from Amen Woods would agree to any job, provided it didn't involve shaking Mitch's sticky paw or Leo Blue's cold hand. Nils was thinking about only one thing: providing work for his men.

The woodcutters had therefore sawed up several centimeters of dense thicket, and great parasols of cut lichen were strewn across the path that led to the Crater. It was June, and it was hot. The lichen was dry and light.

When Nils heard the thunderstorm rumbling, he knew that everything was about to change.

Lichen has the special property of drying out in the sun but springing back to life at the first drop of rain. This was what Sim Lolness called anabiosis: an incredible capacity to adapt according to the climate. Nature is a magician. In the rain, the lichen soaks up water and regains its color, but it also becomes sticky and untransportable.

If the path to the Crater wasn't cleared before the storm, then the access would be blocked for several days. The woodcutters started moving the gray mossy branches. There was at least a day's work here, but the rain was only a quarter of an hour away.

Nils paused for a moment or two. He could see only one solution, and it went against all his principles. Warned by another roll of thunder, he realized he had no choice.

So he sent one of his men to ask for help from the Crater.

Moments later, the woodcutters saw the heavy door to the Enclosure swing open. They heard voices and the sound of whips being cracked. A dozen guards surrounded a misshapen troop. Those who strayed from the group were shoved back into place with sticks.

Nils soon found out that these weren't animals.

"The Grass people . . ." he whispered to his men in a voice choked with emotion.

There were dozens of them on the branch, all huddled against each other. One of Mitch's soldiers came over to speak to Nils. "We're going to help you. It'll all be over in an hour."

"Too late," said Nils. "It's raining. You won't make it. Give these people some shelter."

Nils thanked the sky for sending the first drop. He didn't want to see a people already reduced to slavery suffering even more.

The soldier flashed him a grim smile.

"Are you saying I'm a liar? I said an hour. And it'll be an hour."

"Leave it," Nils repeated. "We'll handle this in a few days, when it's dry again."

"Are you going to keep on insulting me?" asked the thug. "You see if I don't keep to my promises."

He let out a wild shout. The whips started whistling again and the thunder rumbling, as the rain came down twice as hard. And in this hellish atmosphere, the Grass people set to work.

It didn't even take an hour. Between whippings and shouting, the horde of Grass people achieved the impossible: moving hundreds of trunks, as soggy as sponges. Those men who fell were shoved to their feet again. There was no letup in the downpour. Anyone who slowed down got kicked, as together they waded through the green mud that was streaming off the lichen.

Nils noticed a youth who had fallen to the ground: a boy with dark eyes that didn't appear to move. Another young Grass person rushed over to help him. The lash of a whip came stinging across his back, but he continued to try to coax his friend back on his feet, using small reassuring gestures.

Nils guessed that the boy with the unmoving eyes was blind.

Before leaving the Crater, the triumphant soldier came over to Nils Amen.

"If you need help, we're here. All you have to do is ask. They call me Tiger."

The Grass people and the guards disappeared behind the big gate.

As soon as they were out of sight, Nils collapsed in shame and disgust, his face in his hands.

"Mr. Amen?"

A young woodcutter tried to help Nils get up.

"I'll be all right," Nils answered, leaning on the bark.

Back in his hut, Nils had locked himself up for four days.

So this was the independence and freedom his father boasted to him about. . . . Close your eyes; don't see anything; let others suffer at the edge of the forests.

As a result of being hemmed in by other people's prisons, Nils Amen's freedom had become a dark cell.

Nils knew now that he had to fight, but he also knew that you don't attack Joe Mitch or Leo Blue head-on. You don't rise up before them, ax in hand.

Nils was familiar with the traditional woodcutters' recipes for destroying old lichen stumps. You have to attack them from within, by piercing the middle and sliding the acid inside. Poison the heart of the stock.

From that day on, Nils only had one aim: to win Leo Blue's trust, in order to get inside his system and destroy it.

Now Nils Amen was standing right in front of Elisha, and he was staring at her.

She hid her hands in her sleeves. Her hair was very short, and she didn't allow any sign of fear or surprise to cross her face. Nils wondered what this little bundle of courage was made of. *Where does she come from,* he wondered. *Where do girls like her grow?*

He understood Toby's feelings for her.

On Christmas evening, before climbing up toward the Treetop Nest with Leo Blue, Nils had hurriedly gone back to Lola and Lex's home.

He had spoken with Toby, telling him everything. His big secret. The false friendship that he was gently building with Leo Blue.

"I wasn't expecting to tell you about it," Nils had said. "It's my way of fighting back. Danger is something you don't share. Nobody knows about this. Not even my father. But when I found out that . . . that you knew Elisha, I thought I might be able to do something for you two. . . ."

Overcome, Toby had charged Nils with speaking to the young female prisoner on his behalf.

Standing before her, Nils only had one wish: to tell Elisha that Toby was alive, that he was there in place of his friend, that nothing was lost, that life would flow again in the branches.

Up on high, the Shadow was motionless.

It was the figure of a young man, balanced above the arch of the Egg, hands firmly on the shell. There were two boomerangs on his back.

The Shadow of the Tree.

For months now, he hadn't been able to find any

other way of approaching Elisha and weaving something between them.

Something . . . It didn't have to be much. A hint of mystery and intimacy. Anything rather than indifference. He had invented the Shadow of the Tree in order to become Elisha's secret.

At the top of the Egg, Leo Blue was straining his ear, because Nils Amen was about to speak.

Sure enough, Nils opened his mouth to tell Elisha everything. But his eyes came to rest on a circle of sunlight at his feet.

It was midday, and the sun was at its highest point in the sky. The hole in the top of the Egg allowed a perfectly drawn ray to be projected onto the floor.

In this splash of light, a shadow could be seen. It was the profile of a face.

Somebody was listening to them.

Nils swallowed his desire to be sincere.

"Miss, I want to talk to you about Leo Blue. It's my belief that you're mistaken about him."

Elisha's heart dropped.

For a moment, she had thought she'd found a friend.

11
Freedom Music

The smooth-skinned ganoderm is a crescent-shaped mushroom that grows on the bark of the Tree. It forms pleasant terraces with springy floors that put a bounce in your stride.

A long time ago, children would go to the ganoderms to play funnyball on Sundays, lovers would have dates on them, and other people would go to them to dream about their childhood and lost loves.

In *Mushrooms and Ideas,* a slim book you wouldn't be able to get ahold of now, Sim Lolness revealed that each day, as the ganoderm is trampled underfoot, it scatters thousands of millions of billions of spores. The spores are like seeds, all of which should give birth to another mushroom. In theory, you could wake up each morning in a Tree covered in ganoderms. A thousand million billion mushrooms every day. After a week, you could make mushroom soup as thick and wide as the universe.

And yet, strangely, these mushrooms remain rare. The spores get lost in nature. Sometimes it takes years for a ganoderm to produce a second mushroom.

Sim Lolness concluded his book with that curious fact. He claimed that new ideas were a bit like mushrooms: very few of them reproduce.

Nils Amen's revolt could have served as an example for the professor. By being the first to rebel, Nils was changing the face of the Tree. He might sow the good seed of freedom all around him. But it would take a long time for a second person, lower down in the branches, someone who didn't even know him, to take a step in the same direction.

This second mushroom was Mo Asseldor. He was the second son on Seldor Farm.

His story began on Christmas night, during a silent concert.

Ever since they had been banned from playing music, the Asseldor family would gather from time to time in the main room, to play in silence. Each would take his or her instrument: drum, chime, clarinotty, and chelloh . . . Mr. Asseldor always set the rhythm by tapping his foot, and the concert would begin.

The Asseldors knew the music so well, they didn't need it to sound in order to hear it. The bow didn't touch the strings of the chelloh. No air passed through

Lila's clarinotty. Mrs. Asseldor sang without making any noise. The words could be read on her lips.

> *My homeland is a leaf that's died,*
> *Carried off to a world unknown.*
> *Why stay to dance*
> *On a snowy bare branch?*
> *My homeland is a leaf that's died. . . .*

The music was heartbreaking. Lila closed her eyes while she played, and tall Milo had tears down to his neck.

The Asseldors played only tragic melodies now. No more dawn songs or lullabies, dances or serenades.

Mo was suffocating under the weight of all this despair. He didn't recognize his family anymore. Something had disappeared from this house that held so many happy memories.

Mrs. Asseldor continued mouthing the words of the song. There was another couplet that was even sadder, comparing their branch to the gallows. Not exactly a barrel of laughs.

Mo's rebellion began with a silent false note.

Father Asseldor interrupted the orchestra.

"What's going on?" he asked.

Even when it was silent, a false note played in his presence made him feel out of sorts.

"I'm asking you, what's going on!"

"Sorry, Father," said Mo.

"All right . . . Let's pick up again. . . ."

They started playing, but after a few seconds, Mo came unstuck once more.

"Stop playing if you're tired."

"Yes, I *am* tired."

Suddenly Mo took his chelloh and broke it in two.

His brother, his sister, his mother and father all looked at him.

"Do you know what we look like?" asked Mo. "Ghosts. This isn't a farm anymore; it's a haunted house. No noise, no light . . ."

"But if it means that we can stay alive . . ." said his father.

"Alive? Who's alive here?"

Mo pointed to the fireplace, which poor Mano was hiding behind, only coming out twice a day.

"You've even buried one of us alive."

Milo, the eldest son, rushed over to his brother and knocked him down.

Lila tried to separate the fighters.

"Stop!" ordered Mrs. Asseldor.

The two boys broke it off. They had bloody noses.

"What else do you want us to do, Mo? You're speaking selfishly, only for yourself. But what do you want to do? You know the situation very well."

Yes, he knew. He knew that their family had been caught in a terrible trap. The house could be searched at any moment of the night and day, which meant that Mano risked being found. As for poor Lila, she was the victim of the worst blackmail ever. Garric, the Garrison

Commander, had found out about Mano and was abusing this knowledge to secure meetings with the beautiful Lila. The day before, he had kissed her hand, and she had come back into the house trembling all over.

"There are times when you have to risk everything," said Mo.

He was trying to knock some shape back into his hat after the fight.

"Look, if I stake my hat in a bet, I know I risk losing it. If I lose it, I'll be rather sad because I'm fond of my old hat. But for all of us here, what's at stake is our unhappiness. We've got nothing to lose. If we win, we'll be happy. If we don't, all we have to lose is our unhappiness. We have to try to get out of here."

The family had listened attentively to Mo's reasoning. It was true they had nothing left to lose other than their unhappy life of recent years. But they couldn't help remembering the joyous feasts they had held at Seldor, the hunting season in autumn, the dress competitions between sisters and mother, the honey harvest, concerts in the snow, and everything else. They were still afraid of losing all of that, even though it had already been lost, long ago. There's nothing we defend as valiantly as that which we've already lost.

"Lola has left with Lex. Some of us will be able to join them. We have to try to get away. It's not the old bark walls that make Seldor what it is, but joy and freedom. And there's none of that left."

"What about Mano?" his mother asked him.

"Mano will leave too. Just give me a few days."

The next day Mo repaired his chelloh. It was a handsome eight-stringed chelloh, which had belonged to his grandfather.

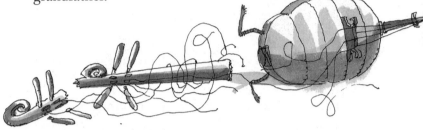

Two more nights went by. Mo's parents thought their son had forgotten about his small rebellion. Both of them told themselves it was better that way. But they couldn't banish a certain disappointment from their hearts. They had secretly hoped that Mo would get them out of there. . . .

One evening, as he passed by the fireplace, Mo heard whimpering sounds. He found his sister crying on the banquette that doubled as her bed.

"It's tomorrow morning," she told him, wiping her face with the sheet. "Tomorrow, before sunrise. Don't tell our parents."

"What?"

"I have to give him my answer. . . . Garric wants to take me with him. I have to tell him if I'll accept."

"Is he crazy?"

"No. He knows I'm going to say yes."

Mo smiled.

"Mrs. Lila Garric. I'd like to see that—with lots of little Garrics all around, chewing your socks. The happy family!"

"Don't laugh! It's terrible."

"A house full of little mites, all crying 'Mom,' all looking like their dad. . . ."

"Stop it, Mo! Stop it!"

She burst into fresh tears. Mo went up close to his sister's ear.

"You're not going to say yes to him," he whispered. "I promise."

"If I refuse, he'll denounce Mano and hand us all over to Joe Mitch."

"You won't need to say no."

"Well, what *am* I going to say? Mo, don't tease me."

"You won't say yes *or* no, Lila," Mo insisted calmly. "You won't be at the meeting."

"I won't?"

"No, you'll already be far away."

"What about Mano?"

"He'll be with you. Just like Milo, Mom, and Dad."

"But what about you?"

Mo's smile became a bit more shadowy.

"You mustn't worry about me. I'll get by. Promise me that you'll take them with you and not think about me. I'll manage on my own. Mom's right, I am a bit selfish, so I'm good at coping by myself. Promise me."

Lila looked at her brother.

"We're not leaving without you," she said.

Mo took his sister's fist in his hands.

"Do our parents know about this?" she asked him.

"No, nobody knows. Except you . . ."

"And?"

"Mano. I've told him all my plans. Otherwise he'd already be dead in his hole."

They heard three knocks behind the fireplace. Mano was listening. This signal made Lila take heart again. They couldn't destroy the hope that was keeping Mano alive.

"Promise me," Mo said again.

Lila put her arm around her brother's neck, and they pressed their foreheads together. Her eyes were welling up again.

"I promise you," she said.

Mo nodded.

"Tell our parents and Milo that I'll join you. Now, go back to sleep. Don't worry about anything."

"When are we going to leave?"

"You'll see. . . . Or rather, you'll hear. When the time comes, don't waste a second, get Mano out, and take all the others with you. The path will be clear."

That night, the Garrison Commander at Seldor was sleeping badly. Garric kept tossing and turning in his bed. He was feeling impatient, and sweating as a result. At dawn, he would have the young woman all to himself. He would put her in his kitchen like a hunting trophy. She would serve him pints of frothing moss and wash his clothes. She would be called Mrs. Garric, and all the other soldiers would be jealous; they'd have drinking songs about her.

He was happy. She had no choice — she would be his.

Garric remembered his first fly; at sixteen, he had killed it in midflight. This was a similar kind of basic pleasure.

Garric had reached this point in his romantic fantasy when he heard an unusual noise. He sat up in his bed.

It wasn't a noise. It was a waltz.

Garric leaped to his feet and ran over to the window.

A waltz. Somebody was playing a waltz in the barracks.

Playing music in the Tree was currently about as permissible as frying an omelet on Joe Mitch's head. It wasn't a small misdemeanor. It was a crime.

If Mitch got wind of the fact that Seldor had been the theater of an extraordinary nocturnal concert, Garric would end his days dancing the waltz in a hole full of vermin. He leaped into his boots and went out. A crowd of soldiers was running across the farmyard from every direction.

"It's over there, by the aviary," somebody called out to him.

"I want to see all men over by the aviary. Stop this nutcase for me!"

There was already a crowd gathering around the cage. The last convict had just been sent off to the Crater, so the cages were empty. The soldiers rummaged in every nook and cranny in their attempt to get to the bottom of where the music was coming from.

This bustling spectacle made for a rather charming ballet by flame light, as the flares came and went to the rhythm of the waltz. From far off it looked like one of the grand illuminated parties the Alnorell family used to give in the Treetop, in days gone by. But close-up, it was no party atmosphere.

"Stop him!" barked Garric.

The musician remained invisible, but his music glided everywhere. It danced in the night, taunting the bars of the aviary and the soldiers' shouts. Music fears nobody. And it refuses to be caged.

Finally, somebody had the bright idea of using a special kind of flare, made of fine cloth rolled up into a ball. They set fire to it before sending it flying into the air using a catapult. It unfurled and glided back down again. The flare was one of the inventions that Sim Lolness had been forced to surrender, along with the feathered wagon and a few others, in order to fend off Joe Mitch, who was holding out for Balina's Secret.

The flare rose high in the night air, lighting up the entire branch. The whole garrison could at last see where the haunting music was coming from.

Pink cheeked and wearing his old hat, Mo Asseldor was sitting, perched at the top of the aviary.

On his knees was his grandfather's chelloh, which he was stroking with his bow. His frozen hands were

wrapped in dishtowels. His feet and chest were icy cold, but he wasn't shivering. Nor was he playing any old waltz. It was "Little Sister," the melody he'd composed years earlier for Lola, when she had fallen sick with melancholy. He hadn't played it again since his little sister had left with Lex Olmech. And as he rediscovered these notes, perched on top of the aviary, he wondered if he would ever hear her voice again.

Indeed, Garric had just decided that the young prodigy in the hat would end up hanging from a hook in his cellar, among his sausages and hams.

"Get him!"

The soldiers started climbing the aviary. Everyone had left their guard posts, and a few stragglers were still arriving.

None of them saw five figures in the night. Five figures who flanked the front of the old house and headed into the undergrowth. Mano was holding his sister's hand as he breathed in great lungfuls of the cold night air. He kept on asking Lila, "Are we leaving? Are we really leaving?"

"Yes, Mano," she whispered over and over again, but still he couldn't quite believe it. Milo was listening to his brother's music. He had understood right away when he heard the waltz in the middle of the night. He'd let himself be talked into leaving.

Mr. and Mrs. Asseldor were walking huddled against each other. They were thinking of the son they were leaving behind. But not once did they turn around to look at Seldor Farm.

The house didn't hold it against them. It watched them leave with the self-effacing manner of old buildings.

The waltz stopped abruptly.

What had they done to Mo?

Lila tugged at Mano's hand a bit more forcefully. Milo started singing the tune of "Little Sister." The others joined him, humming. The lichen forest bowed to let them pass. They had just left the Low Branches.

"Are we leaving?" Mano asked again. "Are we really leaving?"

Three days later and numerous branches away, little Snow found a walnut in a hole in the bark. She wasn't sure whether to tell her parents about this extraordinary discovery. The walnut was thirty times bigger than she was.

Snow had no idea what this giant ball of wood could be, wrinkled as Grandfather Olmech.

Age three, Snow was forbidden to go far from the house. In any case, what's the point of going far if you can find marvelous dangers close at hand? Which is how she managed to risk her life every day with the most familiar objects and places. Her parents remembered the cooking pot that she had gone to sleep inside, after putting the lid back on. Lex Olmech was about to light the fire beneath it when he had found her.

She also liked to roll down the snowy slope of the roof to make a bigger and bigger ball around her that would smash open down below. Snow would let out gleeful shrieks and start all over again.

This time she had found something better. A walnut balanced in a hole, ready to fall on top of her at the first movement. A walnut as tall as thirty little girls with their arms in the air. Bliss.

Snow noticed that the strange object was made up of two sections gently pulling apart. This created a slit through which one might be able to see the inside of the ball—enough to arouse the curiosity of the little girl who was getting ready to climb up. She put her foot on the first vein of the walnut. And this tiny person, lighter than a speck of dust, made the shell wobble right away. Snow had no idea that the ball of wood was about to roll on top of her and crush her. She kept on climbing.

The walnut tipped slowly. This globe, one hundred footsteps high, started moving soundlessly. . . .

At the point where Snow was about to disappear, a

hand grabbed her by the collar and pulled her sharply back. The walnut completed its rotation and came to a standstill.

The little girl looked up at the person who had caught her. It was an old man. He hugged her in his arms. Snow looked at him reproachfully. There was always somebody trying to stop her from having fun.

"What are you doing here, little one?" asked the man.

Snow would have liked to ask him the same question.

They heard a whistle outside the hole. The man answered and two women appeared, followed by two young people, one of whom was very pale.

"Have you found something?"

"This!" the man answered, pointing to the little girl.

The Asseldors looked at Snow as if they'd never seen a three-year-old before. They looked intimidated. Mrs. Asseldor ended up stepping forward, emotionally, and touching the little girl's cheek as she said, "I think you can tell us where Lex Olmech's house is, miss."

Father Asseldor glanced disapprovingly at his wife. When you're a fugitive and you're looking for the house of other fugitives, you don't ask just anybody the way.

Snow smiled and did a twirl, at the end of which she found herself on Mr. Asseldor's shoulders. She wasn't just anybody. She gave a tiny kick to invite her mount to start walking. They exited the hole.

The journey lasted five minutes, but this short trip changed a lot of things for old Mr. Asseldor. Feeling this bundle of gentleness on his shoulders, he realized there was nothing else he wanted but this. That his children would have children and that he would have the right to look after them.

As for everything else, he had given a lot. Work, challenges, he'd had enough. . . . He wanted rest and grandchildren who clambered all over him.

Sometimes he could feel Snow's hands in his hair. He was jealous of the grandfather who could be with her every day, introducing her to things just for fun: log cabins, never-ending stories, and music . . .

The family members were walking one behind the other and only left a single line of tracks.

At a bend in the path, they saw someone coming, far away in the snow. Lila was the first to recognize Lola. She let go of Mano's hand and ran toward her sister.

After a moment of disbelief, Lola started running too. The snow was deep. They could barely make their way through it, and it seemed as if their reunion would never happen, but the two sisters ended up out of breath and in each other's arms. The rest of the family followed.

They formed a little huddle of arms and faces all

mixed up together. The snow reached their knees. They were holding on to each other by the shoulders.

"And Mo?" asked Lola.

"He'll join us," Lila replied.

Snowflakes were falling from the lichen trees, tickling their necks and melting on their backs. The Asseldor family could have stayed there all winter. They'd have been found again at the thaw.

At one point, Mr. Asseldor said, "What about this little bundle I've got on my back—do you know who she is?"

He revealed Snow.

"No . . ." said Lola very seriously.

Mrs. Asseldor looked surprised; she could have sworn that this little one was . . .

Given the furious face Snow was making, Lola gave up on the joke. "Of course, Dad," she said to her father. "She's my daughter!"

"Your daughter . . . Your daughter!" he repeated, sniffing.

"Snow," Lola said to the little one. "This is your grandfather."

He felt Snow slide down from his shoulders. She landed in his arms and wouldn't leave his side from that moment on.

12

The Silence of the Flying Woodcutter

Everybody in the group of Flying Woodcutters liked newcomer 505. He didn't say much, but he was helpful, competent, and agile, and he volunteered for the most dangerous tasks. The men appreciated the sparkle in this young man's eyes and his attentive ear. They also liked his silences, shrouded in a mystery, which he occasionally punctured by giving out a few details about his life. He had no name, no family, and a vagabond existence that was neither easy nor particularly unhappy.

Within a few days, he had won the trust of his new companions.

The section of Flying Woodcutters had been created in response to new kinds of lichen appearing, which no longer just formed thickets or woods on the bark of the Tree but cascaded down in creepers at vertiginous heights.

There were fifty-one Flying Woodcutters, who had all volunteered for the job, and they worked in groups of three. They had stopped counting the number of fatal accidents that had occurred in their ranks.

Number 505 had turned up a little before Christmas. There were few candidates for this kind of job: you had to be in extremely good shape and fearless. Toby had been adopted from day one. He didn't say much, and he worked hard. Above all, it was fascinating how at ease he was in the most difficult situations. They had seen him climb through cascades of moss as fragile as lace.

"Why don't you have a name, 505?"

"When you don't have a family, you don't have a name. Nothing I can do about that."

"If it was me who didn't have a name, I reckon I'd feel lost."

The three Flying Woodcutters were working in a green ravine that was hanging from a branch. They were suspended by silk cables, and the snow was falling all around them.

"I've had nicknames in the past," said Toby as he put his ax back into his belt.

"Like what?"

The creepers were swaying in the wind as the Flying Woodcutters slid down.

"Some people called me Little Tree."

"Can I call you Little Tree?"

"If you want."

The two others were named Shaine and Torquo.

They were ten years older than Toby and had been in a team with him since Christmas. Shaine was married to Torquo's sister. They lived in a hamlet a few hours away from Joe Mitch's territory. Like all the Flying Woodcutters, they went home only one night and one day per week.

Toby had managed to get them to talk about the situation in the Tree.

Woodcutters have a certain reputation. To put it politely, they find it hard to tackle sensitive subjects with any sincerity and are generally known to joke about their clumsy "wooden tongues."

What Shaine and Torquo confided in Toby gave him a better idea of how the Tree had been ruined since he'd left. Joe Mitch and Leo Blue were allies without being friends. They hated each other with a vengeance, but had managed to come to an understanding on common ambitions and interests.

Leo didn't mind using Joe Mitch's Crater as an excuse to make the Grass people "disappear." Mitch, for his part, was satisfied to see new hands appearing to dig his big hole.

Similarly, the imprisonment of certain people in the Tree suited Leo Blue and prevented a new resistance movement. Joe Mitch was hoping to benefit from these captive brains to make people forget that he hardly had any himself and to improve his destruction techniques.

So the arrangement between these two bosses was like one of those balances you find in nature, where one bug tolerates another because it's eating the fleas off its back.

Barely were these words out of their mouths than Shaïne and Torquo regretted them. Their hands moved as if to erase everything they'd just explained, and they kept insisting to Toby, "That's just what people say, but it's not our problem. With our families, our work, our friends, we've got enough to be getting on with. . . ."

"My son," Shaïne said with a laugh, "doesn't even know that fat Mitch exists. He gets him muddled up with the Big Bad Bug in the stories I tell him!"

"We take care of our own," Torquo concluded. "If each person could make the twenty people around them happy, then the Tree would be a small paradise."

Toby could almost hear Nils Amen: *I take care of those around me.* It sounded good in principle. But what about those who weren't surrounded by anybody?

The first time Toby went back to the Olmechs' refuge after a week's work, he found a noisy, happy household. It was December 31 and dark.

Before going inside, Toby saw the candles framing the doorway and remembered the old tradition of celebrating the New Year. He rubbed the snow off his boots on the threshold, realizing he'd completely forgotten about people marking this kind of date.

In the Grass, celebrations are rare, and they never depend on the calendar. They just pop up in the course of the small pleasures of life. Sometimes you would say "What a celebration!" as you plunged your head into a drop of morning dew. No need for garlands and streamers. But Toby had occasionally felt nostalgic for ritualized celebrations, for long dresses and kisses at the stroke of midnight.

Toby pushed the door open. There were ten at the table.

Finding the Asseldor family reunited again, with the Olmechs, little Snow, and the smell of roasted meat and melted wax, Toby felt as if he was traveling back in time. The reunion was silent and misty eyed.

There was now a real island of humanity in the Tree.

In the depths of Amen Woods, between the lichen thickets, a family was coming back to life.

Lila hadn't changed, although her red hair was perhaps a little darker. Toby kissed her hello. She had grown thinner, but she still had those high cheekbones. And Milo still gave off the air of the overserious older brother. Mr. and Mrs. Asseldor were standing tall with smiles that crinkled their eyes and furrowed their brows.

But Mano . . . When Toby took Mano in his arms, he realized that life hadn't spared him. Poor Mano seemed as fragile as a frozen droplet on the end of a branch. The flapping of a butterfly's wing would have been enough to break him.

"I thought about you a lot, Toby Lolness. . . ." Mano told him in a reedy voice.

Toby found a place to sit in their midst. Everyone's

shoulders touched. The heat was rising up around them. A gnat, stuffed with fresh walnut, was being spit-roasted in the fireplace. And walnut wine was being served, the smell reminding Toby of nights in the Low Branches when he and his father, lying under the roof of their house, would listen to the Tree whispering.

Little Snow was very proud to see everybody feasting on the walnut she had found. She had filled her pockets with pieces of sweet fried walnut, and there was a trail of butter all the way around her mouth. Sitting on the windowsill as the mistress of the household, she watched the celebrations.

At dessert, Lex whispered into Toby's ear, "Mr. Amen came by yesterday. He wants to talk to you."

Toby didn't waste any time getting up from the table.

"Happy New Year!" everyone called out.

It was the middle of the night when Toby reached Nils's remote hut. He was about to enter when he heard a loud voice from inside. Toby slid under the floor and listened.

"Where were you, my son?"

"I was traveling."

"You were spotted in the Gray Moss, leaving the Treetop."

"Am I being watched?" asked Nils with a smile in his voice.

Silence.

"Aren't you celebrating this evening?"

"No. I've brought the layouts from up there. I have to make headway on the great map of the forests."

"You work a lot, my son."

"What about you? Aren't you celebrating tonight?"

"I'm on my way," Norz Amen explained. "I'm invited to a party with the Flying Woodcutters."

"Shaine?"

"Yes, Shaine and his brother-in-law. Would you like to come?"

"I'm working. Say hello to them from me."

"Shaine has a sister who isn't married," said Norz.

"Really . . ."

"I think you'd like her. You should see her from time to time. . . ."

Toby heard a dull thump. Father and son must have been giving each other a pat on the back.

"Well, give Shaine's sister a kiss from me, Dad."

"With pleasure," said Norz happily.

The wooden floor creaked, and Norz Amen's voice resonated again. "I'm proud of you, Nils. Sometimes I think of El Blue, that nutter's father. If he was still alive, I don't know what he'd make of his son, but I'm proud of mine."

"If Father Blue was still alive," said Nils, "his son wouldn't have turned out the way he has."

"If it was me," grouched Norz, "and my son had been a traitor like that, I wouldn't be answerable for my actions."

Norz Amen's footsteps headed over to the door.

Toby saw his huge shadow climb down the ladder, which groaned under his weight. Norz was so solid that he was nicknamed the Twig; he was as wide as a piece of wood.

Once he'd reached the bottom, Norz called up loudly to his son, and Nils leaned out his window.

"Why do you live up there?" asked his father. "Eh? Wouldn't you like a proper house on the bark? What girl is going to climb up to your perch? Have you thought about that? Someone wearing a skirt, with ribbons in her hair, isn't going to climb ladders."

"I don't like easy pleasures," Nils answered.

Then came the sound of father cursing son, but he ended with "You silly sausage," and it was stuffed full of tenderness.

Norz headed off.

Toby walked into the hut a moment later.

Nils looked at him and smiled.

Toby's face seemed to be asking, "Well?" But he kept quiet.

Eventually, Nils admitted, "I saw her."

Toby's chest puffed up. He wasn't touching the floor anymore.

"She is . . ." whispered Nils. "She's wonderful, Toby."

Toby looked down.

"Are you sure it was her?"

"No." Nils smiled again. "She didn't say a word to me. She's stubborn as a pickax. She doesn't answer. She looks at you without moving, and you feel like your bones are going soft."

"That's her all right," said Toby, overcome.

He could see her. He could imagine her. He was experiencing that slightly giddy feeling again from the last time they'd met. They'd rushed down the slope, all the way to the lake.

They'd found themselves standing, back to back and breathless, on the bark beach. They couldn't even speak. A wave of joy encircled them, brushing against their skin.

And now the story was starting up again. Three years later.

"Have you told her I've returned?" Toby asked.

"No. Someone was listening to us. Leo's happy with me. He wants me to go back. He wants me to spend time with Elisha. But . . ."

"What?"

"I have to be careful. If I'm seen in the Nest . . ."

"You have to go back, Nils."

"What can I say to this girl, if I'm not allowed to talk about you? It's pointless, Toby."

"No, it's not. You *can* talk to her about me, and I'll tell you how. But first of all, promise me you'll beware of Leo. He's smarter than you think. Ever since I was little, I learned something, Nils. There are two energies in life. Hate and love. Most people live on one side or the other. But Leo has both of these in him. They run in his veins at the same time."

As he spoke, Toby thought about Ilaya, the girl in the Grass. She was also troubled by those contradictory waves that caused storms.

"How can I talk to Elisha about you, if I can't even say your name?"

Toby sat down next to his friend.

"What I'm about to tell you is something that she taught me. There are false bottoms, underneath words, just like there is below the wooden floor of your hut. You can hide secret messages in there, which can only be found by certain people."

Toby explained to Nils what he should say. He talked for a long time, until morning. The roof of the hut was creaking under the snow, and the two friends breathed in the sweet smell of the oil lamp.

At the end, Nils said to Toby, "Why do you trust me?"

"Because I don't have any choice."

Nils shook Toby's hand.

"I'll go back to see Elisha."

Day broke. There was a golden light in the branches.

"It's the first morning in the world," said Toby,

staring up at the arch of the Tree, a stained-glass window of sun and shadow. "Come with me. Don't be on your own today."

He patted Nils on the shoulder and laughed.

"My poor Nils," he went on. "We haven't even warned you that you're hiding five more people in your shelter deep in the woods. Come on. The Asseldors have arrived. You'll like them."

When Lila Asseldor woke up on the first day of the year, on this first morning in the world, she had no idea that it would be any different from any other day for her.

She opened her eyes. Her parents were sleeping next to her, along with her two brothers and little Snow, who was rolled up inside a blue blanket.

Lola and Lex had their bedroom just above.

When they had arrived, a few days earlier, Lila was worried about seeing Lex again, because she had been secretly in love with him for so long. But she'd barely set foot in the house when she saw how much of a couple Lex and her sister were, saw gentle Snow at their feet, and she realized then that they were made for one another.

Lila no longer felt as if happiness had been stolen from her. It was just that there was Lola's happiness, on the one hand, and her own, on the other, and hers was taking a longer, windier path.

But who says the best voyages are always the shortest ones?

So Lila arose with this new feeling of lightness that she'd felt for the past few days.

She slipped out of the loft, grabbed her raincoat, which was hanging from the door, and headed down to the kitchen.

The Asseldors were gradually rediscovering the simple outward signs of freedom.

Lila walked into the kitchen. First of all she saw Toby, his head bent over a steaming bowl of black bark juice. Then, opposite her, she saw another boy drinking the same brew.

"Hello."

"Hello, Lila," Toby answered.

She went behind Toby's chair and kissed him on the cheek.

"This is Lila Asseldor," Toby announced to the stranger. "Lola's big sister."

"Hello," said the young man.

Lila grabbed a cup, went outside, and returned with snow in it. She sat down and poured a drop of sugar syrup into her bowl of snow.

"What are you eating?" asked the stranger.

"Snow with sugar. I love it."

"For breakfast?"

"Yes."

"Don't you want something hot?"

"No."

Toby enjoyed this crazy streak in the Asseldor sisters. He pushed his warm bowl toward Lila.

"Try that. It's good, it's hot, and it's pure happiness."

Lila refused, smiling. She looked at Toby and said in a serious voice, "I don't like easy pleasures."

Where had Toby heard that expression before? He could swear he'd heard it the very same day. . . .

He turned sharply toward Nils.

"Lila," said Toby. "I haven't introduced you to Nils Amen. . . ."

Nils couldn't utter a word. His eyes were already lost in Lila's red hair.

13

The Old Man
with a Pancake on
Top of His Head

"Stay there."

That's what Mika had said to him, drawing a circle with his finger on the palm of his hand and making a dot in the middle. The circle and the dot meaning, "Stay here. I'll be back."

But Mika hadn't come back.

So Liev had stayed there, even though he was fully aware that it had been night for some time now. Blind people aren't stupid.

And even though he was deaf, he could still sense that it was almost completely silent around him.

Even without being able to see or hear, Liev had millions of indicators that told him what was going on around him. He would put his hand on the ground, sniff the air or taste it with his tongue. He was far from being a terrorized creature locked inside his own box. Liev was a strapping young man who had grown up in the middle of the Grass, honing his survival instincts.

But there was no denying the fact that he needed Mika.

A few centimeters away, Mika was waiting for him. He had crawled and climbed until he was in the thick of the tangled spikes that formed the Enclosure. He was catching a cold.

The Crater was crisscrossed with this terrible spiked barricade. If you tried to get over it, you risked being impaled on the oversize pins. No contact was possible between the old scholars and the Grass people.

And yet for several days now, Mika, Moon Boy, and the others had been taking turns to go and lose themselves, one by one, right in the middle of the barricade, like a single straw in a mass of needles.

They wanted to speak with the old man.

The old man with the round disks in front of his eyes.

The old man with the pancake on top of his head.

Moon Boy was the first to mention it. And all of them remembered seeing him when they arrived at the Crater. An old man, with disks in front of his eyes and a black pancake on top of his head. This was how they saw Sim Lolness's glasses and beret. An old man who seemed kind and clever and who might be able to help them. They also knew that this man had spoken to Moon Boy about Little Tree's emblem, which he wore around his neck.

The Grass people, who have a tradition of weaving their tufts together at the beginning of winter, know the importance of counting on others. On the other side of the barricade were more prisoners, who might be ready to link their poor destinies to those of the Grass people's.

"I saw Old Trees with white hair who were digging all day just like we do," Jalam had said. "I only saw them briefly, but in the middle was the old man with the pancake on his head."

Some of the Grass people didn't want to believe they could count on anybody in the Tree.

"Trust nobody," they said.

But Jalam and the others replied, "Remember Little Tree. . . . You'd have trusted him with your own daughter's linen belt, wouldn't you?"

This question was met with a favorable buzz. Even those who were the most worried had to admit that the example set by Little Tree proved that all was not rotten in the Kingdom of Branches.

So, one after the other, they spent their nights in the barricade, trying to see the old man passing by.

Mika suddenly remembered that Liev was waiting for him. The old man wouldn't pass by again tonight. He turned around, ripping his brown pajamas on a spike. The Grass people had been outfitted in convicts' uniforms, which suited them about as well as suspenders would a lizard.

The moment when their linen tunics were taken away and they were made to wear the regulatory uniform resulted in scenes of general hilarity. It was perhaps the only episode in a long time that had made the Grass people laugh out loud. Bent double from laughing so hard, they kept looking and pointing at each other. They definitely found trousers the funniest. The idea of these two tubes, linked at the waist, was highly comical to them. Why not put covers over your ears?

The guards were exasperated by so much giggling during what was meant to be a humiliating exercise. In fact, the Grass people never ceased to surprise and irritate their guards. It wasn't that they were insubordinate, on the contrary, but there was something insulting about their good humor, patience, and solidarity, as far as the officials who wore themselves out persecuting them were concerned.

Not being able to see or hear, Liev didn't know where exactly he'd been for the last six months, but he did understand the rules of the game.

A prison. Good guys. Bad guys. Work to be done.

Having to stay standing.

In the beginning, Joe Mitch's men had taken him for an idiot. Liev didn't answer questions; he just smiled, and his dark eyes remained unfocused. Mitch's men had wanted to eliminate this useless simpleton or use him as a target for darts practice. But Mika had demonstrated that Liev was capable of carrying loads all by himself. With five canvas buckets full of wood shavings strapped to his waist and two on his shoulders, Liev could climb up and down the Crater following a rope. He was in shape enough to do the work of four men.

So he had been given a second chance while they waited for him to wear himself out or break an arm. When the day came, they would settle his account for him.

Liev felt a distant vibration. Someone was coming. He recognized the soft-footed tread of a Grass person, then Mika's hand took his.

They went to lie down for the night near the others, and Moon Boy sat up in the dark, leaning on his elbows.

"Is that you two?"

"Yes."

"Did you see the old man?"

"No."

"Good night, Mika. Good night, Liev."

"Good night, Moon Boy," answered Mika.

Liev was already asleep. At night he found again in his dreams the supplies of sounds and images, gathered by the basket-load, from when he was very small, before he got sick. His nights were filled with colors, sunsets, faces, gentle voices, songs, and the sounds of rippling streams in the Grass. . . .

At the same time, on the other side of the barricade, a meeting was taking place in Sim Lolness's dormitory. The thirty elderly scholars were sitting up in their bunk beds, looking like they were awaiting the signal for a pillow fight to begin.

Actually, they were waiting for Sim's verdict as he did his clever calculations with his eyes closed.

"Three months. It'll take us three more months."

There were weary sighs and even splashed tears on wrinkled cheeks. A few hours earlier, they had thought they were at the end of the tunnel. Three months!

Every day counts when you're old and tired.

A little earlier in the evening, Zef Clarac, lying in the tunnel, had given the wood a few last shaves, raised a floor slat, and poked an eye outside. He had gone back into the tunnel in a great hurry. Old Lou Tann, who was with him, whispered, "Well?"

The way he was grimacing, Zef's hideous face looked even uglier than usual. The result was abominable.

"It smells horrible."

Lou Tann pushed Zef out of the way and stuck his own head out.

He retracted it just as quickly, pinching his nose.

"What a stench!"

"The sweet perfume of freedom." Zef chuckled.
"What shall we do?"

They heard some strange rumbling noises followed
by explosions.

"I'm going back. I want to try and figure this one
out."

This time Zef stuck his head out to neck level. He
discovered two big shoes, which hadn't been there a
minute earlier. It was impossible to breathe. He understood everything when he recognized the smell of old
cigarette butts mixed in with the rest. He closed the floor
slat back over his head and turned toward Lou Tann.

"The toilets . . ." he stammered. "Joe Mitch's lavatories!"

Lou Tann banged his head against the wall.

"Mighty mites! We got it wrong."

That night in the dormitory, they explained their discovery
to the others and Sim Lolness had done the math. Three
more months! But rather than looking dejected, Sim
Lolness looked elated. He was in a frenzy of excitement.

"That's the best piece of news I've ever had," he said.

Even at one hundred and two years old, Councillor Rolden could happily have punched his friend in the face.

"Why don't you just admit you made a mistake, you old fart?" he challenged Sim Lolness.

"I'm telling you, Rolden, this is good news."

"You think dying here is good news?"

They were about to come to blows. Maya glanced anxiously at her husband.

"You should learn how to count," someone mumbled at the back.

Sim clenched his teeth. "Who said that?"

Nobody moved. Sim took off his glasses and rubbed his eyes. He took a deep breath and turned toward Albert Rolden.

"Quite so, young man, I have made a lamentable mistake. I was counting correctly, but I wasn't counting on *it*."

"On what?"

"It. The thing that carries us, feeds us, dresses us. . . . It!"

Sim gestured by waving his arms around. Nobody understood a thing. The professor repeated himself vehemently three times: "It's fighting back! It's fighting back! It's fighting back!"

"Who?"

"What?"

"What's he saying?"

The detainees were looking at Sim Lolness as if he were a complete nutcase.

"The Tree, I'm telling you! The Tree is fighting back! The Tree is defending itself against us! The Tree is resisting! It's moving. It's putting on its armor. All my calculations were right, but I was forgetting that the huge hole of that Crater is like a scar. The bark is trying to heal its wound. It's creeping to the edges of the hole. That's why we made a mistake. The bark is moving. The Tree is fighting!"

Sim caught his breath. He turned toward his wife and told her, "I've been shouting this in the branches for fifty years now: The Tree is alive!"

Councillor Rolden had gone to sit on his bed. The small dormitory was focused on this big news. But Zef Clarac dared to ask, "What about us? What are we going to do?"

Sim smiled at him.

"We'll dig," he answered.

So there were three more months of work ahead. They would have to extend the tunnel by fifteen centimeters. They would block up the exit to the lavatories carefully, to avoid dying of asphyxiation.

Rolden refused to speak for several days.

Sim intended to take advantage of these extra months to find the little Grass boy who had been wearing the emblem of the Lolness family.

The boy surely knew something about Toby. He needed to find a way of talking to him.

That's when he thought of Pussykinska.

Pussykinska was the only female guard in the Crater. She was twice as wide and tall as the most heavyset of her colleagues. Pussykinska was in charge of Maya Lolness, the only female detained in this part of the Crater. They had already come face-to-face a long time ago, in the most painful circumstances, just a few seconds before Toby had disappeared forever.

Because of this memory, and for many other reasons, Maya liked Pussykinska. She had quickly realized that this mountain had a heart. Their relationship was bolstered when Mrs. Lolness had asked the guard about her childhood.

Pussykinska hadn't answered, maintaining her silence for several weeks, but after a month she had conceded, "I didn't exactly have a pampered childhood. . . ."

As the days went by, Maya discovered that Pussykinska had spent most of her childhood in a cage, at the back of a pantry. It was from there that she got her sturdy appetite, plus a few things that were off-kilter in her head.

The day after the intrusion into Joe Mitch's lavatories, Sim Lolness asked to see Pussykinska.

"I've got a little favor to ask you, dear lady," said Sim.

He'd been rubbing his eyes to make them red. And he kept blowing his nose.

Pussykinska bent down to listen. Despite being nearly two millimeters tall, the professor suddenly felt like a dwarf. She was all ears. This colossal woman could

be incredibly well-mannered, and Sim was sorry he had
to lie to her.

"I've lost something," he explained. "A little carved
pendant. It's a souvenir. My son gave it to my wife, who
asked me to look after it for her. I've lost it, but I don't
want to tell Maya about it yet. It was all she had, the only
thing left from our son. . . ."

He showed her a drawing of the Lolness emblem.

"If you find it, tell me. Someone might have taken
it. . . . I would be eternally grateful, dear lady."

Pussykinska listened to every word of this last sentence.
She didn't even know that kind of language existed.

"Eternally grateful, dear lady . . ."

These four words were a pleasure to hear.

"Yeah, all right, yeah," she said, embarrassed that she
could only use her own poor language to respond to a
real poet.

Pussykinska grabbed the piece of paper between her
fingers, which were as fat as a bundle of logs, and headed
off.

The next day, she appeared before the professor, looking
very embarrassed. She had found the person who was
wearing the emblem.

"But . . . he doesn't want to."

"What?" asked Sim.

"He doesn't want to give it back."

Sim took a few seconds to think this over. Why was

Pussykinska obeying the wishes of that small Grass boy? The woman wasn't merely a mountain but a mystery as well. But Sim had just had an idea.

"Well, explain to him that I am the father of the person who made that medal. Ask him where he found it."

"Yeah," said Pussykinska.

She left Sim feeling astonished by this long-distance exchange that had been struck up with such an odd correspondent. That very evening, the miracle developed further.

"He doesn't want to say where he found it. But he does want to talk to you."

"Where?" Sim inquired.

"He can come here tomorrow."

"Here?" he repeated.

It was all turning into a fairy tale. Sim was at last going to find out.

That evening, Sim gave a lecture on the subject of insects. It was the shortest, simplest, and most brilliant lecture of his career. Good lectures are the ones that make you want to do your own research, verify, ask questions. Good lectures open people's eyes to see the simplest reality.

Basically, lectures are like jokes and illnesses: the shorter the better.

Here is the complete text of the lecture given during the first days of January by Sim Lolness, which bore the following title: "Insects."

"Insects have six legs."

That was it.

After uttering these four words, the professor started tidying up his papers. The lecture was over. His public was in turmoil.

"Any questions?" he asked, distractedly.

Everyone's hand shot up. Plok Tornett had a grin as wide as his ears. He admired his teacher's daring. Sim gave short answers to those who dared ask questions.

"But spiders have eight legs!" Zef called out.

"So they're not insects, Mr. Clarac! They're arachnids."

"And ants?"

"Six legs, so they're insects."

"Centipedes, Professor. Don't tell me that centipedes aren't insects."

"I believe I've been clear. Insects have six legs, not one less, and not nine hundred and ninety-four more. Insects are the only animals in the world to have six legs. The only ones, you understand? And that's all I have to say. Piece of cake!"

Nobody had ever given such a clear, obvious definition of an insect. Others had tortured their minds by differentiating between insects and other species according to their diets, their antennae, their body size, or their eggs.

But, as usual, Sim had cut straight to the point.

He also had to admit to being impatient to get to sleep so that he could meet the young Grass boy the following morning.

"That was a splendid lecture, darling," Maya told him on her arrival in the dormitory.

"When I'm really grown-up," said the professor, "I'll give a lecture with a single word."

Above them, in the bunk bed overhead, a little voice was reviewing all the kinds of insects: "Bees, for instance, bees have six legs. Butterflies, six legs. Beetles . . ."

It was Lou Tann, the shoemaker. He was talking to himself. Sim and Maya laughed softly. Amazed by Sim's revelation, Lou Tann spent the whole night thinking about it.

"Flies, six legs. Ladybugs, six. Crickets . . ."

Poor Rolden, who was digging the tunnel that night, emerged at midnight via the trapdoor in the desk. The class had long been empty. The lesson had finished two hours ahead of time. He was locked in. He knocked hard against the classroom door, and two of Joe Mitch's men came to open it for him; they sniggered inanely.

"Hey, Grand-daddy-o, did you fall asleep at school? A bit slow on the uptake . . . You've got to remember to take your vitamins. . . ."

The centenarian just shrugged. Who would have believed that this man had just spent four hours digging an escape tunnel? He wasn't the slowest of these three.

Sim was waiting for the famous meeting. He bided his time in the minuscule closet he'd been given as his office and laboratory. The door opened. Pussykinska stuck her head around.

"He's here."

Sim came out. He felt his legs go weak.

He appeared outside, blinded by the light. Wood dust was floating in the air. His companions had been at work in the Crater since dawn.

But it wasn't a Grass person standing before him. It was a soldier with a twisted smile. A hefty soldier with a poisonous stare, playing with his harpoon like a scorpion in the sun.

"He's called Tiger," said Pussykinska.

Tiger was wearing the Lolness emblem around his neck. He had grabbed it from Moon Boy on one of the first days. Which meant that Sim had been communicating with this man for a while. Without realizing it, he had been providing him with valuable information.

"This is all very interesting. . . ." said the soldier. "We're discovering new things about you, Professor."

"That's my job," said Sim calmly.

Tiger licked his upper lip and touched the little piece of wood that was hanging from his neck.

"How did that Grass boy find this, if it belonged to your son?"

"My wife lost it. She was wearing it in the Crater. The boy must have picked it up."

"Everybody thinks that Toby Lolness is gone for good. . . ."

"Yes," said Sim.

"But what if I was to start thinking the opposite? Perhaps he's still roaming around. . . . I know somebody who would be more than happy to get that kind of information."

"Yes," said Sim. "I know somebody too: his name's Sim Lolness. Nothing would make him happier."

"No," said the soldier. "I'm thinking of a certain Joe Mitch."

In reality, Tiger didn't intend to reveal his suspicions to Mitch yet; there was too much profit at stake here. If he could find Toby, public enemy number one on the famous Green List, and prove the link between the Lolness family and the Grass people, it would be a double victory. . . . And, most important of all, that would mean twice the reward.

In a murky corner of Tiger's mind, there was also the idea that he might perhaps retrieve the Tree Stone.

"I don't think my son is of this world anymore," said Sim Lolness. "But I would thank you with all my heart if you could prove me wrong."

Sim turned his back. He knew he'd made a big mistake.

"Be very careful," Tiger told him.

"You don't frighten me," muttered Sim Lolness.

"Are you sure? We have a friend in common, Mr. Lolness. He used to say the same thing as you."

Sim stopped. What did this man still want from him?

"I was the guard of Nino Alamala many years ago."

Sim turned and looked Tiger straight in the eye and immediately understood.

Alamala had been a very dear friend of Sim's. Everybody remembered the painter who had been accused of killing his own wife.

Sim had defended his friend in the trial.

It was a terrible story, and one that had changed the lives of the Lolnesses forever.

Beautiful Tess Alamala had been found on a branch with her skull smashed. She was a dancer and a tightrope walker. It soon became clear that she had fallen from her high wire a few branches higher. Nino was inconsolable.

The initial investigations concluded that it had been a stupid accident. Many people insisted that Tess Alamala had brought it on herself. Nobody had asked her to balance on a wire. Why couldn't she walk like everybody else, with her feet on the branches?

Soon the reproaches were directed at Nino, the painter, who had chosen an equally dreamy and pointless vocation and who had been the one to let his wife climb up high like that. People kept saying that it was irresponsible and criminal—they had a baby to look after.

These last accusations had led to an inspector coming

to Nino Alamala's house, to rummage through his affairs. He had found a small painting in one corner. The portrait depicted Tess walking on air, and a sentence on the back served as a title: *I will cut the wire to see you fly.*

The same evening, Nino Alamala was thrown in prison.

The trial began a few months later. Defending his friend, Professor Lolness's speech was brilliant. He claimed that poetry itself was on trial, that life wouldn't be life without painters and tightrope walkers. Sim had said, "If I write to my wife, 'You are my little flame,' I don't necessarily intend to grill her in my fireplace. The marvelous Tess Alamala died in an accident, practicing her art. We can only mourn this loss with Nino."

Nino Alamala looked dignified and handsome, sitting on the bench for the accused. He had been instantly reproached for turning up with paint stains on his hands. People talked about a lack of respect. He had apologized humbly.

Sim became angry. Rather than looking at the hands of a worker, as one inspects those of a child about to sit down at the table, it was his face and his heart that needed reading and, above all, the gentleness of his paintings! Nino was innocent.

Sim liked Alamala's paintings. They were miniatures. And his signature always appeared at the bottom, with its curves like an undulating landscape, a signature so harmonious that you could still read it back to front: *Alamala.*

One night, before a verdict had been reached on the trial, Nino Alamala was killed in his cell. There wasn't really an inquiry into his death, on the pretext that you don't run after the murderer of a murderer. One of his guards was vaguely suspected of having wanted to enact a speedier justice.

The story was sixteen years old, but the memory was intact. Sim knew that long before the arrival of a Joe Mitch or a Leo Blue, hatred was already growing like a grub, ready to leap out.

Watching Tiger walk away, Sim Lolness realized that the killer of Nino Alamala had just been standing before him.

Tiger was satisfied. At nightfall he would pay the Grass people a visit. Moon Boy wouldn't be able to resist him for long.

There are fun ways of making a ten-year-old child talk.

14
I'm Coming Back

Toby and his two team members had hung their net from a disheveled moss garland that swung above the void. They were taking a nap in this hammock, rocked by the *drip-drip* of snow melting around them.

It was the third sunny day they'd had this January. Nature was being duped by things warming up. The whistling sound of insects could be heard, and there were cracklings in the branches as on the first day of spring. Toby wasn't asleep. He was listening to the Tree waking up in the hollow of winter. He knew that the winter fairy would come swooping down again on the branches the following day, sending the world to sleep under its white wings.

In among the water droplets from the thaw, Toby saw muddy streaks passing through the air. Melted snowflakes, perhaps. He also heard the reassuring sound of Shaine and Torquo snoring next to him.

What if, one day, the Tree didn't wake up? Toby wondered.

He knew the danger that weighed on the branches. Last spring, a certain number of buds had dried on the spot. People blamed the moss and the lichen, but Toby, who had lived in the Prairie, knew that lichen could grow even on rocks. It couldn't be accused of sapping the Tree's energy; it simply took advantage of the space and light caused by the disappearance of the leaves.

Moss and lichen are like traveling people who are owed a debt of gratitude for setting up camp on abandoned lands. Who would reproach nomads for colonizing branches ravaged by drought or fire?

Toby could have continued meditating like this for a long time, if he hadn't suddenly heard the sound of his friends' breathing come to an abrupt halt. He stood up and turned his head slowly in the direction of Shaine and Torquo.

Nightmare. Two leeches shaped like long sticky hats were covering the men's heads all the way down to their necks. They were preparing to choke them before sucking them dry and reducing them to bloodless sacks. So that's what these muddy streaks falling around him were: springtime leeches that had come too soon.

Toby hurled himself with his ax onto Shaine's head. The elastic, slippery substance of the leech refused to be tamed. The blade veered off and threatened to break the poor woodcutters' necks. Toby started shouting. Other leeches were raining down around him in the net.

Run! It was the only answer. But even if Toby could escape, the image of his companions writhing in agony would haunt him until his dying day.

A fat leech turned its sucker toward Toby's shoulders. He thought he was done for when, out of nowhere, a flaming arrow pierced right through the sticky beast. The leech pulled back in a sudden jerk and fell to the bottom of the net.

More arrows flew in from all sides. The hammock caught fire, and the animals were struggling. In a flash, the faces of Shaine and his brother-in-law reappeared. The leeches released their hold as they curled up, rolling into the middle of the flames. Toby let out a victory cry, but all that was holding up the three Flying Woodcutters was a line of burnt netting. It suddenly gave way.

The men fell a drop of several centimeters and landed in a brown goo that came up to their chests. Saved! They found their feet again and hugged each other, with their bodies and faces covered in this near-black substance. Toby was watching the strange sauce they were swimming in drip off his hands. Where were they?

"Are we disturbing you?" asked somebody next to them.

Torquo, Shaine, and Toby had fallen into a big tank mounted on a feather sled. They were surrounded by crossbowmen and torchbearers, who weren't looking at them forgivingly. Torquo and Shaine shot each other a worried glance.

"Mr. Mitch is making his black pudding!" Torquo said between gritted teeth.

Toby turned this phrase over and over in his head, thinking it must be a coded message.

"Mr. Mitch is making his black pudding. . . ." he repeated slowly, trying to understand.

Just then, something huge was lifted level with the rim of the tank; it was enormous, it was clothed in a small hunting suit, and it was spilling out of a sedan chair.

Toby froze.

It was Joe Mitch. And he wasn't looking happy.

Studying him properly, Toby thought this man looked more and more like a lump. He didn't have a definite shape at all. Every time he breathed out, there was a shlurping noise as distinguished-sounding as jam going splat between two pieces of toast.

Would the monster recognize Toby?

"Mr. Mitch is making his black pudding," explained somebody next to him.

This phrase was clearly the height of fashion. What Toby hadn't yet understood was that Joe Mitch really was busy preparing his winter black pudding.

Surrounded by a large team, he was out hunting leeches. They were tapping the branches because leeches drop when they feel vibrations. The animals were being killed with flaming arrows and were squeezed on the spot to harvest their coagulated blood.

Toby and his friends had fallen into the tank of blood that would be used as the chief ingredient for large black puddings, long and thick as a woodcutter's arm. Even without the coating of black liquid on his face, Toby wouldn't have been unmasked by Joe Mitch. He had changed too much. But somebody who was squeezed onto the running board of the sedan chair had recognized him instantly.

This person was attached to a leash held by Mitch. He was being treated like a domestic animal.

When he saw Toby Lolness, his hunted-animal expression suddenly lit up. Toby recognized him instantly. It was Plok Tornett, the grubber from the Low Branches, Vigo Tornett's mute nephew. The two of them exchanged glances.

"We're woodcutters," Torquo said to Joe Mitch.

This sentence seemed to vex Mitch, who had been counting on integrating these three vermin specimens into his black pudding. He snorted and scratched his ear, then signaled to one of his team. The man leaned over, in order to hear his boss's whispered, slobbering message. He stood up, looking very pale and embarrassed at having to contradict his boss.

"Friendly Neighbor, I . . . You will recall that we don't touch woodcutters. . . ."

Fresh rumbling from Joe Mitch.

"It was an accident," said Shaine. "We were being attacked. It won't happen again."

Mitch tugged on the leash and rubbed Plok Tornett's hair. For the time being, the corporation of woodcutters was untouchable. Joe Mitch looked forward to the day when he'd make a big kebab out of this bunch with ideas above their station. Just thinking about it relaxed him. He also liked feeling young Tornett's small head trembling beneath his hands.

After a few minutes of negotiations, the Flying Woodcutters were allowed to leave the vat, and Joe Mitch's procession swung off, abandoning them there.

The three woodcutters found a puddle where they could rinse off the blood before all the predators in the Tree swooped down on them.

Wringing out his woodcutter clothes, Toby watched the tiny dot of Plok disappearing at the end of the branch. Anger flared in his eyes. When would the hour for revenge come?

And then he thought of Elisha.

Would she remember? She was so wild. Why would she have waited, when she didn't want to belong to anything or anybody? It was as if Toby had left a living butterfly on a bud years earlier and expected to find it again in exactly the same spot, with powder on its wings! Impossible . . .

Nils had gone back to the Treetop with Leo Blue. Perhaps he was talking to Elisha right now. Toby was suddenly very scared. Did he still exist for her?

Yes, Nils was talking to Elisha. But she wasn't listening.

She looked down her nose at him. She would rather spend time alone with the Shadow that was back in its observation post at the top of the Egg. The Shadow was less tedious company; there was always something unsettling about its arrival. Whereas Nils never stopped muttering inanities.

Elisha stroked the sole of her foot. It seemed a long

time ago now since she had hidden the luminous blue mark drawn on her at birth in caterpillar ink.

Her mother had spoken to her about it one day, in the Low Branches, just before their animals had been massacred.

"I never thought it would come to this," she had said.

On that day, after a silent supper, beautiful Isha had held her daughter's face in her hands.

"Elisha, I've never tried to hide from you where we come from."

Elisha made a face. She knew she came from the Grass, that her mother had grown up among the Grass people. But what else did she know about her origins? How had they both arrived in the Branches of the Tree?

Elisha hung her head a bit. She had never asked her mother anything about it and didn't feel she could start that evening.

"You know, Elisha, the world is becoming a dangerous place for us."

Isha had taken a bowl filled with brown dye.

"It's powder from a moor moth."

Elisha watched her mother catch her ankle and smooth the brown, slightly greasy powder over the soles of her tiny feet.

The glow in the luminous ink went out. The marks had disappeared. Elisha shuddered. She felt naked. Isha held out the bowl of powder to her, and the young girl took it: now it was her turn to smooth the moor powder over her mother's feet.

Both of them felt the seriousness and sadness of this act. The sole of the foot is sacred for the Grass people. It's called the "sole of the foot" because it's the sole (or only) body part that enjoys this constant relationship with the surface of plants.

Erasing the line was an extremely rare act, one that recalled the great tragedies of this people.

That night, Elisha and her mother slept lying against each other in their house of colors. They thought they could hear the lugubrious wing beats of an army of moths out on their night flight. The mournful sound made them feel even more alone.

As a prisoner in the Treetop, Elisha was now looking at her extinguished feet. She knew that her mother had saved her life that evening by erasing the sign.

"Are you listening to me?"

"No," said Elisha.

Nils Amen was in front of her, giving her a long lecture about Leo Blue.

"You've got the wrong idea," he continued. "We always tend to have fixed ideas about people. I know Leo well. . . ."

Here we go, thought Elisha.

She had gotten the message and was starting to wonder if this boy was completely stupid. She glanced up at the top of the Egg, with a look that begged the Shadow perched up there to free her from this total bore. But, as usual, the Shadow didn't move.

"Leo Blue isn't what you think. Leo Blue . . ."

"I've understood!" exclaimed Elisha, exasperated. "I've understood! I've understood!"

Nils went quiet. He knew the moment had come.

Elisha breathed again. How could Toby have been friends with this dolt? Leo Blue, Nils Amen . . . She tried to comfort herself with the thought that perhaps it was better Toby was no longer around to see what had become of his old friends.

A strange sensation suddenly took hold of Elisha. Was it because she had just been thinking about Toby? She closed her eyes and realized that Nils had started talking again.

But not in the same way.

He was talking slowly, hanging every word on a thread of voice that was touching and fragile. Nils Amen was unrecognizable.

"Life is an abandoned bees' nest, Elisha. You walk around. The light looks like honey. The weather's nice.

You're lost. You can smell the wax. You call out. Your voice echoes. You're looking for the person you've lost. And that's life."

Nils took another breath.

"And then a big worker bee buzzes very close to you. You lie on the ground, with your arms protecting your head. The bee passes overhead. You get up; your dress is covered in honey. You're frightened. You hear a voice. It's the other person. He's there. You run down the hallways of the nest. You find him again. You don't tell him you were frightened. And that's life, Elisha."

Elisha turned her head away to hide her tear-covered face in the darkness. What was happening? What was going on?

Standing directly above this scene, Leo Blue had just imperceptibly squinted his eyes. What did these strange, incomprehensible words mean? Where did this emotion come from that rose up to reach him?

Nils didn't know whether his message had reached beautiful Elisha, its target. He was simply saying what Toby had asked him to say.

"And there's a heavy downpour over the moss forests," he continued. "You think you'll hold out, clinging on up there, right until the end, right until the last drop. Down below, you're being asked to climb down. You're shivering. You're going to be ill. You have to stop, to go and find shelter, Elisha. But you stay there. And even your clothes are melting. You're too stubborn, Elisha."

Up above, Leo Blue was thinking about Arbayan's suspicions. His hand was trembling lightly on the shell of the Egg. Who was Nils Amen really?

As for Elisha, she didn't know where she was anymore. That voice was going around inside her head.

It was no longer Nils Amen's voice. It was another voice that had returned from far away, a forgotten voice, hidden beneath years of sadness: the voice of Toby Lolness.

Memories weave a secret, inviolable language.

The bees' nest. The great downpour. Nobody but Toby and Elisha could recognize these faraway memories. They were some of the most intimate things they had shared.

She was sure about it: Nils was speaking to her in Toby's name.

Listening to Nils Amen's voice, in the wretched solitude of the Egg, Elisha could hear Toby's silent message, his coded message, stitched between the words. A message that lifted her off the ground and transported her elsewhere.

Everything suddenly became possible again, because this message was "I'm coming back."

PART TWO

15
Betrayal

Two months later, winter was still lingering in the Branches. But what had plunged Norz Amen into despair, what wrenched at his guts, was the fact that there could no longer be any doubt about it.

As Norz had known deep down for some time, Nils had gone over to the side of the enemy.

On the first day, he had refused to believe it.

It was an evening in the middle of autumn, and Norz was eating supper in the open air with big Solken, his oldest friend. Despite its being November, a warmish wind was blowing. The two woodcutters were listening to the night: the rustling of the last leaves, the chirruping of a May beetle that had lost its way.

They dined on bread and moss beer.

Norz Amen considered his friend to be the truest of the true. Solken had been the best man at his marriage to Lili, witnessing their joy on that day, watching the wedded couple's traditional dance, nose to nose until daybreak, and sharing Norz's horrifying despair when Lili had died giving birth to Nils the following year.

At the time, Solken had felt powerless to console his friend. He wasn't even able to console himself over the loss of Lili, who was like a sister to him and to so many others.

Lili Amen was a diminutive young woman, very kind and gentle, with green eyes. Beauty makes people seem immortal. Nobody could ever have imagined that Lili might one day disappear—and still less in giving birth to her first child.

It took several weeks before big Solken, who was overcome with grief, could stand before his friend and say, "We all loved her dearly, you know. We'll help you, my old friend."

But Norz had remained stiff as a twig, refusing any help or support. He brought Nils up all by himself. Or rather, he watched him growing up all by himself.

Solken knew that it wasn't Norz's coarse voice and hearty slaps that had turned Nils into the exceptional person he was, but rather an ethereal, invisible hand: the hand of someone absent. And it wasn't until that day in the Great Clearing, when Nils had saved Toby Lolness's life, that Norz truly understood what a man his son had become.

Now, three years later, Solken was sitting opposite

Norz Amen in the Clearing. And everything was about to crumble.

"Why don't you say something?" Norz asked.

Solken looked at his friend. He could no longer find the strength to say what he'd come to say.

"Speak, you wood louse!" Norz burst out laughing.

"Your son, Nils . . ."

"Yes?"

"Where is he?"

"Don't look so gloomy, Solken. My son's at home in his hut," said Norz. "If you want to ask him a favor, he'll do everything in his power to help you."

"I don't want to owe anything to a traitor."

Norz stood up, fist clenched, and went to attack Solken. His fist stopped just a hair's breadth from his friend's face.

"Repeat what you just said."

Solken's voice was trembling with emotion.

"I said I don't talk to traitors."

Norz closed his eyes to stop himself from beating his best friend to a pulp. His fist was still clenched and trembling, ready to spring into action.

"Forgive me, Norz, but what I'm saying is the truth," Solken continued. "I saw your son up there, near the Nest. He goes there often, to meet with Leo Blue in secret."

"Nils?"

"Yes, Nils. I saw him. If you can prove to me that I made this story up, then go ahead and kill me with your fist."

Norz opened his hand, looked at his palm, and passed his hand over his face, as if to chase away a ghost. Then he turned to Solken and looked at him questioningly.

Brave Solken shook his head. He wasn't lying.

The next day, Norz saw Nils's sin with his own eyes. He even saw Leo shake Nils's hand at the exit to the Nest. Norz had to bite his lip to keep from calling out his son's name.

Solken swore that he wouldn't say anything. He and Norz were the only witnesses to Nils Amen's crime.

Norz knew what he had to do. Deep down, he knew. There is only one punishment for traitors.

For a long time now, he had warned Nils about choosing between freedom and death. The lives of hundreds of woodcutters depended on it, as did the survival of the Tree.

Norz would have to eliminate the traitor, even though it was his own son.

He planned to act alone, in order to keep Nils's reputation intact. He'd lead people to believe it was a fatal accident. Nobody would find out about Nils's treachery.

On the last night of the year, Norz had nearly gone through with it. He had been with Nils in his hut, and there was a weapon hidden in his belt. But he couldn't find the strength to kill his own son.

You can ask anything of a father, except that.

After leaving Nils that evening, Norz hadn't gone to join the feast with Shaine and the others. He had run off to hide in a hole and cry as he'd never cried before.

Two more months went by. And now it was March. Without even realizing it, Norz was avoiding his friend Solken, who had simply said, "I understand if you can't do it. If that's the case, I'll take care of it."

Norz replied that he was waiting for the right moment. Solken looked at him and pointed out, "Is there ever a right moment to bring about your own son's death, my poor Norz?"

As for Nils Amen, he couldn't have been happier.

Having gotten himself assigned to Elisha, the plan was going perfectly. Leo Blue seemed to trust him completely, and Toby was thrilled.

So everything was turning out for the best.

But there was something else. An event that set the young woodcutter's head spinning and knocked him off balance. It was as if the Tree had suddenly found itself upside down and had started dancing on its Branches.

For Nils, the whole world had changed since the arrival of the divine Lila Asseldor.

Throughout the winter, Nils only saw her once a week when he went to visit Toby in the house deep in the heart of the forest.

"Have you come to see Toby, Mr. Amen?"

Nils didn't dare say no, even though Lila was his main reason for coming.

He would watch the young woman washing her niece in a tub. She poured jugs of hot water over Snow's head as the little girl splashed about.

Lila had her sleeves rolled up and an apron tied around her waist. Between the scalding showers, Snow shivered. Faced with this tender display, Nils felt horribly clumsy. He always asked how old Snow was, and Lila would answer, "Three. Just like last week."

"Ah, yes . . . She looks younger."

"Toby's at the other end of the house."

"Ah . . ."

But instead of leaving, Nils went over to the window and gave a running commentary on the weather. Lila would smile to herself behind the veil of steam. She didn't understand how someone as important as Nils could be so shy. He had a thousand woodcutters under his command and oversaw forests that went on forever, but even so, he still blushed when he spoke! Lila was sensitive to this more vulnerable side of Nils. Her hands slowed down in Snow's hair, and she joined in, "You're right—it's been cold since last night."

"I'll bring you some blankets," answered Nils.

Sometimes he plucked up the courage to offer to fill the jug with water from the big cooking pot. He worried he might faint if he touched Lila's fingers while handing over the jug. So he put it down next to her, on the ground.

When Nils eventually left, Lila always felt as if she was floating. She would start rubbing Snow's tummy with the blue towel, and Snow would stare deep into Lila's eyes with a little smile. She didn't take her eyes off her aunt until Lila had rolled her up inside the towel and started tickling her.

"You don't miss a trick, do you, little one? You don't miss a trick!" Lila would laugh.

Oh, yes, the little one spotted everything. After they'd had a good laugh, Snow would put her index finger to her lips and whisper, "Shhhhh." And Lila, playing the game, would copy her niece, dreaming that one day there might be a real secret to hide.

Nils regularly updated Toby on his visits to Elisha, but there wasn't a lot to say.

"I caught her eye for a moment today. At one point, she moved her hand."

He repeated the same thing every time: "I'm sure she's understood that you're behind my visits."

Toby was only worried about one thing.

"Leo. Doesn't Leo suspect something?"

"No. He seems happy with me. Even old Arbayan smiles at me from time to time."

Toby went quiet for a while. He didn't trust Leo one little bit.

"Leo will never be happy with anybody. If he's happy, that means he's up to no good. I should know—he used to be my best friend."

Toby pointed at Nils.

"The day he gives you a hug, it'll mean he's found out about everything. You'll have to get out immediately! Vanish! Don't stay a second longer in the Nest."

"I'll remember, Toby." Nils smiled. "But for the time being, it's all going fine. Maybe Leo's changing."

"People don't change without a reason," Toby reminded him.

"He loves Elisha. He's changing because of her," Nils suggested one day, and immediately regretted it.

Toby turned away sharply and headed off.

At precisely that moment in the South Egg, a gleaming dagger landed on the mattress, just missing the sleeping face of Elisha Lee. She opened her eyes and rolled off her bed.

For a long time she stayed still, panting against the Egg wall.

The bad news was that somebody had just tried to kill her. But there was good news too. With a weapon, she might be able to escape—if she could stay alive for long enough.

Elisha started crawling on her back. The knife must have been thrown from the gap at the top of the Egg. If she kept an eye on what was happening up there, perhaps she could avoid further attacks.

Hands and feet flat on the soil, she made her way like a spider to the middle of the Egg. She was on the lookout for the tiniest shift in the light. She tipped her head back and glanced at the dagger that was gleaming in the dark.

Finally, she was level with her mattress. Without taking her eyes off the gap directly above her, Elisha shot out her arm to grab the weapon.

She repeated this move several times, before turning her head.

The dagger was gone.

At this point, she leaped backward, landed on her hands, and pressed down on the ground with all her strength to land back on her feet, upright, in a defensive position.

Somebody had retrieved the dagger. He had to be there, lying in ambush in the gloom. The assassin might pounce on her at any moment.

A minute went by. Nothing moved in the Egg.

Elisha went over to the mattress again. What magician had been able to retrieve the weapon without revealing himself? Elisha found a square of pierced paper, which she hadn't noticed before. It must have been on the tip of the dagger. There were a few words written on it, so she held it close to her face and read slowly.

I am . . .

A flash of light. Elisha looked up at the opening to the Egg. She was sure she'd seen a shadow passing overhead.

She read the message again.

I am a friend of Nils Amen.

Elisha wasn't a confident reader or writer. She had learned in secret, never confessing to Toby this gap in her knowledge.

Isha Lee, her mother, didn't know how to read or write at all.

Elisha could remember the times when Toby had shown her a piece of paper or a notebook with long sentences written on it. It was always painful for her. After a while, he would ask, "Well?"

Elisha couldn't read, so she would answer, "It's not really my kind of thing."

Given that she was interested in everything, it hurt her to have to say that.

So, little by little, she had gathered a few of the secrets of writing. Pol Colleen, the old poet of the Low Branches, had taught her how to read and write.

The proof of Colleen's talent lay in quickly dismissing his student with a little note that read:

If you can read these words, then you don't need me anymore. Farewell.

But Elisha still felt clumsy and unconfident in herself,

so she read the sentence for the third time before whooping with joy.

Nobody was trying to kill her. On the contrary, somebody wanted to help her. The Shadow was on the same side as Nils and Toby. They were busy organizing her escape. Perhaps that Shadow might even . . . Elisha imagined Toby's face.

For the first time in years, she asked for something. She let all her tough masks drop and whispered in the silence of the room, "Help me. Tell me what I should do."

The Shadow seemed to listen to these words before disappearing.

Elisha collapsed onto her mattress. She would do everything she was told to. She was no longer alone.

She lifted her hand. There was a damp patch at the top of the mattress, close to her face. She smiled. She finally understood the mystery of the dagger. These March nights were still very cold, so the message must have been attached to a knife made of ice. The warmth of the room had melted it.

Not far away, the Shadow slipped under a footbridge, avoiding a few noisy guards, and pushed open the door of the East Egg. Crossing this threshold and entering the light, Leo Blue had just enough time to drop his black coat before Arbayan walked in.

"You called for me."

Leo looked at his adviser, "Perhaps you were right."

"What?"

"Perhaps you were right about Nils Amen. He's not on our side."

Arbayan put his hand on the sheath of his hornet's stinger sword.

"I take no pleasure in this news," said Arbayan. "I would have preferred to be wrong."

Leo Blue was no longer in any doubt. All winter long, he had listened to the mysterious words uttered by Nils to Elisha, but he had lacked proof.

After several months, he'd had an idea. By making the Shadow seem as if it was Nils's friend, he would get his proof. If Elisha asked for help from the Shadow, that meant Nils was an enemy to Leo.

"The next time Nils Amen comes," Leo Blue declared feverishly, "I don't want him to leave this Nest alive."

Arbayan saluted and left the Egg.

Poor Nils, whose heart was dancing joyfully because Lila had just said to him, "See you soon. . . ." Poor Nils, who was heading home at that very moment . . . He had no idea there were at least two death warrants hanging over his head.

16
The Bride Wore Green

"There's a man outside with his daughter. He wants to talk to you."

Arbayan knew this wasn't a good time to bother Leo Blue. But he also knew he mustn't go against the wishes of these important visitors, who were close friends of Joe Mitch.

"Kick them out," said Leo.

"He's a Master Worm Rearer. It's in our interests to listen to him."

"What does he want?"

"He's offering his help."

"His help . . ."

Lying in his hammock slung in the gloom, Leo started laughing quietly. He had barely left his Egg in three days. This business with Nils Amen had plunged him into a violent, despairing mood. He had trusted

Nils, allowing him to get close to Elisha, and Nils had abused this trust.

"I'll show them in," Arbayan ventured. "I'll explain that you don't have much time."

Leo didn't answer, which was his way of agreeing. He was deep in his thoughts again.

A few moments later, Arbayan introduced two rather extraordinary characters into the East Egg.

The father was on the plump side and wore a shirt with a ruffle from another era. His hair had been greased back and combed using fly gel, which gave his hair blue glints. His white shoes were polished, and he kept blotting his face with a big polka-dotted handkerchief. He looked suspiciously like one of those glowworm rearers who had gotten rich quick when fire had been banned in the Treetop.

It was hard to behold his daughter without wincing. She was as dull as he was shiny: a sort of fourteen-year-old doll who had been decorated with a bow or two, a few ribbons, and a bit of lace on her dress. The expression on her face was as blank as blank could be.

"Dear sir," said the visitor, who sensed Leo's presence in the gloom. "I bring you good news."

Leo sat up gingerly. There wasn't much in the way of good news just now.

"Please forgive my indiscretion," whispered the man in the white shoes, "but I understand that you're currently experiencing a few romantic problems."

This time, Leo nearly fell out of his hammock. Nobody had ever dared to speak to him on this subject.

"Mr. Blue, I am here to put an end to your troubles once and for all."

Leo tried to stifle the urge to strangle this nitwit.

"If you follow my advice, you'll be married tomorrow. Your situation is completely ridiculous. I mean, you're a laughingstock throughout the region. . . ."

Leo leaped to his feet.

"There's a very simple solution," his visitor continued calmly. "And I'll tell you what it is in just a moment. . . ."

Posted at the door, Arbayan was listening in. He knew this would all end very badly; he could see it in Leo Blue's eyes.

"The solution," said the man, "is right here. Marry my daughter, Bernice."

Poor Bernie (for it was indeed the unforgettable Bernie) tried to curtsy, but she snagged her right heel on the bow of her left shoe. She slid to the floor without a sound. Gus Alzan rushed to her aid.

"Bernie-wernie, my little . . ."

He was trying to pick her up by the collar, but she kept falling back down again. It looked like he was cleaning the floor with a mop.

In just a few years, the terrifying Bernie had changed. The girl who used to knock out prisoners by the handful in the ball of mistletoe at Tumble, the girl who used to bite the neck of anyone who bent over to kiss her, the girl who used to spend her life chewing on the toenails she kept in her pocket . . . Well, terrifying Bernie had become as expressionless as a toilet seat. And her father almost missed the Bernie of before.

Following the fire at Tumble, Gus Alzan had left the prison where he had been governor and applied himself instead to raising glowworms. He had become Master Worm Rearer in the Treetop, but he still had one obsession: marrying his daughter off to someone respectable.

Gus had dozens of employees to look after his glowworms. But out of all these workers, only one had put themselves forward as a prospective marriage candidate. His name was Tony Sireno, the very same assistant who had betrayed Sim Lolness. Sireno had worked for a while for Joe Mitch but was thrown out when he failed to get the professor to divulge Balina's Secret. That was when he was taken on by Alzan Lighting.

It was impossible not to be dazzled by the farm at first sight. The eggs, the larvae, the adults . . . when it comes to glowworms, *everything* is shiny. Visitors entered an incandescent warehouse that prompted them to coo with admiration, but these coos quickly became shouts of terror.

Glowworms paralyze their prey with poison, and all the worm workers came under regular attack. Little by little, they got weaker.

Tony Sireno became a shadow of his former self, as floppy and sleepy as Bernie, who had also teased the glowworms rather too much for her own good. Their engagement had only lasted one and a half days.

"Well?" asked Gus Alzan.

Leo didn't react.

So Gus bumbled on, "You're not going to get yourself worked up like this for three Grass people and a girl with a shaved head!"

Gus was sniggering now. In a few months, ever since people had heard about Leo's misfortunes, this had become a common expression. Three Grass people and a shaved head: they were all Leo thought about.

Leo walked over to Gus Alzan; his body was perfectly still, but his head swayed from left to right, as if to get rid of the rising tension. He whispered something in Gus's ear.

"What? I can't hear you!" inquired Gus, delighted by the familiarity struck up between them.

Closing his eyes, Leo repeated his message in Gus's ear. The latter smiled, thinking he'd heard, "Thank you, my dear."

"That's quite all right. Delighted to be of assistance."

"I said, get out of here!"

Stupefied, Gus let go of his daughter, who had been tilting dangerously in the direction of the floor for a while now. She collapsed in a heap.

Arbayan could see that his boss was on the verge of doing something that couldn't be undone. But Bernie was Joe Mitch's goddaughter, and an "incident" was to be avoided at all costs. Arbayan gave a warning signal to Leo, who suddenly managed to restrain himself from giving the head butt that the back of his neck was itching to give and instead walked slowly out of the Egg.

Poor Bernie stared at her swollen feet.

Dumbstruck, Gus Alzan pointed at the door through which Leo Blue had just disappeared.

"Where's he going?" asked Gus.

"This is very emotional for him," Arbayan explained. "Mr. Blue is overwhelmed by your proposal. He just needs a little time. . . ."

"Do you really think so?"

"We'll keep you informed."

"My daughter had that effect on him?"

"The greatest effect."

"Has he fallen for her?" Gus inquired with an impertinent wink.

"He's fallen, all right, Mr. Alzan. Allow me to accompany you."

Gus caught hold of his daughter's hand. "Come on, my little rag doll."

He dragged her to the door, said his farewells to Arbayan, and bumped into somebody who was entering in a great rush.

The person, who had just appeared out of nowhere, apologized flatly.

Gus's eyes nearly popped out of his head.

"Clot?"

Clot froze. He couldn't even speak. The only man he'd vowed never to cross paths with again was standing before him. Gus Alzan turned toward Arbayan.

"Don't tell me you trust this scoundrel," said Gus.

Clot's arrival at the prison at Tumble and his educational services to little Bernie . . . All these memories brought back a terrible period in the Alzans' life. Bernie had never been the same since those misadventures.

"You're dealing with the worst riffraff here," said Gus, pointing to Clot. "Beware of his grand words. I'm warning you now that if my little chick is to marry and make her home in this Egg, I don't want a rogue like that on the scene."

Gus clicked his heels and headed off, dragging Bernie by the hem of her dress.

Arbayan gave his soldier a questioning look. Clot, who was in no fit state to answer, turned red and stammered.

"I—I promise you that . . . I don't know what he's talking about. . . ."

Arbayan put his hand on Clot's shoulder and said indulgently, "Of course not. I have no reason to listen to what that man says, dear Clot."

Clot started breathing again.

"Thank you. I was scared that—"

"You've been irreproachable," Arbayan interrupted him. "You guard our prisoner with the greatest dedication. But there's something I recall you saying. . . ."

"Ah?"

"You've always said we can never be too careful. And you're absolutely right."

Clot smiled and shook his hand.

"You're very greasily with me, Mr. Arbayan."

His hard work was at last being recognized. His eyes brimmed with tears. He took a step toward the footbridge, but Arbayan went on, "And seeing as we can never be too careful . . . I must ask you to leave the Nest before tomorrow evening."

Clot stopped dead. He didn't turn around, or he would have thrown himself into the void.

Elisha didn't hear Clot come in. She was crouching down, holding a message that she had just received. The Shadow had sent it to her, on the tip of a second ice dagger.

Say yes to Leo.

That was all the message said.

Say yes to Leo.

These words had made her feel profoundly sad. Was this the route she had to take in order to regain her freedom? Of course, she'd been toying with the idea for a long time. Give in to Leo, marry him, and then escape; leave and never come back.

But her pride had always banished this idea from her mind.

"Ah . . . It's you. . . ." she said in a small voice.

"Yes," answered Clot. "I've come to bid you farewell."

"You're leaving?"

Clot couldn't manage an answer. He hadn't realized how attached he'd become to this girl. . . . He wiped his sleeve across his eyes.

"When are you leaving?" Elisha asked gently.

"Tomorrow."

They stayed there in silence for several minutes. Clot's sniffing was the only sound. Elisha fiddled with her message in the sad, gray light.

"It's not fair," said Clot.

The prisoner and her guard looked like two old branches growing far apart.

Elisha called out in a feeble voice, "Clot . . ."

He took a step toward her.

"Can I ask one last favor of you?"

The rumor landed on the Nest like a flock of birds.

"No . . ."

"Oh, yes!"

"No . . ."

"I've just heard."

"Her?"

"Yes, her."

"With him?"

It was a most unexpected piece of news, and the inhabitants of the Treetop had to keep repeating it to convince themselves that it was actually true.

"No . . ."

"I'm telling you, yes!"

The prisoner had relented. Elisha was going to marry Leo Blue.

Within a matter of hours, nobody could escape the frenzy of preparations. The marriage ceremony would take place the very next morning, on March 15. It had to be conducted promptly, since there was some concern about the bride changing her mind.

She had requested to marry wearing green, in the purest tradition of the Tree.

"As for everything else, do whatever you like," she told Arbayan, who had decided to make it a grand event. That same day he launched a campaign to renovate the Third Egg, which was being used to store leaves.

He had the interior repainted in a golden powder. He hung an enormous round chandelier that shone with a dozen glowworms. And last of all, he summoned the guests for the next day. Arbayan took it upon himself to persuade the Great Candle Bearer himself to conduct the ceremony.

The Great Candle Bearer was still bitter about the

way he had suffered at Elisha's hands. But he eventually accepted, once he realized that he would be stripped of his position if he refused.

The only person who wasn't caught up in these feverish preparations was Leo Blue. He didn't leave his bedroom, choosing instead to nurse his melancholy to the rhythm of his swinging hammock. The momentous news had made him turn even paler. Arbayan watched Leo bury himself in his silence. He didn't understand this despondency on the eve of such a happy day.

But Leo Blue knew: he knew why Elisha had finally agreed.

After the visit from Bernie and Gus, Leo had rushed over to Elisha's Egg. He had climbed up onto the top and abused the young woman's trust by giving her the signal to say yes: a simple message on the tip of a blade of ice.

Elisha had followed the Shadow's advice, believing the Shadow to be a friend of Nils Amen.

Leo knew that she was only hoping for her freedom; there wasn't even the tiniest space for a speck of love between the three letters of her YES.

Elisha was just slipping this YES through the gap in her cage, to force it open and then fly away.

Leo was paralyzed with shame. He had acted in this way in order to show a modicum of pride to his people and himself. Gus Alzan had said that he was a laughing-stock, and this was something that Leo couldn't stomach.

His whole life had been a battle to protect his honor, as well as that of his father.

But this marriage was just an illusion, like a *trompe l'oeil* painting. Leo was fully aware that he would be forced to keep his wife a prisoner until the end of her days. He had even quietly given Arbayan the order to position the entire guard from the Nest around the Third Egg, in case Elisha tried to escape during the ceremony.

Nightfall. Elisha could hear the sound of preparations. The footbridges between the Eggs were being reinforced. Spring was just a few days away, but it was snowing again. Men were exchanging orders.

Elisha looked up at her great green veil, which was hanging from a string above her head. They had brought it to her in the evening, freshly dyed; she had rinsed it herself and now it was drying. She was drinking a bowl of hot water as she listened to the snow sliding down the Egg.

Where did this sense of peace come from that seemed to wash her clean of worry? Her hair now formed bangs just above her eyes. She had tied two ribbons to the back of her head, like braids.

One thing was sure: she would be free tomorrow.

It began as the finest wedding of the century. The bride's veil was magnificent, covering her entirely. She left the Egg alone. Dozens of soldiers formed a guard

of honor as she made her way through their midst, over snow that had barely been swept. Her emotional state was visible from the way her dress trembled from time to time.

The Egg was filled with guests: poor people whom Arbayan had brought in from the different regions of the Treetop. In exchange for a meager bowl of soup, there were plenty of people willing to say "bravo" on command. They were sad-looking men, women, and children forced out of the worm-eaten branches where they lived in cramped conditions. They were stunned by the beauty of the chandelier and by how handsome Leo Blue looked in their midst.

Leo stood like a sleepwalker, in his dark jacket of bumblebee fur. Deep down, he knew it was impossible to feel any joy in the course of this great day. Everything was fake, including the guests. And yet . . . Elisha *would* have to take his hand. It would only be natural for him to tremble: he had never been allowed to touch her before. Perhaps this young woman didn't really exist at all? Perhaps his fingers would go straight through her as he tried to put his hand on her shoulders?

Leo no longer held out any hopes of taming this ghost. His only goal was to keep her close to him. Might she love him one day? He didn't really think so, not now.

The Great Candle Bearer crossed the crowd to collect the bride from the door. He greeted her with a little grimace before positioning himself beside her and guiding her through the public, toward Leo Blue.

For Leo, the whole ceremony happened in a shroud
of mist. He couldn't hear a word the Great Candle Bearer
was muttering as he shook a cube of peppery-smelling
incense. The words became distorted as they reached
Leo's consciousness. He couldn't quite believe she was
there at last. The ceremony went on for some time.

"Do you, Leo Blue, take Elisha Lee for your wife?"

The Great Candle Bearer's voice was like a distant
hum. Leo didn't reply. In the last row, right at the back,
Arbayan never took his eyes off his boss. He sensed that
something was going on. Perhaps Leo was just overwhelmed by the emotion of it all. . . .

But Leo wasn't so much overwhelmed as thoroughly
distracted. He had a doubt. A major doubt. Leo was staring at the bride who was right beside him, but he didn't
feel anything.

The Great Candle Bearer coughed.

"Do you, Leo Blue, take Elisha Lee . . . ?"

The crowd dared to let out a murmur of astonishment. Leo Blue still wasn't reacting.

"Mr. Blue? Mr. Blue?" inquired the Great Candle Bearer.

Suddenly, Leo took a step toward Elisha. Pushing the Great Candle Bearer roughly aside, he caught hold of a corner of the bride's veil and pulled it off in a single tug. The public let out a gasp.

It was Clot.

Elisha was running barefoot between the white feathers. She threw herself from branch to branch, and her arms rose like wings as she leaped through the air. She felt drunk on freedom.

Elisha had left the South Egg just after the solemn departure of the fake bride. There was nobody in the Nest alleyways, because everybody was at the wedding. She had run through the White Forest.

When the Shadow had asked her to say yes to Leo, she had instantly realized that this piece of advice didn't come from a friend, but she had decided to turn the situation to her advantage.

Elisha was amazed by Clot's courage. "I've got nothing left to lose. Tomorrow they're throwing me out." He had blushed a bit and added coyly, "Anyway, I've always dreamed of a big wedding."

And sure enough, while she was dressing him up

in his veil, Clot didn't look like a man who was down on his luck. Instead, he was almost meditative. All he asked for was to be allowed to wear his slippers.

"I just want to end up in my slipperties," he had said, brave and upright to the last.

As she bounded down the pathways of the Nest, Elisha recalled the expression on her friend's face as he had pulled the veil over it.

With this memory fresh in her mind, Elisha noticed two figures at the bend in the path; they were heading her way.

She jumped to the side and hid behind a bush of white down.

Elisha was stupefied by what she saw. A bride passed by who was absolutely identical to the one in the Third Egg at that precise moment. And behind her, a man Elisha immediately recognized: Gus Alzan.

"Hurry up, Bernie-wernie. Your husband is expecting you."

The bride was Bernice.

On hearing that a marriage was to be celebrated with Leo Blue, Gus Alzan had convinced himself that his own daughter was the betrothed. He was therefore leading her proudly toward the ceremonial venue.

His final advice to his daughter was clearly audible: "You just have to say yes."

"Yes," said Bernie automatically.

"Not now, you know that. We've rehearsed it all.

When you're asked if you'll marry him, you'll say yes."

"Yes."

"Not now, no."

"No," Bernie repeated after him.

"No! Whatever you do, don't say no!"

"No."

"Yes!"

"No."

Elisha waited for them to disappear before continuing on her way.

Clearly, nobody was expecting poor Bernie. But Gus Alzan's unfortunate mistake won Elisha some precious time. Shortly afterward, when the first men who'd been sent out to find the escapee discovered this young bride lost in the White Forest, they naturally mistook her for Elisha. They didn't hesitate to take her prisoner, despite her father's protestations.

The three or four unlucky men who triumphantly delivered Bernie to Leo Blue immediately saw from the look in their boss's eye that they would regret their mistake.

Elisha stared at the black hole that gaped in front of her. Clot had told her to slide down it. At the exit to the White Forest, the Nest was crisscrossed with long pieces of straw that formed tunnels. This straw tube would lead her toward the Branches.

Elisha launched herself down the slope.

Lying on her back, with her arms around her knees, she shot down the tunnel at top speed.

At last, she could let herself go. . . .

At last, she could stop fighting and resisting.

Happiness might just be at the end of this long golden tunnel.

And despite the strongest desire to find Toby alive one day, Elisha's first thought was of her mother's arms.

17
The Last Grass Person

The noise was so loud that Sim thought the dormitory had collapsed. Someone had just broken down the door.

In the darkness, Maya gripped her husband's arm.

"Don't move," Sim whispered.

The sound of boots was rattling around. Guards had entered carrying torches and proceeded to fling off the blankets to see the prisoners' faces. They were searching for somebody.

A flame was brought dangerously close to Sim's face.

"Here he is!" the torchbearer called out. "Hurry up and follow me. Things are sizzling for you this time, Sim Lolness."

"Yes, you've singed my eyebrows."

"What?"

"Could you keep the torch away—you're burning my eyebrows."

"You won't be making jokes for much longer."

The soldier grabbed Sim by his pajama collar and set off, dragging the professor behind him.

"I believe I've forgotten my glasses," the professor managed to utter. "They're under my pillow. . . ."

"Shut your mouth, you'll see better like that."

They disappeared in a deafening din.

Once the door had closed behind them, someone whispered, "I think they've found the tunnel."

Their tunnel was practically finished, and their escape was planned for the following week.

Darkness and silence returned to the dormitory.

Maya put her head between her arms: she couldn't bear it anymore. So much violence . . . So much stupidity . . . So much fear.

Maya Lolness no longer felt she had the strength to go on. Once again, her husband had been ripped away from her. With her face buried in the old mattress cover, she started crying. She did what she could to avoid being heard, but she was crying her eyes out.

It was so hard to keep fighting all the time. This had been going on for so long, and the hope on the horizon was so slim. . . . Who would she be able to count on if her husband disappeared for good one day? She was all alone at the bottom of the Crater.

Maya was very fond of the other prisoners, but how could she lean on them? And, anyway, had a single one of them said a word to her in her moment of suffering? Had a single one come over to comfort her in her moment of loneliness, even though they all knew what she had just been through? Men. At the end of the day, they were just a bunch of rusty, thoughtless men! Men who didn't know what a difference small gestures made, who didn't know about being sensitive and tender. . . .

Maya wept for a long time, with her eyes closed. And when she felt a little calmer, after an hour of tears, she turned onto her back with a sigh.

It took her a few seconds to see the crowd of men surrounding her.

The thirty dormitory inmates were all around her. Barely a moment after Sim's hasty exit, they had gathered, one by one, to form a group around her bed. Lou Tann's head was sticking over the mattress above her, Rolden's was next to Lou Tann's, and all the others had been watching over her for the last hour, shoulder to shoulder.

Yes, they were a bit stupid and clumsy, and they had no idea what to do or say, but they were there.

"If you need anything . . ." Zef Clarac offered.

Maya started laughing, very gently, and it was a laugh of genuine joy. They were all there, around her.

"Thank you," she said. "You're very kind."

The thirty elderly rebels returned to their beds.

When he realized that they were taking him in the direction of the classroom, Sim Lolness had a sense of foreboding that they had found out about the tunnel. He had no idea how he was going to get himself out of this one.

Joe Mitch was sitting in the professor's study with a napkin around his neck, eating. Sim had never witnessed one of Joe Mitch's meals before, and it was an experience he could have done without.

There was more food on Joe Mitch's napkin than there was on the plate, and even more on his knees and the ceiling. Razor and Torn were standing at some distance, to avoid the flying squirts of sauce. Even without his glasses, Sim was instantly relieved to see that the trapdoor over the tunnel wasn't open.

The professor was flung into a chair.

"Piece of cake!" He smiled.

Razor became the spokesperson: "The Friendly Neighbor is tired of your stories."

"I'm glad to see that they're not putting him off his food," said Sim.

"Be quiet!" shouted Torn.

He kicked the chair to drive the message home.

"You asked for time before revealing Balina's Secret,"

Razor went on. "You told us you still had some work to do on it, before . . ."

"The equinox," said Sim Lolness.

"The what?"

"The spring equinox."

"We don't give a fig about your knoxes!"

"March 20 . . . That's the spring equinox."

"Be quiet!" Torn roared. "Nobody asked you!"

Razor got a splash of grease on his cheek and looked up at the ceiling to see if it was raining. But Mitch had just sunk his teeth into the meat on his plate.

Razor coughed and started explaining again. "The Friendly Neighbor is very patient. But the Friendly Neighbor isn't stupid."

Sim looked astonished, as if he had just heard some shocking news. "Really?" he said.

"Be quiet!" yelled Torn.

"Could you confirm for me that you are indeed working properly on the Balina project?"

"I can confirm that," said Sim.

"And this? What is this?"

Razor picked up a box full of papers, which he proceeded to empty over the professor's knees. Sim looked at a few pages, almost gluing his nose to them, as he could hardly see without his glasses. The pages all showed the same drawing: a tree.

"Mr. Lolness, we have emptied your laboratory. It is full of these pieces of paper. There is no sign of a single piece of work on Balina."

Sim smiled amiably.

"I said that if I didn't give you the secret on March 20, you could do what you like to us. But until then, I don't think you're qualified to judge my work. Kindly put all these drawings back in my laboratory."

Mitch held out his dirty hand. He was given a bundle of drawings. He looked at them slowly as he sucked on a leftover bit of insect shell. Greenish juice dribbled from his fingers onto the paper.

Sim was seething. This handful of drawings, which they were getting filthy, was the fruit of research that had fired him up since his arrival in the Crater.

It had all started with a crack in his glasses. They had fallen, and the cracked section of glass created the shape of a tree. Sim had meticulously copied this design. The next day a storm had broken, and Sim had noticed the shape of the lightning. Trees! Always trees! Day after day, by observing a stream, cracked ice in a bucket, the veins in his arm, the veins in the leaves, Sim had found this pattern everywhere.

The shape of the Tree was following him. He didn't know exactly where this discovery would lead him, but he was amassing the evidence. And this new heavy file was keeping him alive. It was like a secret garden at the bottom of a mine.

Joe Mitch tossed the bundle of papers across the room. Sim got up to collect them but was sent back to his chair.

Mitch pulled out his napkin and wiped his face. He was spreading the sauce right up into his hair. Charming!

"Professor, don't forget that you have a wife," said Razor. "It would be a shame if anything unfortunate happened to her. You need to apply yourself seriously to your work. We want results."

Sim returned to the dormitory a little before dawn. He was clutching a bundle of greasy sheets of paper. Maya hugged him tight.

"Piece of cake . . ." said Sim, overcome with emotion.

"What did they want?"

"They wanted to know how I'd managed to charm you."

"So what did you say?"

"I said I didn't know."

Maya smiled sadly. Sim decided it was the moment to talk to her about Toby.

"Maya, I don't normally say anything I can't prove.

This time, I can't be certain at all—in fact I have virtually no evidence—but I believe Toby is alive. I don't think he's far from here."

Maya couldn't manage to speak.

"I'm telling you," Sim whispered, "because this hope is helping me."

"I got the impression that Plok Tornett wanted to talk to me about Toby a few weeks ago," Maya answered her husband. "He saw something. I didn't dare believe in it. But if you think that . . ."

Through his gestures, Plok had indeed tried to tell Maya about his encounter with Toby during the great leech hunt.

Sim and Maya were lying next to each other now.

At the first glimmer of dawn, they heard the voice of old Rolden, who was two beds away from them. "Professor, I'll be one hundred and three tomorrow."

"I know, Albert."

Councillor Rolden had been very tired for several weeks now. He kept reminding people that he wasn't sure about holding out until his one hundred third birthday.

"We'll have a party," said Sim. "Maya will bake her white tart for you."

Rolden knew all about Maya's white tart. But he also knew that there was no more chance of a white tart being baked in Joe Mitch's Crater than of poetry being created out of fly dung.

Maya wanted to set the record straight. "I'll make you one soon, Albert."

"Tomorrow," Sim insisted. "It's his birthday tomorrow."

Maya poked her husband with her elbow, but Sim got up and went over to stand in the middle of the dormitory.

"Friends, tomorrow night we will be outside. Get ready. We're leaving this evening."

On the other side of the Crater, in the Grass people's shelter, nobody had slept a wink all night. At one o'clock in the morning, two male captives had been brought to the edge of the prison area: two Grass people who had made it that far.

They had set out from the Grass in the middle of winter. They had overcome every obstacle but had been caught in the snow while snowboarding down a branch in the middle of the night. Every evening, Joe Mitch's men set their nets to catch prowlers and gnats.

They had caught these two Grass people.

Room was made for the newcomers in the freezing shelter where the other prisoners were sleeping. They had no strength left at all.

"Why did you come this far?" Jalam inquired sternly. He didn't like pointless heroes.

"We had no choice," the man said.

Moon Boy stood between Mika and Liev, staring at the new arrivals; they didn't know that the worst was still ahead of them, in the Crater. Back in the Grass, they referred to this as walking into the flea's den.

For several months, Moon Boy had been persecuted by a soldier called Tiger. This Tiger wanted to get him to talk about Toby and interrogated him behind the other guards' backs. Moon Boy was the only Grass person who knew Little Tree's real name.

He was hopeless at lying, so Moon Boy had to find other ways of telling the truth, without betraying his friend: "I've never called anybody Toby" or "There's nobody we address by that name in our country." Time and again, Tiger had nearly skewered him on his harpoon, but he didn't want to get rid of his only witness.

"Setting out in the middle of winter like that!" complained Jalam. "You didn't stand a chance!"

"It wasn't about chance," said the second Grass person.

"We had no choice," the other one repeated.

"What were you coming to do?" asked Moon Boy.

"Someone left the Grass with the first snows. We were looking for her."

"Who?" asked Moon Boy.

"It's unforgivable," said Jalam. "You shouldn't have left the Prairie."

"Who were you looking for?" Moon Boy asked again.

The two new prisoners looked at each other before turning toward Moon Boy.

"Your sister, Ilaya."

All the Grass prisoners fell quiet.

"Nobody understands why she left."

The fields of snow, the bark mountains, the vertiginous Trunk, all this and more flashed before Moon Boy's eyes. Could Ilaya have crossed all of that alone?

"We saw her very close to here three days ago," the man explained. "She nearly killed me when I tried to speak with her. I don't know what's happened to her. I don't know what she wants."

"Your sister has been full of anger since you left," said the other Grass person. "And since Little Tree left."

Moon Boy thought about his sister, only a few years older than him, who had taught him about the world, who had been his mother, his father, his whole family. He thought about Ilaya singing in wintertime, in their ear of wheat. Where had all that gentleness gone? What was Ilaya coming to do in the Tree?

"They'll catch her," said Moon Boy.

There was a hush.

"It's already happened, little one. They caught her at the same time they got us. But she put up such a fight that they imprisoned her a little higher up. We heard her cries as we went past."

"My sister's here?" whispered Moon Boy.

∽

That evening, in the classroom perched above the Crater, the thirty elderly students were awaiting the hour of their escape. A great silence hovered above them. Wearing warm undershirts under their pajamas and carrying food in their satchels, they were all ready to leave. Rolden's hands were trembling a little.

Seeing as nobody else felt up to teaching the class, Zef Clarac had offered his services. Everybody had looked at him in astonishment: Zef had no area of expertise whatsoever and had always been a bad student. He had succeeded in his career as a lawyer only because of chance circumstances.

One of the prisoners had advised him to give a cooking or embroidery lesson or to recite the times tables, but Zef had apologized for his lack of knowledge in those disciplines.

It was Maya who had eventually whispered a helpful suggestion.

And so Zef Clarac — the ugliest man in the Tree, the scarecrow of the Treetop — had just started giving a talk on "Inner Beauty."

Nobody, apart from Maya, knows what he said on the subject, because nobody was listening. Everybody's ears were strained toward the sound of footsteps coming and going in front of the classroom window.

Zef was talking into a void. He wasn't even thinking about their imminent escape anymore; quite simply he was telling the story of his childhood. He had regressed to the tiny misshapen Zef who had made the midwives faint the day he was born, the repugnant-looking little boy who had learned day by day to shine from the inside.

Maya thought it was an excellent lecture.

Sim finally gave the signal for them to leave. He got down on all fours and made his way over to the trapdoor.

At precisely the same moment, the main door to the room opened softly. Zef stopped talking. Sim quickly lay down on the floor. He heard footsteps coming toward him and then Zef's voice mumbling, "The professor is having a little snooze."

"I'll wait for him," came a loud voice overhead.

It was Pussykinska.

She stood there for a while in silence, very close to Sim. Zef picked up his lecture again, as a fascinated Pussykinska listened. She had never heard of inner beauty before.

When Sim realized that Pussykinska wasn't going to leave, he stretched, yawned, and sat up a bit.

"Another Grass person has arrived," said the female guard. "You're needed."

"Again?" answered Sim. "There were already two newcomers this morning."

"You have to come and see."

There was no way for Sim to escape these confrontations. Every Grass person that entered the camp was presented to him. He shrugged. He would get it over with quickly and be back in no time. Desperate to hear more of what Zef Clarac had to say, Pussykinska followed him with some reluctance.

"I'll be right back," said Sim before walking out of the door. "Wait for me. There's no change of plan."

The elderly students let out a long sigh. Rolden was trembling more and more. In two hours, he would be one hundred and three years old.

Sim entered a small room, where Pussykinska left him alone. He waited for the Grass person, but he was surprised by a second catch in one day. It was rare for a Grass person to be taken alone: usually they were caught in groups.

Sim waited impatiently for several minutes as he ran

over the escape plan in his mind. Sunrise was at seven o'clock. Even if they escaped at midnight, they would still have several hours of walking under the cover of darkness. That was enough time to reach a safe place and embark on the second phase of Operation Liberty. Thirty old people escaping from a prison as well guarded as this was an insane idea, but Sim knew that he could pull it off.

Nothing would stop them now.

The Grass person was shown in. The room wasn't lit, and all that could be seen was the blue mark on the soles of his feet.

"Do you know this old man?" asked the guard.

Sim's glasses shone in the gloom. There was a long silence as the two prisoners stared at each other. They grew accustomed to the dark, and Sim's eyelid started twitching. The shadowy face of the Grass person was motionless. Finally he said, "No, I don't know him."

Sim was very pale when he returned to the classroom. He sat down on a small chair and whispered something in his wife's ear. Maya's face was equally pale as she smiled and lay her head on Sim's shoulder. Her husband enjoyed the moment, the weight of her forehead pressing against his neck. He could feel hope, on velvet paws, finally returning to this low point of his life.

Zef was trying to carry on with his lecture, in spite of his distracted public.

Sim leaned forward and whispered a few words, which spread around the classroom from table to table.

These words finally reached Zef Clarac.

"Sim and Maya aren't leaving anymore. It's because of the boy who's just been captured among the Grass people. Sim recognized his voice: he says it's Toby Lolness."

A little flame had rekindled in Maya's eyes.

Sim kept staring at old Rolden. He was trying to make him understand how sorry he was.

But deep down, Sim was sobbing with joy.

Albert Rolden ran his hand through his beard and wrote a few words on a sheet of paper. This new message was passed along the rows. Eventually it reached the hands of Sim and Maya.

Some departures can wait. All of us here know that we won't leave without you.
Albert Rolden

Out of the silence, Maya started singing "Happy Birthday," and the others joined in as they surrounded Rolden. Their departure was only being delayed. They would all leave with Maya, Sim, and Toby.

Some guards appeared to make them hush. Their boots rang out on the floor.

It was almost a relief for old Rolden when the singing stopped.

He alone knew that, at the age of one hundred and three, he had another great, very great departure to fear, and no surprise would ever be enough to delay it.

18
Fugitive

Elisha felt as if a well-wishing wind was supporting her from behind, pushing her across the branches of the Tree. Her epic slide down the straw tunnel had thrown her out onto a jagged branch in the Treetop, from where she had quickly entered a lichen forest.

There were signs of spring peeping through, but the cold and snow were still holding out. Elisha didn't stop.

She came across wandering vagabonds who took no notice of her. She skirted around the edges of several sad estates, which looked deserted but where she noticed whole families hidden in the cracks of the bark, watching her pass by. She picked up the pace, impatient to find nature and the cleaner air lower down in the Branches.

The only pause she allowed herself was to watch an earwig tending to its eggs. It was a female, of course, since the husbands don't survive the winter. Elisha knew how much care the mother earwig took over its little ones.

One spring, she had watched a brood growing up near her house in the Low Branches. Every day, Isha took some food to the earwig family. As a little girl, Elisha had clung to her mother's skirts, scared of the earwigs' pincers.

Gradually Isha had taught her daughter not to be afraid. She passed on her understanding of the world: a simple understanding handed down not through words, but everyday gestures. Elisha would have liked a few words as well, but she knew that trust and tenderness were the finest gifts.

Right now, Elisha wanted to see her mother again. To do this, she needed to go to the place where she had left her, back to Seldor Farm, at the entrance to the Low Branches. Isha was bound to be there, with the Asseldors.

And so Elisha had taken the path down to the Low Branches, running for several days and nights. She knew that Toby had undertaken this great journey when his parents were already in Joe Mitch's hands, so she felt as if she was following fresh in the young fugitive's footsteps.

Throughout the winter, Nils Amen's visits were all that Elisha had lived for.

It was always the same ceremony. Arbayan would enter the Egg to announce Nils's arrival.

"Your visitor is here."

Arbayan looked permanently suspicious. He never left the pair of them without first casting a dark look in Nils's direction. These glances bolstered the trust that Elisha had put in the young woodcutter.

For the first few minutes, the visitor would recite a moralizing lesson that Elisha barely listened to. He would talk about Leo Blue, about how upright and honest he was, about his courageous battle against the Grass people, who had killed his father.

"You know, for a long time I didn't have a good impression of Leo either," he would say. "But all it takes is for you to hold out your hand to him. . . . Just give him a chance. . . ."

Each time Elisha would watch out for the moment when Nils started talking in the secret language. The language of memories. It would begin gently, without Elisha quite realizing. . . .

"For now, you're a prisoner," he might say, for example. "You're alone in the heart of winter. You've painted the walls of your cave with all your memories, but you are alone. Someone will come to find you. Someone will chip away at the ice that blocks the entrance. Someone will make you dance on the branch, by the shores of an immense lake."

Nils often referred to this lake imagery, which made Elisha feel as if she was listening to Toby's voice. She resisted the urge to turn to Nils and instead kept her back to him. But, with her eyes shut, she saw Toby's face.

ᵔᵔ

Elisha was traveling in the middle of the night; she was exhausted by now and level with Joe Mitch's Crater. She knew all about the dangers of this region, but she had to maintain her lead over those who were surely on her heels. Elisha was hoping to arrive ahead of them, before the news of her escape could spread.

She didn't dare stop.

Weariness was spreading through her body, and her step became less assured. She was making a concerted effort to get away from this area before morning. At dawn, her head started spinning; she fell to her knees and rolled into a bark ditch.

She had lost consciousness.

A strange tapping noise woke Elisha several hours later. It was broad daylight. She leaned on her elbows to see who was passing by on the narrow footpath that she was lying under.

A platoon of wild ants.

The ants were advancing very slowly, pushing an object as big as they were.

Elisha recognized a trap cage: hunters laid these kinds of traps to catch aphids. It was a large, ball-shaped cage that would be left open, camouflaged in the moss; its two halves snapped shut on any animal that ventured inside.

The ants had seized the cage together with the creature that was presumably trapped inside. They were transporting the cage back home, to force its lock and share the spoils with their sister ants.

Elisha wasn't very fond of red ants, which sting you before they devour you. They were one of the few insects that genuinely terrified her.

She was about to dive back into her hole and let the crowd of ants pass by when she witnessed the cage getting stuck on a wooden stalk. There was a certain amount of agitation among the rows of ants, who weren't sure which maneuver to perform. They were debating the matter in ant fashion, which is to say by tickling their antennae politely.

Intrigued, Elisha poked her head out.

She stuck her hand over her mouth just in time to stop herself from shrieking and immediately disappeared back into her hole. What she had seen made her heart pound in her chest.

The prey caught inside the trap cage wasn't a bug or an aphid or even a little beetle. It was a fifteen-year-old girl whose panicked wide eyes had met Elisha's.

The ants were having trouble getting the cage out of the rut it was stuck in. Elisha could hear them impatiently rubbing their legs together. Without thinking twice about it, Elisha leaped out of her hole and ran into the middle of the ants. Before they'd had a chance to notice her, Elisha had climbed on top of the cage, where she proceeded to swing a stick around her.

The young prisoner watched without reacting.

"I'll help you," Elisha called out to her.

There were already ten ants surrounding her, and they had started to climb up the rungs. Elisha shouted as

she hit the first beast on the head; it slithered down the cage and collapsed onto the bark. The strongest kick she could manage sent another ant tumbling, dragging two more in its wake.

The prisoner still hadn't moved. Behind the bars, she was much safer than the person risking her own life to free her.

Elisha's stick whipped up the air around her, but there were more and more ants. They were advancing relentlessly toward her. When Elisha pushed two back, four more set out to attack her.

After several minutes of putting up a fight, Elisha realized she wouldn't be able to hold out much longer. She gave a last thwack with the stick, which shattered on the cage between two ants. She was now unarmed and exhausted as she watched the red-skinned warriors around her. Then she looked up at the sky.

Elisha thought of her father.

She'd never allowed herself to give a face, a name, an outline to this father. But for the first time, she felt as if she could hear his laughter echoing in a hallway of her memory. It was a very gentle laugh. She didn't know anything about him; her mother had never talked to her about him. But his laughter was so clear in her ears that Elisha thought she must have gone over to the other side.

With her head still thrown back, she opened her eyes and saw a green shape hovering above her. She heard something that sounded like a blade cutting through the air. The shape brushed against Elisha and landed on an ant, which it seized and chopped cleanly in two. At the same time, the shape was dragging another ant off by its head. None of the ants was trying to escape this monstrous green force, which was about to destroy them one by one.

But at the next attack, they started scattering.

It was a praying mantis. The calmest and most violent of all insects.

Mantises can eat any creature, even one their own body size. This particular mantis extended its elongated foreleg to catch a fleeing ant and slit its abdomen. As it brought its victim back to its mouth, the mantis shot out its back leg, which made the cage roll.

Elisha clung to the bars.

The mantis's head span around one hundred eighty degrees to contemplate the trap cage that was sliding down the slope. Letting go of the ant it was holding, it started moving like an articulated monster. Sending out one of its pincers, it grabbed the cage and brought it close to its big dull eyes. The prisoner had fainted, but Elisha was still clinging to the outside.

The mantis tore off a few bars, and Elisha managed to slip inside. The insect stared at the two girls for a while before putting the cage back on the ground. A vibration ran the length of its green frame. Its antennae and hind legs collapsed, and the mantis rolled onto its back, dead.

Elisha stayed still for some time. By a freak of nature, this mantis had survived several months of snow, forgotten by the winter. It had hidden itself away somewhere, living off its hunting spoils. It had saved these two girls' lives, and now it had collapsed, without ever touching them.

This miracle made Elisha feel hopeful again. She dragged the young prisoner, who was still unconscious, out of the cage and covered her with Clot's coat. The girl's long, tangled hair fell over the garment's mud-splattered shoulders. Elisha realized this was a Grass person: every now and then, she caught a flash of the blue lines under her feet.

Apart from her mother, Isha, this was the first time she had seen someone of her own race. The girl finally opened her eyes to find Elisha scrutinizing her.

"I'll stay with you for a while," Elisha told her, placing her hand on the girl's forehead.

The girl pulled the coat over her face.

Elisha stood up and walked a few steps to fetch some water.

She came back and crouched down next to the girl.

"Do you want to drink?"

No answer. Elisha lifted the coat by the collar.

The girl had disappeared.

Elisha looked all around her. No movement in the lichen forest; the silence was almost troubling. Where had the girl come from, this apparition that had just vanished?

"Come back!" she called out into thin air.

She heard a noise behind a thicket and went over.

Elisha discovered hundreds of busy ants, who had come back for the mortal remains of the mantis and were starting to devour it. Ants always win in the end.

Feeling chilled to the bone, Elisha backed away and grabbed the coat. *That girl won't stay free for long,* she thought as she started to run.

Ilaya was caught the very next day, in fact, by one of Joe Mitch's patrols.

Elisha was soon close to Seldor Farm.

It was still dark, but a few rosy patches were beginning to spread across the sky.

Entering the Low Branches had brought a great rush of emotions and memories for Elisha. The sharp cold brought back all the smells of her childhood: in the air was the steam from a leaf-tea infusion, the taste of the first mornings of spring, and the smell of wood fires that makes the memory of winter live on.

Elisha knew exactly what she had to do, and she also knew how risky her plan was, but she didn't have any choice. Seldor Farm was so well guarded that she wouldn't be able to infiltrate it secretly in a bid to free her mother.

She needed to arrive with a fanfare, no holds barred.

Her coat was lined, so she turned it inside out to make herself look like a grand lady wearing a yellow-and-black fur coat. With her finger, she ran some black dust around her eyes.

Elisha approached the first guard post, took a deep breath, and launched into the adventure.

"I'll have them thrown to the birds!" she shouted. "Where are my stupid idiots of attendants?"

The two guards who heard Elisha coming toward them were dumbfounded. She was cursing her shoes at the top of her voice, because their heels had broken and she'd had to leave them behind.

"You're as stupid as starlings, as wretched as wrens, as limp as linnets!"

These insulting birds' names rang out in the lichen forests until, eventually, Elisha noticed the soldiers and called out to them, "And as for you, you're no help to me either, you bunch of good-for-nothings. I demand to speak with your boss!"

Intimidated, they began by taking off their caps.

"I . . . We . . . Let's see what we can do. . . ."

"You'll do what I'm telling you!" shouted Elisha.

One of the guards nudged the other one with his elbow.

"Have you seen who it is?"

"No . . ."

"It's the girl prisoner from the Treetop."

"D'you think?"

"I recognize her. I was here when Blue came to get her."

After a moment's hesitation, they pounced on Elisha, each of them grabbing an arm, and marched her off.

Elisha didn't call out. She just gave a small disturbing smile and allowed herself to be led away. Who could have imagined that this was exactly what she'd been hoping for?

The garrison at Seldor woke up immediately. The Garrison Commander, Garric, needed to be informed.

Elisha looked at the farmhouse out of the corner of her eye. It was a ruin now, and it no longer looked as if anyone was living in it. Elisha turned up her fur collar to hide how distraught she was feeling. Where could the Asseldors have gone? And above all, where was her mother?

Garric appeared in the farmyard, rubbing his hands. Ever since the Asseldors' escape, which had made a lot of noise, he'd been looking for a way to improve his reputation with Mitch and Blue. The capture of Leo Blue's fiancée boded nicely for such an opportunity.

"I didn't even know that you had escaped." Garric chuckled.

"Me neither," Elisha came straight back at him.

"I'd heard that you were going to marry Mr. Blue at last."

"So did I."

"So what are you doing standing between these two men like a fugitive?"

Elisha gave a glimmer of a smile and shrugged.

"I ask myself the same question, Mr. . . . . Mr. what?"

"Garric."

She held out the tips of her fingers toward him, to have her hand kissed.

"Delighted to meet you, Mr. Panic. Leo Blue has told me a lot about you."

Garric was flattered and confused at the same time. This young lady almost looked like she was enjoying herself. She had changed a lot since he'd last seen her and now resembled more of a princess with airs and graces.

"I shall return you safely to Leo Blue," he said without daring to touch her out-held hand.

"He'll be delighted to see you, because for some time now he's been wanting to chop your head off."

Garric nearly choked.

"I beg your pardon?"

"I'm saying that I don't think your head will count for much," Elisha explained, "when Leo finds out how you've treated . . ."

Brushing the dust off her fur collar with the back of her hand, she took her time before finishing her sentence.

" . . . when he finds out how you've treated Mrs. Elisha Blue."

The soldiers flanking her stared, goggle-eyed at their boss. Was it possible that . . . ?

"I know that Leo was terribly offended that you didn't attend our wedding, Mr. Panic."

"Garric," Garric corrected her between gritted teeth.

"Yes, Garric. I'm sorry, I really should remember your name. Leo is always talking about a certain Garric who'll never make it through the winter."

"You are . . . You are Mrs. Blue?"

"I suppose my husband hasn't arrived yet?"

"No, madam."

"What a pity. Could you instruct these two soldiers to let go of my fur coat?"

"Let her go," sighed Garric, who was almost in tears. "I am really, totally, absolutely . . . I am . . ."

"Don't apologize, dear boy. Why don't you just tell me if there's anybody here who actually has a brain in their head."

Garric didn't know how to react.

"A . . . ?"

"A brain. I have an important question. But I don't want to ask it to the wrong person."

"I can . . . perhaps . . ."

Elisha started laughing. Garric tried to join in, but Elisha broke off to say, "You?" She laughed even more. "You *are* joking?"

Garric turned red. He had never seen such insolence.

"Well, I suppose we could always try," Elisha finally conceded. "Do you happen to know, Mr. Panic, where the people who used to live in this house are now?"

Garric started twitching and squinted nervously.

"Those people lift, Mrs. Bli . . . I—I mean . . ." he stammered. "Those people have left, Mrs. Blue."

"Really? Isn't there a single one of them left?"

"No . . . Well, actually . . ."

"Yes?"

"There might have been a little one left."

"A little one?"

"A little one who did some stupid things."

"Where is he?"

"In my cellar."

"Show him to me!"

"He won't be a pretty sight. I've rather . . . forgotten about him."

Elisha insisted on being taken to Garric's cellar. It took a while to find the keys, because the trapdoor hadn't been opened for months.

"Smash that lock for me," Elisha ordered.

When Mo Asseldor was brought out, he couldn't even bear the daylight. Garric had locked him up after his family's escape. Mo had eaten the provisions in the cellar, thinking they'd never let him out of there. He recognized Elisha's voice, but he was too weak to react; he just heard her giving orders.

He didn't understand anything.

Mo was thrown onto a bench. He could feel the fresh air on his face, and he could smell the forest.

They were taking him on a sled somewhere.

Mo Asseldor didn't wake up until the next day. Elisha's big eyes were hovering right above him. He was lying on a feather sled with a blanket.

Back at Seldor Farm, Elisha had promised that she wouldn't say anything to Leo about Garric's monumental mistake.

"Really, do you mean it?" Garric had implored.

"On one condition, Mr. Panic. Let me take this little one out for some fresh air."

Elisha had stopped with Mo in a completely white clearing, and she was making him drink tepid water under a sky of entangled branches.

"Where are we going?" Mo managed to ask.

"We're going to my mother's," answered Elisha.

And once again, she started dragging the sled over the melting snow.

19
Butterfly

It was the third day of Isha Lee's fever. She was lying down in her house of colors. She knew she needed help but didn't expect anyone to come to her rescue.

Nobody had been inside the house for months.

Isha had caught a fever when she fell into the lake. The ice had cracked under her feet, and she had been shivering so badly from the cold that she'd barely been able to drag herself all the way back home.

She knew the remedy for her suffering.

Isha knew every single remedy.

But her body lacked the strength to go as far as the thicket that was growing close by in the bark, which could cure even the most violent fevers.

Isha wasn't afraid. Clasping a little portrait in the palm of her hand, she was shivering on her blue mattress. She had managed to get up to throw more wood on the fire, and now, to her eyes, the burning flames were distorting the light and casting strange shadows. Slowly, these shapes were being transformed into landscapes and people.

Isha saw the Prairie of her childhood again, an endless expanse that sloped toward the sun.

She heard the buzzing of wasps in the morning.

Isha used to sleep inside a flower in those bygone days, and sometimes she would be woken by the flight of a bee at dawn. She would open her eyes as the tiny tornado approached: the deafening noise of the insect, the air stirred up by the beating of wings, and the smell of honey. The pollen lifted by the bee made a little pink cloud all around her as she got up.

Isha wasn't afraid of wasps or bees or large hornets. All she had to do was leave the place to them, with a curtsy. She would slide between two petals and drop down the stem.

Isha sometimes liked to linger around the butterflies. She would stroke their bellies with the palm of her hand: nothing is more ticklish than a butterfly.

Isha had been the most beautiful and the wildest of the Grass girls.

The fever had thrown Isha Lee back into her memories. For a while she tried to resist, to hold on to her grip on reality.

But when she had no strength left and was crushed by the fever, she let go.

The years flowed over her. She found herself back on the day after her fifteenth birthday, the day that had determined the course of her whole life.

Isha was taking a nap on a wide blade of grass that towered over the Prairie, in the shade provided by a butterfly. She had just argued with her father, who had asked her to choose a husband.

Isha always had a dozen escorts around her, and they all dreamed of marrying her. The young girl didn't do anything deliberate to attract them. But just catching her eye was enough for any beholder to join the army of sighing men.

Some of them had done extremely stupid things in a bid to attract her attention. Nouk had leaped from his ear of wheat, using a dandelion seed as a parachute: he had broken both his knees.

Actually, there was nothing Isha enjoyed more than being on her own, and she would disappear for several days without anyone knowing where she was. Her father had gotten used to it in the end, because each time, Isha came back.

On this particular day, she was thinking about her next trip, when the butterfly that was shading her from the sun suddenly flew off, revealing a man on the other side.

He was carrying a large basket on his back.

"Hello."

Isha didn't answer him right away. She could see that he was different. His clothes didn't look like anything she was familiar with. He had an injured arm tied up in a sling.

"I'm sorry," he said. "It's my fault for making it fly off. I didn't see you."

Despite the fact that he was clearly tired and his eyes were sad-looking, there was something very solid about this man.

Multicolored butterfly powder had spread all the way up into his hair.

Isha had never paid much attention to men, but this one made her curious.

"I come from the Tree," the man said. "I'm working on butterflies."

"Working on butterflies." The expression sounded peculiar to Isha's ears. The words didn't fit together.

The traveler wanted to take the basket off his back, but he stopped mid-movement. His arm was hurting.

Isha got up and went over to him. For the first time in her life, she paid a tiny bit of attention to how she put one foot in front of the other, to how she walked in her dress. With her fingertips, she adjusted her linen cloth that was too tight at the hips.

She looked at the wound, running her hand delicately over it. "You're in pain," she said.

"It's nothing. A mosquito attacked me three nights ago. Are you a Grass person?"

"That arm needs taking care of."

The traveler looked at her and smiled.

"If you knew what gets said about your people . . ."

"Come with me."

"They say you eat your visitors."

Isha started laughing.

"Right now, you're spoiling my appetite with your gross arm."

Isha was laughing, then suddenly both of them were laughing: it was all decided in that one moment.

The butterfly passed by again overhead.

Isha led the traveler to her father's ear of wheat. They looked after him, keeping him in their home for the first week. The Grass children came to watch him for hours on end.

At first, they didn't dare draw near, but little by little the stranger tamed them as he showed them the contents of his bag. He was carrying long boxes, each one divided into compartments containing thousands of colors. The Grass people were familiar with a few only simple colors: red, yellow, and green, which they never mixed. They took all their colors from the Prairie plants.

But this visitor from the Tree was on a quest for butterfly colors, of which there is an infinite number. The hues went from golden to black via every kind of brown, ocher, silvery gray and orange.

The variety of all these colors fascinated the Grass people, who referred to the traveler among themselves as Butterfly.

They would file past, one by one, and Butterfly would put a dab of color on the tip of their nose.

Isha didn't disappear off on her trips anymore. She sat in the corner and never took her eyes off the man. Sometimes he turned toward her when he was talking to the children. She would lower her gaze as she tried to rekindle the wild look in her eye that she'd always had before. But, faced with this man, there was nothing wild about her anymore. She could have stayed there forever, like a pet animal, in her father's ear of wheat.

After two weeks, the wound had unfortunately healed.

"It's not perfect yet," Isha insisted, as she looked at the arm.

"You think not?" asked Butterfly. "I can't see anything. . . ."

"It's . . . It's inside. . . ." Isha explained clumsily.

The two of them were alone that evening, and, lit by the flames from a straw fire, Butterfly was showing his forearm to Isha.

"I can't feel anything anymore."

"We don't always feel what hurts us. You need to rest here some more."

He looked at her in silence.

"I have to leave, Isha. I have to get back to the Tree."

"But you're not cured," she insisted in a voice choked with emotion. "It's serious; it's very serious. You need to rest."

This time, Butterfly noticed her long eyelashes laced with tears.

"What is serious?" he asked gently.

Very close to the fire, Isha answered, "I'm the one who'll hurt if you leave."

Cracklings, rustlings, the sounds of night, everything fell quiet to mark this moment.

Isha put her head on Butterfly's shoulder.

How many men in the Prairie would have dreamed of being in Butterfly's place?

Neither of them dared move now.

"Me too. I'll hurt if I leave," said the man. "But there's something I haven't told you about, Isha."

He let the little fire in front of them hum to itself for a few moments.

"I had a life in my Tree. I was married to someone. I lost the person I loved. It'll take time."

"I like taking time with you," Isha whispered in a broken voice.

Butterfly decided to stay on a little longer. They kept this secret to themselves, and things carried on this way until the end of the summer.

The Grass people went on treating their guest with great kindness.

The old people invited Butterfly to sip violet nectar with them. The young ones followed him on his butterfly hunts. The women combed his colors into their hair. Small children hid in his basket when he set out on a walk.

They had all gotten into the habit of passing by the ear of wheat belonging to Isha's father to receive their little dab on the nose.

One day, however, things changed. Somebody saw Butterfly walking hand in hand with Isha at the foot of a clump of reeds.

The rumor spread through the Prairie as fast as wildfire.

Nobody was allowed to touch Isha: she was the favorite, the Grass princess. Nobody could imagine a young stranger from the Tree coming to harvest this forbidden flower, this wild flower with its scent that not a single man from the Prairie had been allowed to breathe.

Something that had never happened before took place among the Grass people: malicious tattle-tale, mumblings, secret meetings. Lee, Isha's father, didn't enter into this game. As soon as the old man approached, people fell quiet.

Children were instructed not to visit Butterfly anymore. The old people sipped violet nectar among themselves. Women no longer cared for Butterfly's colors.

But the worst happened at the very end of summer, when a small assembly summoned the stranger and ordered him to leave.

The next morning, the lovers disappeared.

They had gotten married without telling anybody. Now they were setting off in the direction of the Tree.

Alone, Isha's father bid them farewell in the middle of the night. There was a bitter taste on his lips. Did he know that he would never see them again?

The old man stayed for a long time at the foot of a clump of clover. He watched the two shadows disappear, together with their secret.

He had just learned that his daughter was expecting a child.

Remembering this departure from the Grass, sixteen years earlier, Isha, who was burning up with fever, felt the heat reach her belly, in the place where her baby had grown. Just at that moment, she heard a voice saying, "It's me. . . ."

Isha knew that she was sinking into a delirious state.

She had relived these memories with an overwhelming clarity. She was finding it more and more difficult to breathe.

But there was still this heat on her belly, this insistent voice. "It's me, Mom."

A strong light fell across her eyelids.

She opened her eyes to see that the flames were high now. Someone had thrown dry wood onto the fire beside her. Isha tried to raise herself a little.

"Who's there?"

Somebody had put their head on her belly.

"It's me," came the voice.

It wasn't until then that Isha recognized the face that was so close to hers. The short hair gave those features a strange energy.

"Elisha."

Elisha buried her head in her mother's neck.

"I'm going to look after you. I've come back."

Elisha wasn't alone. The figure of Mo Asseldor was waiting behind the fire, thin but smiling. He watched the embrace between mother and daughter.

Isha was still holding the portrait of Butterfly tight in her fist.

At exactly the same time, but much higher up, at the point where the Tree touches the sky, Nils Amen was walking into Leo Blue's Nest.

He wanted to see Elisha.

He didn't know anything about the last few days' adventures, or about Elisha's marriage and her escape, because he had been traveling through the Boughs of the North, deep in a jungle of lichen and creepers. He had been looking for a group of Flying Woodcutters.

Nils had been trying to find Toby, who hadn't visited the home of the Olmechs and the Asseldors for a long time. The families were worried about his disappearance. Nils had promised Lila that he'd find Toby again quickly.

"Can I count on you?" asked Lila.

Nils and Lila dared to look each other in the eye.

"I am your man, miss," Nils had answered.

He'd immediately realized there was another meaning to these words, but Lila didn't seem to be upset by this. She pushed back a lock of hair that was falling in her eyes, tucked it into her black velvet hair band, took off her glove, and shook his hand.

When it was time to let go of Lila's hand, Nils held on to her fingers for a second longer. There was as much tenderness in that second as in a kiss.

When they left each other, both of them felt as if they were seeing a little piece of themselves walk away.

Nils couldn't make up his mind whether or not to turn around. He told himself he'd feel disappointed if she'd already gone back inside the house rather than staying to watch him leave. But he decided to chance it. On the crest of the damp bark hill, he turned around slowly.

There was nobody left outside.

He smiled ruefully and set off walking again.

Behind the window, with her face and hands pressed against the windowpane, Lila's emotions were welling up inside her. She had seen him turn around, and she was starting to wonder if he wasn't a tiny bit in love with her.

Nils spent several days searching for Toby. He ended up tracking down his group of Flying Woodcutters, but Shaine and Torquo explained that Toby was no longer with them.

As a result, Nils was feeling distinctly concerned by the time he reached the Treetop Nest. He didn't want to miss his regular meeting with Elisha, but he was impatient to get to the bottom of Toby's mysterious disappearance.

Nils entered Leo's Egg. There was nobody there.

"Leo!" he called out.

He walked slowly into the dark Egg, headed over to the pyramid-shaped cage where the glowworm was shining, and pulled off the piece of material covering it. The spurt of light illuminated a general mess in the middle of which Nils recognized Elisha's yellow mattress.

Something must have happened.

"I didn't have time to straighten up. I was on my balcony, up there."

The voice coming from the shadows belonged to Leo.

"I'm here to speak to Elisha," said Nils.

Leo's breathing was audible, and he was behaving very oddly. Nils tried to stay calm and upbeat.

"I've come to see her. I think she's getting better," he went on. "She listens to me now."

Leo headed toward Nils Amen.

"I trust you," said Leo in a voice of ice. "If you think she's getting better . . . I trust you."

"It will have taken a winter," said Nils.

"Yes. A long winter. Do you know what I just was thinking?"

"No."

"I was reflecting on the fact that you're the first person I've trusted in a long time."

"Thank you, Leo. I'm your friend."

Leo Blue couldn't suppress a slight chuckle. Nils tried smiling as well.

Eventually, Leo went right up to Nils, stared hard at him, and opened his arms.

"My friend."

He hugged him.

Nils closed his eyes, before saying, "Can I go out on your balcony? I've never been up there before."

Leo made a sweeping gesture, as if to say, "Make yourself at home."

Nils turned his back on Leo and climbed the staircase that spiraled around the interior wall of the Egg. Leo watched him, following his every move.

When he had disappeared, Arbayan burst in with ten men.

Leo didn't even look at them.

"He's up there," he said. "Do what you have to do."

The men headed in the direction of the first steps. Leo signaled to Arbayan, who came over to him.

"Well?" asked Leo.

"I'm worried she may already be far away. All our troops have been in action since the first day, but the Tree is so huge."

"If you don't find her, I'll look for her myself."

With a bang, the men pushed open the door that led to the balcony.

Arbayan was the first one out. He had unsheathed his hornet's stinger sword, which was hanging from his belt.

Nobody.

The Treetop landscape stretched as far as the eye could see. The little balcony that was attached to the shell of the Egg towered over the Nest. It gave a view over the White Forest, the bundles of sticks that formed the Nest, and, farther off and pointing toward the sky, the buds whose snowy tips stood out clearly against the light. But Nils Amen had disappeared.

"After him, guards!" roared Arbayan. "He can't have gone far."

"Over there! His glove!"

A glove had been left behind on the shell, just below the balcony.

"He must have gone down that way."

The soldiers threw themselves onto the slope of the Egg and slid down the shell. Arbayan stayed for a moment on the balcony, before going back inside the Egg and closing the door.

A few seconds went by and then Nils appeared. Having hidden himself just above, he now jumped back down onto the balcony.

The moment that Leo had given him a hug, he had remembered Toby's words: *The day he gives you a hug, it'll mean he's found out about everything.*

Immediately, Nils had decided to escape.

"I thought it was rather surprising that you'd leave your glove behind."

Arbayan had pushed open the door and was standing just behind Nils, holding his weapon in his hand.

Nils stepped back. Arbayan was pointing his hornet's stinger sword at him.

"I knew you were a traitor," said Arbayan. "I knew it from the start."

"You're the traitor," said Nils. "You're the one who's betraying everything you stand for, Arbayan."

The two men stared at each other.

"When I was a small boy," Nils recalled, "I used to see you going through Amen Woods, to collect your colors from the butterflies' wings—"

"Be quiet, Nils Amen."

"You were the man I wanted to become. You believed in what you were doing. Now you've become a sidekick. A madman's sidekick."

Arbayan threw himself at the young woodcutter.

Nils stepped to the side, and Arbayan's weapon just missed his neck as Nils got ready to throw himself into the void. Arbayan saw him letting go of the balcony, bouncing and rolling down the wall, then getting crushed at the foot of the Egg. He thought it was all over. But after a couple of seconds, Nils got to his feet with some difficulty and headed off down a hallway of dry wood.

Arbayan gave orders from the top of the Egg. The troop spotted Nils, who was making headway toward the White Forest.

Nils had enough of a lead to escape the front line of his pursuers, but a few soldiers also rose up on either side, blocking his way. The stem Nils was advancing down was narrow, and he forced his way through the middle of the soldiers, sending them tumbling between the branches of the Nest.

Nils crossed the White Forest. His leg was hurting, and he could feel himself slowing down as his pursuers gained ground. Nils was almost out of the Nest. Suddenly, overcome by exhaustion, he felt as if his limbs were no longer responding. He collapsed to the ground. He could hear the voices of Arbayan's men drawing near. Nils knew he was done for.

The soldiers stopped just behind him.

Nils was resting his head against a lichen stem. He was thinking about Lila, her voice, her gestures, and her gentleness, which would be lost to him forever. He should have told her how he felt once, just once.

"We've got you, you filthy piece of scum," said one of the men, gasping from having run so hard.

He went over to Nils, but just as he was about to put his hand on Nils's shoulder, he heard, "This man is ours!"

Nils looked up. It was the booming voice of his father, and there were fifteen woodcutters by his side.

"This is our forest you're in," said Norz Amen.

There was a moment of general consternation.

Arbayan's soldiers looked at one another and quickly realized that there was nothing they could do. Those were the rules. They weren't allowed to touch the woodcutters.

Nils saw them waver a few seconds longer. Then they spat on the ground and headed off.

Nils turned toward his father. A huge smile lit up the young man's face.

All the woodcutters looked away, some of them discreetly dabbing their eyes.

Norz put his hand on the ax that hung from his waist. He looked at big Solken, who was standing right next to him, unflinching, and said, "The truth is, Nils, you're no longer one of us. You're our prisoner, awaiting sentence."

They grabbed Nils Amen like a common thief and dragged him off.

Norz tried to hold his head high, but his heart had been split down the middle, like a log.

20
In Tiger's Claws

The only person who could have vouched for Nils Amen's innocence, the only person who knew about his real plan and intentions, was down at the bottom of Joe Mitch's Crater digging wood in a cloud of dust.

Toby was wearing the Grass people's layer of mud on his body again and had set off to wander around the Crater. The blue lines on his feet could be spotted from a ways off. They'd caught him at nightfall.

This was exactly what Toby had intended. He'd handed himself over to the enemy.

Moon Boy, Jalam, and all the others were delighted to see their Little Tree again. Mika was trying to communicate to Liev the fact that Toby was once more among them, but Liev had already understood. He ran his fingers through Toby's hair and ruffled it, the way he used to in the Prairie.

A smile returned to the Grass people's faces.

"I saw my father," said Toby. "They stood me in front of him and asked me if I recognized him."

"Your father?"

All the Grass people stared at each other. The old man with the pancake on his head . . . So that was Toby's father.

"He's a good man," said Jalam. "One can tell that you're his son."

Toby nodded. Sim wasn't his biological father. Toby knew about this from Pol Colleen's revelations. But he was happy that Jalam should mention a family resemblance.

"We're all going to get out of here," said Toby. "I've come to help you leave, you and my parents, and everybody else who has to dig in this Crater."

The Grass people whispered among themselves, then Mika asked, "Do you know the way out, Little Tree?"

"Not yet," Toby apologized. "But there's always a way out."

"There's no way out of here," said Moon Boy, who could feel the tears welling up.

Jalam explained quietly to Toby how a character named Tiger came every day to interrogate Moon Boy. He told him about the story of the pendant.

"I don't have much more time," said Moon Boy.

"What does he want?" asked Toby.

"He wants to find you."

Toby remained silent for a long while. "I'll make sure

I'm careful. Nobody must recognize me. There's always a way out," he repeated for his own benefit.

Before going to sleep that evening, Moon Boy turned to Toby and whispered, "I've got something to tell you, Little Tree."

"What is it?" asked Toby, yawning.

"My sister is here."

Toby tried to hide his astonishment.

"Where is she?"

"I don't know. I think they've put her to work in the kitchen. Mika saw her up there."

"Your sister mustn't know that I'm here," Toby managed to say.

"Why?"

"I can't tell you. It's very important. Your sister mustn't see me."

Moon Boy didn't realize how serious this request really was. He thought it was one of the rules of that incomprehensible game that grown-ups call love.

Toby stayed awake all night long. What was being played was another game altogether, the game of life and death. Ilaya was now his greatest threat in the whole camp.

During the days that followed, Toby experienced what working life in the Crater was like.

He learned to blend into the group of Grass people. Not one of the guards recognized the person whom everyone had been looking for three years earlier.

Toby suffered with every swing of his pickax. The tool forced its way into the wood with a dreadful squeaking noise, and when a drop of sap rose up to meet Toby's feet, he couldn't help thinking about the Tree's pain.

One morning, he was lined up with a dozen Grass people, at the foot of a cliff of ravaged wood, when Tiger rose up in their midst. Jalam signaled to Toby. "That's *him*."

Tiger had a whip that had just grazed the convicts' shoulders.

"Look down, Little Tree," said Jalam. "Or he'll recognize you."

But Toby deliberately turned instead to catch the soldier's eye. He needed to be sure he wouldn't be unmasked. Tiger didn't react at all; he just kept on cracking his whip.

On the other side of the ravine, Liev was perpetually climbing and descending the side of the Crater. Saddled with several sacks filled with shavings, he guided himself by pulling on a rope that was destroying his hands. When the other workers were allowed a brief pause, Liev

didn't stop. Instead, a guard made sure that he was even more laden down.

The Grass people were alarmed to see him wear himself out in this way. They watched him climbing at his regular pace.

"I saw his hands and feet," Toby told Mika. "They bleed every evening. He won't be able to hold out for much longer."

"Liev is strong, Little Tree."

"He's got to stop."

"If he stops," said Mika, "they'll get rid of him."

Toby was always thinking about his parents, who were living right there, on the other side. How could his mother survive in this hell?

He had to act quickly, Toby knew. He observed the way things worked in the Crater, the customs, the changing of the guards. He was looking for a weak link in the organization that would allow him to communicate with his parents and all the others.

Once again, events sped up Toby's plans.

Every evening, the Grass people received a bowl of crimson soup with bits of boiled sponge floating in it. Basically, a disgusting large mushroom was tossed into a big cooking pot, and it stained the water red. This meal was doled out at the entrance to a den, which doubled as a kitchen. The Grass people would stand in line, one behind the other, and hold out their bowl to an old guard who stood behind the cooking pot.

The canteen server looked exactly like a sponge, and he must have thought he was seeing his own reddish reflection when he peered at the surface of the soup.

On this particular day, as they arrived for their meal, Moon Boy nudged Toby's shoulder.

"Look!" he whispered.

Next to the old canteen man, there was Ilaya.

She was kneeling at the foot of the cooking pot, blowing onto the fire. Toby shuddered. Without wasting a second, he left Moon Boy and let the person behind him go ahead as, little by little, Toby made his way back down the line. Slowly, he was getting closer to the end of the long line of Grass people, all waiting their turn.

Toby preferred to go without food than be seen by Ilaya.

"Why is this one acting up?"

Toby had accidentally bumped into two guards who were bringing up the rear.

He realized he couldn't retreat any farther. Obediently,

and looking ahead now, he advanced toward the cooking pot. Some way in front of him, Moon Boy had just been served. He had smiled at Ilaya but hadn't recognized anything in his sister's gaze. Her eyes were wild and violent, and the features of her good-looking face didn't move.

Toby was only a few paces away. One by one, the three Grass people ahead of him were served. He moved forward.

Toby held out his bowl and looked away. Ilaya had started to blow on the embers again. Only her hair tumbling down her back was visible. The cook filled up the bowl, and Toby headed off.

He had gotten away with it. He lowered his eyes, trying to make himself invisible.

All of a sudden, something tripped him up and he stumbled. A great peal of laughter accompanied his fall, as the boiling soup spread across the floor.

"You don't even look where you're going, you savage!"

The guards who had tripped him were treading their boots into the reddish liquid.

"You're always wanting to roll around in the mud, you bunch. . . ."

"Hey, girl!" the canteen man ordered. "Collect his bowl. He's eaten enough."

Ilaya obeyed. She left her fire and took a few steps toward the body that was writhing around on the floor. Toby got up at precisely that moment, and when he opened his eyes, he saw that Ilaya was looking at him.

She was beautiful, but something about her beauty inspired fear.

And she was smiling.

"Hello," she said.

Toby went to join the others.

At nightfall, Toby found Moon Boy curled up, his face buried in his knees, crying. Toby sat down next to him but didn't dare say anything. The others were keeping their distance, lying on their sawdust carpets. Some were pretending to sleep so they wouldn't disturb the two friends.

"Why didn't you tell me the truth?" Moon Boy sniffed.

Toby gulped. There was nothing he could say.

"Answer me! She wanted to kill you, that day when I saw you both. . . ."

"Yes," whispered Toby.

"What are we going to do?" Moon Boy sobbed.

"It's too late," said Toby.

Sure enough, there were footsteps at the entrance to the Grass people's shelter — slow, booted footsteps drawing near. Moon Boy had heard these footsteps all too often in the evening. They sounded like the steps of a casual stroller, but they were actually the steps of an assassin.

"That's him," Moon Boy whispered. "He's coming."

The man whistled as he walked through the middle of the Grass people, who were all lying down. His terrifying shadow grew bigger.

He came to a halt in front of Toby and Moon Boy. The whistling stopped. A dull sniggering could be heard.

"Well, this really is marvelous. . . ."

It was Tiger's voice.

"I'm a genius. . . ."

He stopped laughing, bent down, and grabbed Toby by the hair to turn his face toward him.

"I don't know what you did to that young girl, but she doesn't like you."

Toby kept quiet. Tiger let go of him and kicked Moon Boy.

"As for you, it's not like you were any help in finding him. I'll take it out on your sister."

Moon Boy leaped on top of Tiger, who struck him with the handle of his harpoon. The little boy crumpled at his feet.

"Nobody dare lay a hand on me! The sentry knows I'm here. If something happens to me, you'll all be massacred one by one."

Then, turning back to Toby, he said, "Come on. Uncle Mitch will be pleased to bits to see you. And I'll get to pocket my million."

The Grass people no longer dared to breathe. Moon Boy was watching his friend. What else could he do?

In the silence of the shelter, the sound of quiet chuckling could be heard, followed by outright laughter. It was Toby.

Tiger struck him on the knees, but Toby couldn't stop

himself. He received several more blows. Each time, he laughed more. He was choking from laughing so hard.

The Grass people were horrified. They thought their friend had lost his mind. Only Moon Boy realized that something was going on. He started chuckling in turn. Tiger sent him rolling onto the ground. But at the other end of the shelter, there was more laughter. In the space of a few seconds, all of the prisoners had burst out laughing.

"Be quiet!" ordered Tiger, blocking his ears and belching. "Or I'll crush you all."

When he was at last able to contain his giggles, Toby said, "I'm coming. Here I am. Sorry . . . It's nerves."

Tiger watched him stand up. Toby walked through the middle of the Grass prisoners, who were all drying their tears of laughter.

Tiger followed him, vexed, but after a few steps he made Toby stop and pressed the spikes of his harpoon against his neck.

"Would you mind telling me what made you laugh?"

Toby smiled.

"Nothing. It's nothing, really."

"Speak!"

"I'm worried you won't find it funny."

"I'm ordering you to speak."

"It's your reward of a million." Toby chuckled.

"You don't believe me?"

"Yes, but . . ."

"You don't think Mitch will pay?"

"Of course he won't pay, but . . ."

"But what?"

"But that's not the funniest part."

"Stop!" roared Tiger. "Stop mocking me!"

The tips of the harpoon touched Toby's throat.

"Four billion . . . You call that mocking someone?"

"Four . . . ?" Tiger choked.

"Four billion, yes."

Tiger retracted his harpoon. He was breathing heavily. The Grass people didn't understand much of what was going on, but they were watching Little Tree intently so they could copy his reactions. The word "million" didn't exist in their country. Nor did the word "billion," for that matter. You just counted up until twelve and after that you said "a lot."

"The Tree Sto—" Tiger managed to articulate.

"Yes, the Tree Stone," said Toby.

Tiger turned toward Moon Boy, who nodded proudly,

even though he understood less and less of what was going on.

The sound of more boots—someone was coming. Tiger looked nervous.

"Tiger!" the new arrival called out. "Now, Tiger, it's time to leave!"

"Wait for me outside," Tiger roared back.

The man retreated. It was Elrom, the guard at the gates, the one who held the keys. He had let Tiger in, and he knew it was forbidden. He was always uneasy about letting this brute be alone with the Grass people.

Toby felt the spikes of the harpoon on his neck again.

"Have you got the Stone?" whispered Tiger.

"Yes," said Toby.

Tiger turned around nervously. He was concerned about his colleague being so close.

"Give it to me!"

"Tomorrow at the same time," Toby said. "We can come to an agreement."

Tiger rubbed his hair. He was dripping with sweat. Toby continued calmly. "Tomorrow I'll give you the Stone if you don't let on that I'm here."

Tiger took a step back. The billions were flashing before his eyes. All that money was munching on what remained of his brains. He tried to resist for a few more moments but ended up giving in to temptation.

"Tomorrow," he said, backing away. "Tomorrow evening. Or I'll chop you into little pieces."

Tiger's footsteps grew fainter. All the Grass people

surrounded Toby. How had he magically made the man give in?

"We no longer have any choice about it," said Toby. "We have to leave before midnight tomorrow."

Then he went on to say, "I'll warn my parents and all the others. We'll take them with us."

"Have you found the way out, Little Tree?" asked Jalam.

Toby smiled. "I think I've found the way out for us, but as for them . . . I'm still not sure what we're going to do. I'll speak to my father about it first. Right now, we need to sleep and get our strength up."

They lay down on their carpets of sawdust and shavings. Sleep carried them away.

The silence of the night filled the shelter. Only Moon Boy's eyes still shone in the gloom.

A few minutes went by.

His tiny figure sat up. He stayed there, motionless for a moment, and then leaped to his feet. Nobody had noticed anything.

Without a sound, he glided between the sleepers.

Moon Boy shivered when he got outside. It was a clear but freezing night. He went in the direction of the barricade.

A ten-year-old boy walking barefoot under the moonlight through a ghastly work camp . . . His delicate shadow looked almost surreal.

Moon Boy was walking with a steady stride. His sister was the cause of all this. He had to fix things. He would

go himself to talk to the old man with the pancake on his head. He was the smallest, so he could squeeze through the barricade.

At four o'clock in the morning, Maya left the dormitory. She had just spent two hours in her bed staring at the plank of wood above her, unable to close her eyes. She went to sit down on a step in front of the door.

For the last few days, she had been living on the verge of tears. Knowing that Toby was alive, knowing that he was so close to her . . . To begin with, she had felt extra-ordinary joy. But then the joy had stupidly given way to anxiety. She felt responsible as a mother again, that fear that niggles its way into a parent's happiness — fear that something might happen, fear that the happiness might go away one day.

She remembered the day when Sim had turned up with a little bundle of swaddling clothes under his coat. A tiny baby wrapped in a blue blanket.

"He needs us," Sim had said.

Maya had only asked herself one question: "How will I know what to do?"

She had held the little boy clumsily in the bend of her elbow, and from that moment on everything had seemed so simple.

"His name's Toby," said Sim.

Before he'd even told her where the child came from, Maya had adopted him.

Now, as she sat at the bottom of the Crater with her chin on her knees, her gaze was lost in the night. She didn't feel the cold. She just closed her eyes a few times to remember how tiny Toby's feet were, when she had taken them for the first time in her hands to warm them up.

Opening her eyes again, she discovered an amazing little character. He was about ten years old, and he was standing in front of her in the cold night. His teeth were chattering and his purple lips trembling. His clothes were ripped, and the skin on his arms was streaked with a thousand tiny cuts.

Maya smiled at him. "Are you lost?"

"I am a friend of the person you call Toby," said Moon Boy.

In the white light of the half-moon, the scene looked like a painting. Maya put her hands together as if to pray, then she got up and kissed Moon Boy.

"Come with me, my dear."

She made him cross the dormitory on tiptoe and

then she woke Sim, who opened his eyes and grabbed his glasses.

She wanted to introduce the little boy, but Sim stopped her.

"I know who he is," he said. "I'm happy to see you here, my young friend."

He shook Moon Boy's hand vigorously.

Maya put a blanket over Moon Boy's back. She sat him on the mattress and rubbed his feet.

Moon Boy was quaking with this newfound sense of well-being. So this was what parents were. They rubbed your feet and called you "my dear." Luckily, he hadn't known what he'd been missing, up until now.

"He says to be ready," Moon Boy explained. "He'll come to find you tomorrow."

"What about you?" asked Sim.

"He's got an idea to get us out."

Sim took the time to ponder all this.

"Tell him not to worry about us. It'll be too risky for all of us to escape together. We've built a tunnel. We can leave from our side tomorrow night. It'll be a nice surprise for Joe Mitch."

Moon Boy agreed. "So, will I see you again?"

Sim gave him a hug.

"Yes, my little one. We'll find each other again."

Maya tried to keep hold of Moon Boy for a while longer, but it was nearly dawn. The little boy got down off the bed, flashed a smile at Sim and Maya, and disappeared.

Jalam found Moon Boy at dawn, sleeping in front of the Grass people's refuge. His clothes were in tatters and his skin grazed rough as a cheese grater. He hadn't even had the energy to drag himself inside.

"What happened to him?" asked Mika when he saw Jalam walk in with the little boy sleeping in his arms.

"I don't know."

Toby rushed over to his friend.

"Moon Boy!"

The latter found the strength to open an eye.

He muttered something.

"What?" whispered Toby.

"Your parents are very nice," Moon Boy murmured.

Toby immediately understood. Moon Boy had gone to the other side.

"I'll lend them to you," said Toby.

21

Escaping on the Equinox

It was a calm day on both sides of the Crater. The guards had relaxed their treatment of the prisoners, subjecting them to fewer blows and insults.

The last night of winter was Joe Mitch's birthday. Preparations for the big event took place all day long, and Mitch's men were ordered to celebrate as if the memory of his birth was a cause for rejoicing. Since the man himself found it hard to blow straight, they put only one candle on his cake. Not that anybody knew the exact age of the ugly oaf.

Strangely, Mitch loved sharing his enormous cake, the only thing he ever shared. But his men could happily have done without this rare show of generosity. Nobody wanted to eat a cake that Mitch had blown, spluttered, and spat all over for half an hour trying to snuff out a single candle.

Every year, the cake-tasting ceremony prompted grim faces and pinched noses. Barely concealing their disgust, Joe Mitch's men chewed the thick snot that covered their portion.

For this reason, the guard on duty at the night school that evening felt relieved to have escaped the birthday party. Most of his colleagues had volunteered to swap places with him, but he had generously swept such offers aside.

"I don't mind making a personal sacrifice," he'd said.

He glanced through the classroom window to make sure that the lesson was running normally. Sim Lolness was standing behind his desk, and all the elderly students were looking very attentive in their seats. Little Plok Tornett was wiping the blackboard.

The guard settled down for an evening of sitting peacefully outside the classroom, watching the time go by. He'd never really understood what exactly he was supposed to be keeping an eye out for. Did anyone seriously think there was a risk of this bunch of old madmen escaping?

He chuckled to himself.

On the other side of the Crater, the sentry who was guarding the Grass people didn't complain about his assignment either. Elrom, who wore little round glasses, had tasted Joe Mitch's cake the year before and had no desire to try it again.

"Who goes there?"

The guard squinted through his glasses, trying to recognize the person approaching in the dark. Elrom hadn't been expecting any visitors this evening.

"Ah! It's you. . . ."

Big Tiger was standing in front of him. Elrom fiddled nervously with his glasses. He was scared of Tiger. What did he want with the Grass people, tonight of all nights?

"Open up for me."

"Again? Have you got . . . permission?" stammered the sentry.

"I've got permission to squash you if you put up a fuss."

"But I—I mean . . ."

He started to open the gate but kept on muttering, "I was told that . . ."

"Shut it!" roared Tiger.

Elrom promptly shut the gate again.

"Open up!" shouted Tiger.

"Er . . . am I closing it or opening it?"

"Shut your mouth and open the gate," growled Tiger, grabbing hold of his harpoon.

The guard realized there was no point in arguing. He unlocked the gate to let Tiger through, closing it behind him.

"Don't stay too long," he called out to Tiger.

"I told you to shut it!"

"I already have," said Elrom, turning the key in the lock a second time.

Tiger often paid visits to the Grass people. Only

the day before, Elrom had begged him to leave because he was lingering in the shelter. What dubious plot was he hatching?

The guard knew all about Tiger's cruel streak. The rumor among some of the guards was that Tiger had killed Nino Alamala, the famous painter. Every evening, Elrom liked to draw in private. He had always been a great admirer of Nino's works.

Elrom knew there was a risk of Tiger's visits to the Grass people ending badly, so it was with a degree of anxiety that he awaited the return of the soldier with the harpoon.

The noise from the party could be heard in the distance. Stupid shouting, laughter, stamping feet . . . A real hullabaloo. You'd have thought it was a fly taking off. This was an expression used by one of Elrom's friends, a bumblebee tanner. In his job, he was familiar with the deafening racket flies make when they take off.

Elrom was trying to imagine what the atmosphere was like up there. The presents, the muted applause, and the big banner with the obligatory: HAPPY BIRTHDAY, JOEBAR K. AMSTRAMGRAVOMITCH! This was Mitch's full name, the one that was used on important occasions, but the big tyrant could only get his tongue around the first and last syllables. He didn't have room for twenty-four letters inside the small empty box of his brain. So he'd only ever been called Joe Mitch.

When Elrom realized that an hour had gone by and Tiger still wasn't back, he decided to find out what was going on. He grabbed a torch and opened the gate, then locked it from the inside and put the key in his pocket.

The light from the torch disappeared into the Crater. Elrom was grumbling into his beard that it wasn't his job to guard the other guards, and, anyway, how come Tiger got permission to leave the birthday party?

Elrom was now at the entrance to the shelter, where the Grass people slept. He swapped the torch into his left hand, freeing his right hand to grasp the knife that hung from his belt. The Grass people didn't really frighten him, but Tiger did, a lot. He had a nasty sense of foreboding.

"Tiger!" he called out.

Nobody answered.

He took a step toward the narrow opening.

"Are you there?"

He thrust the torch ahead of him, came to an abrupt halt, pushed his glasses back up his nose, and held his breath.

He went in.

"Ooohhhh . . ."

The cry he tried to let out fizzled into a feeble whimper on his lips. In no time at all, his face was covered in drops of sweat and his eyes got progressively wider than the lenses of his glasses. Was he hallucinating?

Elrom nearly dropped down like a dead leaf.

What he saw was hideous. The corpses of the Grass people were piled up in the middle of the room, bathed in a pool of blood. Behind them, wiping his harpoon on a box and with his back to Elrom, sat Tiger.

Elrom staggered toward him, holding his scarf over his mouth as he tried not to gag.

"What have you done?"

Tiger turned around.

But it wasn't Tiger.

It was a much friendlier face.

Elrom was dealt a powerful blow to the head—a blow that made him crumple and that took him to a faraway place, among the stars.

"Thanks, Jalam," said Toby, emerging from the shadows.

He was still holding the beam that he'd used as a weapon. He looked at brave Elrom.

"I feel sorry for him. He wasn't the worst . . ."

Jalam agreed. He'd rather enjoyed playing the part of Tiger. They both turned toward the pile of Grass people.

"Are you coming?"

A body on top of the pile was the first to stir. Then, one after another, the Grass people started moving. In a matter of seconds, all the corpses came back to life. They gathered around Toby.

His idea had worked. He searched Elrom's pockets and produced the key. With the help of three men, he rolled the unconscious guard toward Tiger, who was also out for the count.

Tiger had fallen for the same trick of this nightmarish spectacle, mistaking the famous canteen red soup for blood. All the Grass people had kept their rations from the previous evening to smear over themselves.

It had been easy for Toby to take a horrified Tiger by surprise.

At first, Jalam had needed some coaxing to play the part of Tiger. He wasn't sure about putting on the soldier's coat. He didn't like the idea of trying to pass himself off as somebody else.

"But I'm not him. . . ."

"No, you're not him, but you can pretend to be."

"No, I can't, Little Tree, because I'll still be me, so I can't pretend to be someone else."

"You don't stop being you; it's just that you make people believe you're him."

"But then I'd be doing something that wasn't true."

"Yes!" Toby had concluded angrily. "We need you to do something that's untrue in order to save all of our lives. There are times when the truth doesn't matter, Jalam."

Jalam had been won over, though Toby already regretted what he'd said. For him, the truth always mattered.

Right now, old Jalam was still wearing Tiger's coat and strutting around the room like a star actor. He kept making all sorts of faces, playing the bad guy, imitating Tiger's accent to terrify his friends.

"Let's go!" said Toby.

The group of Grass people formed a line. Silent as a breeze, they walked out of their shelter and stood by the edge of the Crater.

Toby opened the gate with Elrom's key: this was the second time he'd tried to escape from the Crater.

The first time he'd been thirteen years old, back when the Crater was just a few woodpecker holes deep. Now it was an abyss that gutted the Tree, gnawing away at its heart. In the brilliant moonlight trickling through the branches, Toby surveyed the extent of the damage.

"Do you know the way out?" asked Mika, who was leading Liev by the arm.

"Yes, I do," Toby replied.

A few years earlier, also on the run from Joe Mitch's barbaric ways, Toby had escaped with Mano Asseldor. He headed for the spot in the Enclosure where he'd been lucky the first time.

Liev's smile expressed complete understanding. He didn't need eyes or ears to sense the wind of freedom. Freedom has a smell; it has a taste. Freedom is something you feel in your body. Mika could feel Liev's hand pressing on his wrist.

Meanwhile Moon Boy reached the front of the column of men, having worked his way up the line of Grass people, followed by Jalam, who was still playing the part of Tiger. Moon Boy walked quickly to keep pace with Toby, because he wanted to have a word with him.

"I'm not leaving without my sister."

"What?"

"Go on without me," Moon Boy insisted, panting. "I'm staying here to rescue my sister."

"Don't talk nonsense," said Toby, without slowing down at all. "You'll do what I tell you to do. And I'm telling you to come with us."

Jalam backed up Toby's words with a stern look.

"I'm staying!" Moon Boy sobbed.

It broke Toby's heart to see Moon Boy upset in this way, but this time it was his duty to behave like a big brother.

"It's not up to you to decide, Moon Boy. There's nobody left here to rescue. Your sister isn't a prisoner. She denounced me. She's with the enemy."

Toby's hard voice echoed inside the small boy's head. He stopped and looked down. Toby didn't turn around. Surreptitiously, Jalam followed Moon Boy, pretending to rejoin the Grass people bringing up the rear.

They reached the Enclosure. The hole had been blocked with only a thin layer of lopped-off branches, and in a few minutes they'd cleared a passageway. This wasn't an escape; it was a stroll by moonlight.

Toby stood there, watching his Grass friends crossing the Enclosure, one by one. He knew there was still a

long adventure in store, but for now he was enjoying this peaceful victory.

Toby thought about his parents, who had promised to escape at the same time. Perhaps they were already out ahead. . . .

The last Grass person stepped into the breach with a small boy on his back. It was old Jalam, who was bright red and didn't dare look Toby in the eye.

"I . . . I hit him. . . . I could see he was trying to leave, so I hit him."

Moon Boy had fainted, with his head on Jalam's shoulder. Toby gave the old man a flicker of a smile.

"You did that?" he asked.

Jalam could hardly believe it himself.

"My hand just shot out."

"It's your costume," Toby explained. "You're still play-ing the part."

"Do you think?"

"Without you, Moon Boy would probably have been captured by those oafs. You did the right thing."

"I didn't want to hurt him. . . ." Jalam sniffed.

He was stroking Moon Boy's forehead.

The Grass people were free.

A second later, the night-school guard got up to check that everything was in order and the classroom was calm. He had just spent the last hour sitting against the class-room's only door, so he stretched as he trod the few steps separating him from the window.

Calm? Yes, the classroom was calm.

Perfectly calm.

So calm, in fact, that there was nobody in it.

The guard didn't move. He stared at the big empty room, without even noticing that he was munching his hat. He couldn't believe it. Panic paralyzed his body: the only movement came from his chattering teeth and his eyes rolling in every direction.

Several minutes and half a chewed hat later, he finally reacted. He opened the door, praying that by some miracle the thirty old students would be back in their places.

But there wasn't even a wisp of a white hair.

Down in the tunnel, progress was very slow. Sim had sent Plok Tornett out in front, followed by Councillor Rolden. The professor was immediately behind them, because Maya had refused to go ahead of Sim. She'd been too frightened of losing her husband in the past, and now she never wanted to take her eyes off him again.

The rest followed.

Zef Clarac brought up the rear of this line of heroic old people, whose combined ages added up to two thousand years. But if you added up the collective experience crawling through that tunnel, you would never have room for all the different occasions, the laughter, the moments of anger or grief, the regrets and joys, the loves and blunders that had filled these individual lives.

They were making their way on all fours, soundlessly. From time to time, Sim could hear Councillor Rolden breathing. The old man had clasped him for a long time before entering the tunnel.

"I'd stopped believing in it," Rolden had said. "Now anything is possible. Perhaps I'll even enjoy a bit of freedom in my twilight years."

Sim had smiled at him.

"When you get to one hundred, the counter goes back to zero. You're the youngest among us."

But Sim felt worried every time he sensed old Rolden slowing down ahead of him. This time, the old man was trying to turn around to say something to Sim.

"There's something sliding down my back."

"It's nothing," said Sim. "Go on."

"I can't," Rolden answered. "The ceiling's coming down on my back."

"Don't worry," the professor repeated. "Keep going, my friend. We have to keep going."

This had been Sim's only concern since the start: making sure that Albert Rolden didn't lose his mind. On the nights leading up to their escape, the councillor had experienced panic attacks in which he thought he was fighting off moths. Each time, Maya had sponged down his face with water and he'd eventually calmed down.

Someone from the back of the line called out, "Can't we go any farther?"

"No," whispered someone else. "They think Rolden might be losing his mind."

"Rolden never loses his mind!" exclaimed a furious Lou Tann.

Out in front, Professor Lolness was insisting, "Just follow Plok Tornett—he's right in front of you. . . . Trust me, old friend."

"I trust you completely," said Rolden. "But I'll say it again: I've got the ceiling on my back."

Maya was the first to notice.

"Sim," she whispered. "Why don't you listen to what Albert's telling you? Perhaps the ceiling really *is* falling on him."

In a flash, everything fit into place in Sim's head. He realized exactly where they were. Albert Rolden hadn't lost his mind—he was spot-on. A splintering noise broke the silence.

"Get back!" roared Sim. "Everyone move back!"

The professor grabbed Rolden by the feet and gave him a sharp tug. The tunnel collapsed ahead of them in a crash of broken floorboards.

An oversize mass blocked the passage, a pink slug that writhed around on its back and roared. It was a nightmare. Sim was holding Rolden in his arms as Maya helped them to edge backward.

"What about Plok?" Vigo Tornett called out. "Where did Plok Tornett go?"

Sim didn't have the strength to reply. In his arms, the councillor was making desperate whimpering noises: "I'm begging you . . . Pleeeease . . . Don't tell me we're going back there. . . . I can't take it anymore. . . ."

The slug, which was still writhing and wriggling

around at the far end of the tunnel, was none other than Joe Mitch.

Mitch had just walked across his lavatory floor.

Responding to an urgent call of nature in the middle of his birthday celebration, he'd staggered to the cramped room with the fugitives' tunnel running directly underneath it. He'd barely had time to undo his pants and stamp his boots when the floor had given way.

A few months earlier, Zef Clarac and Lou Tann hadn't done a very thorough repair job in replacing some missing slats from the wooden floor. And they'd immediately started digging in another direction, without realizing that this section of the tunnel was now vulnerable.

When all the old prisoners emerged in single file through the classroom trapdoor, crestfallen and dusty-eared, there were fifty soldiers waiting for them.

Sim and Albert Rolden appeared last. Maya noticed Sim's inscrutable gaze. He would never be able to forgive himself for this failure. She wanted to take his hand, but the two of them were roughly separated.

Joe Mitch was roaring as he came in, carried on a stretcher by eight exhausted men. Someone turned to him with a pale expression and said, "I've counted. . . . There's one missing."

One of Joe Mitch's eyes was closed because of a plank that had landed on him when he fell. He closed the other and bellowed with all his strength.

"It's Plok Tornett," the guard specified.

Mitch's bellowing turned to a howl.

"Ploooooook!"

Razor and Torn entered quietly. They had come from the bottom of the Crater and looked pallid as the moon. Each was trying to hide behind the other, to get out of having to speak.

"Er . . ." Razor managed in the end. "There's a few more than one missing."

Joe Mitch stared at him with his huge bulging eye.

"The Grass people have escaped. All . . . the . . . Grass people . . ."

Torn showed a man in: Tiger was still recognizable beneath the big bandage that covered his head.

"It's Toby. . . ." said Tiger. "Toby Lolness has returned, and he's led them all away."

Joe Mitch fell off his stretcher.

Maya and Sim Lolness looked at each other. Toby's name formed a bubble on Maya's lips, which floated gently over to Sim, who received it with closed eyes.

A little lower down in the Branches, Plok Tornett was running in the open air, through the moss forests. He was alone, disorientated, and in shock.

But for the first time in a very long time, and despite being out of breath, he was talking.

22
Toward the Low Branches

Toby and his Grass troop came to a stop after one day and two nights. They might have continued their brisk march if fog hadn't descended in the middle of the second night. They huddled between the stalks of a lichen thicket.

At last, the Grass inhabitants could sleep perched on high again, something they'd sorely missed in the Crater. They liked to feel the air circulating beneath them and their bodies swaying with the leaves.

Toby managed to close his eyes for a few hours, before rising early and signaling to Mika.

"I think I know where to find some food for these sleepyheads. Follow me."

Mika was trying to work out what time it was, through the thick mist.

"Let's take Liev with us," he said.

The three of them set out, with Liev walking behind Mika, holding on to his shoulder. The shadow cast by the lichen made for freezing conditions, and the snow was still holding out against these first few days of spring.

Toby knew he wouldn't be able to accompany the Grass people for long. He was just waiting for the right moment to set out in search of Elisha. As far as he knew, she was up in the Treetop, still in Leo Blue's Nest. But first he wanted to lead his friends to a safe place; then he'd embark on his journey across the Tree alone.

Sensing Liev let go of his arm, Mika had come to a standstill. Toby turned around at the same time. The fog was like a wall hemming them in.

Liev had disappeared.

Mika was moving frantically in every direction.

"Liev!"

He knew that calling out like that was pointless. The greatest danger his friend faced was getting lost. When you can't see your way or hear anyone calling out, all it takes is a momentary lapse of concentration and you're lost forever. Mika had already thought he'd lost Liev for good on one occasion. It had happened one evening in the Grass, but luckily Mika had found Liev sitting calmly in a muddy crevice.

We won't always be so lucky, he'd reflected at the time.

Toby couldn't understand what had happened. He was going around in circles, looking for Liev in the mist. Just then he spotted Mika being raised into the air, as if sucked up by a whirlwind. Toby threw himself at Mika, grabbing hold of his legs at the last moment. He was hauled off the ground as well but managed to snag both feet on a loop of moss that was firmly fixed to the bark. Their ascent came to a sharp halt.

"They're lifting me with a rope," Mika called out. "It's around my waist!"

"Cut the rope!"

Toby's feet were still clinging to the moss, but he was close to losing his grip. Mika wasn't having any luck cutting his makeshift belt. He looked up and saw a man shinnying down the rope. He just had time to see him wielding an ax and cutting the cable, before tumbling with him to the ground.

Toby came crashing down at the same time, hitting his head on the bark. As he got back up again, he heard, "I've got him. Don't worry."

Toby was ready for a bare-knuckle fight. He advanced through the dense mist toward Mika's attacker.

"What are you doing?" roared the man as Toby threw himself at him.

Toby deliberately rolled to the side, having just recognized one of the Flying Woodcutters.

"Shaine!" he called out.

"We've been following you since this morning. I know these two Grass people are holding you prisoner."

"I'm not anybody's prisoner! Let the man go!"

"Torquo's got the other one!" answered Shaine, who had no idea what was going on.

"Let the man go, Shaine! He's my friend."

Shaine couldn't bring himself to release the young Grass person.

"Let him go," Toby repeated softly, with his hand on the woodcutter's shoulder.

Shaine released Mika, and Toby explained, "There's no reason to be afraid of the Grass people. And it's high time the whole Tree came to terms with this."

"Where's Liev?" asked Mika.

Toby looked questioningly at Shaine.

"Torquo's got him."

Mika grinned as he rubbed his rope-gouged arm.

"I'd be surprised . . ."

And sure enough, they found Liev waiting patiently at the top of the lichen stalk. He was sitting on top of Torquo, who was sighing underneath.

It took a while to make Liev understand he could let Torquo go.

Shaine and Torquo were staring at Toby and his two friends in fascination. They had never seen Grass people so close up.

"Who are you *really?*" Shaine finally asked Toby.

Toby stared back at him. Could he tell these two Flying Woodcutters the truth? He thought back to the long working weeks they'd spent together in the lichen forests. He also reminded himself how much he needed them, along with all the good-hearted people left in the Branches.

"I am Toby Lolness."

If Toby had said he was the Queen Bee, Shaine and Torquo wouldn't have been more surprised.

Toby Lolness was a legend. And without realizing it, the Flying Woodcutters had spent the whole winter with the most famous fugitive of all time.

They looked at each other in silence.

"If they find out you're here . . ." Torquo sighed.

"Everyone thinks you're dead," said Shaine.

"If Leo Blue knew . . ."

"He won't find out," Toby interrupted them.

Shaine frowned. "You should beware of him. People say he's gone crazy since his bride-to-be escaped."

Toby felt the mist close in on him. "His . . ."

"His fiancée," Shaine repeated. "She escaped."

Toby remained silent for a long while and Mika watched. He was the only one to guess at the turmoil inside him.

"I'm going to ask you something. An enormous favor," Toby eventually said to the woodcutters. "Take these men to the place I direct you to. It's a house deep in the woods where two families live. Tell them I sent you and that it'll all be fine."

Shaine and Torquo exchanged looks. They trusted Toby, who proceeded to trace out on the bark the path that led to the house where the Olmechs and the Asseldors lived.

"There aren't any houses in that area," said Torquo. "There's just a forest that's impossible to access."

"Trust me. There's a house on exactly that spot."

Shaine shook his head.

"Everybody knows there's nothing in those woods."

"Well, stop repeating what everybody knows, and go and see for yourselves!"

Toby gave a sign to Mika.

"Mika, bring the others with you."

"The others?" queried a wide-eyed Shaine.

"Yes," Toby called out as he headed off. "I warned you it was an enormous favor."

"Toby!" shouted one of the woodcutters, who wanted to tell him about Nils Amen's betrayal. "Toby, wait!"

"Farewell!" cried Toby, and vanished.

That same evening, Shaine approached the house in the woods by himself. He couldn't believe that people lived in such inaccessible branches.

Milo and Lex watched him get close. How had this stranger come so far?

Shaine raised his hand in a friendly manner. The Asseldor sisters came out of the house, together with their mother and little Snow. Mrs. Asseldor feared bad news involving her son Mo, whom she believed was

still in the hands of the soldiers stationed in the Low Branches.

"I come on behalf of Toby Lolness."

Lila dropped the plate she was holding and ran over to him.

"Where is he?" she cried. "Where's Toby Lolness? I have to talk to him. . . ."

"He's gone."

"Where? Which way did he go?"

Milo put his hand on her shoulder.

"What are you doing here?" he asked Shaine.

"I was going to ask you the same question."

Milo didn't answer. Lex wiped his hands on his vest.

"I worked as a Flying Woodcutter with Toby," Shaine explained. "He's asking you to look after his friends."

"His friends?"

"They're waiting a little lower down. I can call them."

Shaine looked at Lila, who was crying quietly. Mrs. Asseldor went over to give her a big hug.

"Do you know all about the Nils Amen affair?" asked Milo.

"Yes. He was collaborating with Leo Blue. He deserves his punishment."

Lila escaped from Mrs. Asseldor's arms.

"That's not true!" she shouted. "I know it's not true. And Toby's the only one who can prove it. We have to find Toby Lolness. Nils will be killed for a crime he didn't commit. He was never in league with Leo Blue."

Shaine felt moved by this young woman. He looked at her attentively and would have liked to help her.

"Toby left this morning. He's already got a day's head start on us. It'd be impossible to catch up with him now; you know what he's like. He can head down between the branches faster than a snowflake."

Lola shared in her sister's suffering. She hadn't needed Lila to confide in her to realize that her sister loved Nils. The announcement of Nils Amen's imprisonment by the woodcutters had brought this secret feeling out into the open.

Lila wasn't engaged to Nils—in fact, she hadn't even declared her love for him—but she was drowning in a widow's grief.

Like her little sister years earlier, she collapsed with the anguish of it.

"Who gave me daughters like these?" wondered Mr. Asseldor.

"Me," answered his wife, who was secretly the most romantic of them all.

Shaine put two fingers between his teeth and whistled. He was answered by a far-off cry.

Seeing the small crowd of Grass people approaching, Milo thought he must be hallucinating.

"But . . . Who *are* these people?"

"The friends I told you about."

"The . . . Are you crazy?" whispered Milo. "You think we can look after all—"

"You're the one who's crazy, Milo," boomed a deep voice from behind him. "Since when did an Asseldor ever refuse anyone hospitality?"

Mr. Asseldor appeared, and Snow slid down the roof into her grandfather's arms.

"Tell them to go behind the house," he added. "They can help us to build their camp."

Led by Torquo, the Grass people went around the back of the house in the woods. Shaine and Torquo slept in the attic that night, and for some of the time they could hear the sweet songs of the Grass people.

"It's true—they're not the way I'd imagined them to be," Torquo whispered to Shaine.

"They're good singers," Shaine replied.

The next day, just as the Flying Woodcutters were getting ready to leave the house, news broke that Lila had run off.

"She'll be back," said Milo.

But Lola knew her sister, and she was sure that Lila had set out in search of Toby. He alone could save Nils.

Mr. Asseldor went to sit on a bark dike that protected the house from the rivulets of melted snow. Two of his children were out there, somewhere in the wilderness. . . . He felt overcome with a great weariness.

A few paces away, Mrs. Asseldor was watching her eldest son, Milo, who was holding his head in his hands. Of all her children, he was the only one not to have had a stormy time. Or rather, the only one not to have shown it. And the only one to have endured everyone else's tempestuous emotions. Lola, Mano, Mo, and now Lila . . .

People said that Milo was a boy with no problems, which meant that sometimes they forgot to take proper care of him.

Mrs. Asseldor went over to sit next to her son. She stroked Milo's hair tenderly, the way she used to when he was little, and hugged him close to her.

Young Lila didn't waste any time. She had made a promise to herself that she'd catch up with Toby, and she knew the places where she was most likely to find him: the house in the Low Branches and, most of all, the lake. She had as good a knowledge of the region as Toby.

The insects that saw the little russet-colored slip of a girl flash past, dressed in blue and galloping over the black bark, must have thought they were dreaming. The emotion of it all made her even more beautiful. She would have made a black ant blush.

By the next day, she was close to Seldor. Lila was fully aware that since their departure from the farm, the

Asseldors were not welcome in the region. So she hid for a few hours to get some sleep.

As she continued her descent at dusk, she thought of her Nils. What did she know about him? Their entire story amounted to an unspoken conversation that had taken place over a few weeks. Silence, trivial words, their clothes touching by accident. Nothing more. And here she was risking her life for him.

"My Nils . . ."

All she knew was that he was innocent of his crime. She had heard him talking to Toby about those visits to the Nest.

Lila stopped and caught her breath for a moment. She put her hands on her hips to get rid of a stitch.

"I'd given up waiting for you. . . .You're late for our meeting."

The voice came from behind the skeleton of a dead leaf. It was a lugubrious voice, a voice that Lila had heard somewhere before.

When the man appeared, she didn't recognize him right away.

It was Garric, the Garrison Commander of Seldor and the author of those letters. The spurned lover. He had a horrible smile on his face. Lila had humiliated him by running away, and he'd been dreaming of revenge for a long time.

Lila grasped all this in an instant. She turned around and started running. The stitch had returned, but she kept going as fast as she could. She repeated Nils's name as if it was a magic charm that would make her disappear, fly away, vanish into thin air.

"Nils!"

But Lila could almost smell Garric just behind her. With every step she took, he got closer. Blinded by tears, Lila was calling on the Tree and the sky to help her. It wasn't her own life she was trying to save—it was Nils's life. She had a mission. If her life stopped here, then Nils's life would end too.

Garric was puffing just behind her.

When she felt the man's hands grabbing her dress, she let out a scream that made the lichen creepers all around her tremble. She fell to the ground as Garric's hand clutched her throat.

"We could have been happy," said Garric. "We could have—"

A hiccup finished off his sentence. His body collapsed on top of Lila.

A sword had just gone through Garric's back. A sword made from a hornet's stinger, and Lila even felt the tip of it brush against her.

She jerked to shake off the body before collapsing in the snow.

An elegant man in colorful clothes stood beside her. Lila, who had never seen Arbayan before, was completely breathless on the soaking bark.

Arbayan pulled off his glove and held out his hand.

He had been following Garric since the previous day. On learning that the imbecile had let Elisha get away, Leo had charged Arbayan with punishing him.

Lila took the man's hand. It was firm and honest, and he helped her get to her feet.

"Thank you," said Lila.

"I should have acted earlier. I'm sorry, miss."

Arbayan was staring at her, and Lila responded with a tired smile.

She felt safe. He was clearly a kind man; perhaps he could help her find Toby.

Arbayan retreated respectfully with his customary good manners before turning and heading off.

And then it happened: Lila said one word too many. A single word that would change the course of history.

"Wait!"

Arbayan froze. He came calmly back toward her and

looked at her with his blue eyes. Lila drew even closer. Yes, she trusted him.

"I'm looking for somebody," she explained. "Can you help me?"

"I don't know," said Arbayan.

Lila folded her arms and in doing so closed her coat. Her wet hair fell over her eyes.

"I'm looking for Toby Lolness."

Arbayan didn't move. It had been a long time since he'd heard *that* name. And it was a name that would interest Leo Blue.

"Toby Lolness?" he whispered very softly.

"He's got to be somewhere around here, in the Low Branches."

"Perhaps," said Minos Arbayan.

Lila needed to talk. This man had saved her life.

"He's trying to meet up again with the girl he loves. . . . He told me about a lake in the Low Branches."

Arbayan might have looked calm and distant, but his heart was beating fast.

"The girl he loves? Is that you by any chance, miss?"

"No . . ." She smiled. "Her name is Elisha Lee."

Lila had just handed all the keys over to the enemy.

"I don't know your Toby Lolness," said Arbayan without batting an eyelid. "And I'm not sure about any lake in our Tree. Good luck to you, miss."

He headed off, with a strange bitter taste in his mouth.

Leo Blue was waiting for him an hour away from there, wrapped in a black shawl and sitting near a carpet of glowing embers. He didn't even look up at his adviser when he returned.

"It's done," said Arbayan.

Leo's eyes were lost in the fire.

"Garric is dead," Arbayan went on. He crouched down on the other side of the fire, hesitating.

"I've got something to tell you, Leo Blue."

This time, Leo could hear the emotion in Arbayan's voice. He turned to him and said, "Speak."

But Arbayan no longer had any desire to speak. He no longer knew on whose side the truth really lay.

"Speak," Leo said again.

And Minos Arbayan spoke. Once again, he felt as if each word was distancing him from the person he really was.

On the other side of the fire, the poison of hatred and fury welled up in Leo Blue's veins.

Elisha and Toby.

Toby and Elisha.

They loved each other.

An icy gust ran across Leo's body.

The freezing wind made Arbayan shiver and almost extinguished the flames as it passed by.

Alone in the night, Leo set off in the direction of the lake, to meet Toby.

23

Duel Under the Moon

Mo Asseldor held out a bowl to Elisha.

Warm rays of light spread across the floor in the house of colors.

Spring!

On these first fine days, the cacophony in the branches sounded like an orchestra tuning up. Intoxicated by the honey smell of the buds, swallows whistled and the flowing sap sounded a deep note. The bark was cracking in the sunshine. Melted snow ran in rivulets around the house.

Elisha took the bowl in her hands. A silvery powder floated on its surface. Isha had prescribed her own remedy, and in just a few days, the fine fern powder was beginning to save her.

Elisha pressed the rim delicately to her mother's lips. Isha sipped at the infusion, keeping her eyes on her daughter. She sensed that Elisha had changed, that she was both kinder and stronger.

"It's over," Elisha repeated. "We're heading for the good weather now."

Every now and then, Isha turned toward Mo Asseldor.

"He's doing better, the little one."

Beautiful Isha's words made them laugh, because she was the one visibly coming back to life, hour by hour.

Mo was playing at being the man of the house. He blocked up the holes that recent winters had nibbled out of the old door, and he washed the squares of cloth. Mo returned from these epic laundry sessions with weary, multicolored arms.

Sometimes Isha worried about the arrival of spring. She always received a visit from a regiment of soldiers at this time of year. They came down to the Low Branches, when the snows melted, to inspect the ruined homes.

The year before, they had ended up staying the whole night. The hours had gone by slowly for Isha, who was hiding in the wood store. With each log the soldiers took, the pile had gotten lower, and she was frightened of being found out. Luckily, they had left just before the last layer of wood.

Now Mo kept an eye out for what was happening in the distance. He knew they might come looking for them, even in the most remote part of the Low Branches. When he noticed a figure below the house climbing the hill with some difficulty, he flung himself to the ground and crawled as far as Elisha.

"They're here!"

The pair of them helped drag Isha Lee behind the last blue cloth screen. They huddled there, between the cloth and the wooden wall.

"Leave me," whispered Isha. "You can still make your getaway...."

Neither Elisha nor Mo moved.

The door creaked: dragging, unstable footsteps. Isha thought she recognized the limping man from the Great Border, a soldier who sometimes came to get drunk in the house he believed to be deserted.

The footsteps came to a halt. And a dull note rang out. Elisha thought it was a song, a sad tune she'd heard somewhere before. But her mother was the first to recognize the refrain as the music that everybody shares, whatever branch or era you're born into. The only song you hum on the first day of your life through until the last. A sob. A stifled sob.

Elisha appeared gingerly from behind her cloth screen. Finding someone sitting in the middle of the room, sobbing into his sleeve, she went up to him.

"It's you, Plok Tornett.... It's you...."

Plok didn't seem startled. But his tears flowed twice as freely when he heard Elisha's voice, and he hugged her tight.

Just then, Isha appeared on Mo's arm. None of them

knew where Plok Tornett had come from or how he had survived, but they gave him a king's welcome.

For days on end, Plok had fed on the milk of wild grubs. He had chewed on bark and sucked on snow. He didn't seem too weakened by the experience, but he looked more distraught than ever. He had found himself alone, in the middle of the night, at the exit to the tunnel, when all the others had been prevented from going any farther by the roof caving in. He'd careened down the branches without knowing where he was going. His legs had instinctively led him to the Low Branches.

He had looked for the house he used to share with his uncle and found it burned down, with the charred remains of grubs on the ground. Both Joe Mitch's and Leo Blue's men had destroyed everything in their path.

That was when Plok had remembered young Elisha. She had always been kind to him, and he was grateful for that. Perhaps there was some hope for him with Elisha and her mother. So he limped as far as their house. But when he found their home abandoned, he crumpled to the ground.

Which is why it came as such a relief to see Elisha, Isha, and Mo.

"You can stay with us," Elisha told him.

She had always suspected there was a wound at the heart of Plok Tornett's life. Vigo Tornett, his uncle, always insisted that Plok had been cheerful and talkative, both as a child and later as a young man. Plok's loss of the power of speech had been sudden and brutal. In an instant, he had been struck dumb and stalked by fear.

Plok accepted the pancakes Mo Asseldor gave him. He gulped them down, as if worried someone might start eating them from the other end.

That evening, Isha contemplated the three young people in front of the fire. Proud Elisha had repainted the blue lines on the soles of her feet in caterpillar ink. She was staring dreamily into the flames. Mo and Plok were asleep, propped up against each other. There had never been so many people living in this house.

And then Isha thought back to the day when she had arrived on this branch, sixteen years earlier, alone in the world. At the time, she couldn't believe there would ever be any light in her life again. She no longer had anybody. She had left the Grass full of hope and love, and on the arm of her Butterfly, but she had lost everything along the way. Misfortune had swooped down on her.

She had sought refuge in a hole in the bark that would become the house of colors, situated where the path forked, just above the Great Border. With her energy failing, she had tucked herself away. Everything frightened her: the way the wind twisted the branches, even the night sounds, which were different from those in the Prairie.

It was one week before the birth: seven days and seven nights before Elisha. Isha stayed in the hole, listening to the creaking of the Tree and saying her lover's name over and over again.

Sensing the hour of the birth approaching, she had felt terribly abandoned. She had so often dreamed of Butterfly holding her hand when the moment came. There are some kinds of loneliness that make you want to disappear altogether.

But just holding their baby in her arms was all it took to understand that she'd been wrong. She realized that she hadn't been alone for the last nine months after all. When she had found the strength to leave the Grass with her love, and above all when she had seen Butterfly dying in front of her, Elisha was already there and would never leave her.

The four dwellers in the house of colors stayed together all night long. They were huddled against each other, on one side of the flames.

Mo was thinking about his family.

Plok was chasing his perpetual demons as he swayed his head slowly backward and forward.

Elisha was meditating on her plans. She knew she would set out the next day in search of Toby, but she wasn't ready to tell her mother yet. Toby was hiding somewhere in the branches. She had to find him. She would start with the lake.

As for Isha, she still held the miniature portrait of Butterfly in her closed fist.

When he had given her this round frame, Butterfly had explained to Isha that it was the work of a great painter. A man called Alamala. Isha was eternally grateful to the man whose paintbrushes had fixed the face of love forever.

Today Isha had made the decision that it was time to tell the whole story to Elisha. She was going to talk about her daughter's father. During the night, she rehearsed what she would say in the morning. Words that would stick the pieces of the past back together again and put faces to shadows.

When the others dropped off to sleep, she was still watching over them.

Not far from there, a young man with boards strapped to his feet was heading down the snow-covered branches. Despite the way barely being lit by the moon, he was sliding down at an incredible pace, before he side-slipped at the bottom of the branches and then set off again over bark slopes.

Toby was heading toward Elisha. His boards left two parallel tracks that cut out every now and then as he

jumped over an obstacle or a patch of bare wood. The
snow was thin on the ground, but there was still a sufficient covering in the lichen forests of the Low Branches.
He had to stay in the shadows, between the blades of
moss, reemerging in a chance beam of moonlight.

Sometimes a snowy bud appeared in his path before
he'd had a chance to spot it. He used it as a springboard
and felt as if he was flying. Each time, he landed firmly
back on his boards, with no loss of speed. His bluish figure disappeared in a veil of snow.

When he finally came to a stop, day was breaking.
He was exhausted and his breath looked purple in the
morning light.

Toby wasn't far from the lake. He was sure that
Elisha would be there. His eyes were stinging, and
already the smell of dawn was familiar. He recalled their
first meeting. That strong little girl, brown as the wood
of the Tree, who had watched him swimming. He could
still hear his first words to her: "It's beautiful," he had
said, staring at the lake.

Elisha had taught him how to look at the world.

He kicked off the remaining snow from his boards. He still had to head down for another few minutes, and then he'd see their lake.

Toby was about to set out when he heard a beating wing whipping up the air behind him. He turned around and threw himself into the snow to avoid the object. But a second boomerang followed at ground level, and Toby rolled to the side. The cruelly sharp blade brushed against the back of his head. Toby suddenly stood up.

Leo was standing in the moonlight, fifty paces higher up. He grabbed his two weapons as they came back to him and stared at Toby. Any closer and he'd have sliced his enemy's head open.

Toby ran his hand over the small cut on his head. He was bleeding. He jumped back onto the slope and started sliding down again. He had only his bare hands to fight with. He couldn't tackle Leo out in the open.

The two boomerangs, hurled simultaneously from both hands, followed him at top speed. Toby could see that they were about to cross. Their blades gleamed. He side-slipped and stopped dead as the boomerangs passed by, just in front of him, brushing against each other.

Toby continued on with his downward journey. He had listened for the sound of the weapons going back into their sheath. But Leo was chasing him now. As he turned around, Toby spotted his enemy running through a riverbed that followed the snowy slope. Toby bent forward to pick up speed. Leo looked like he was flying over the stream of water. They were both approaching the cliff overhanging the lake.

The snow was becoming patchier. Toby's snowboards were scraping against the damp bark.

He stopped on the edge of the precipice.

Leo hadn't let Toby out of his sight as he followed behind. Toby kicked off his boards and started running down a sheer path between some moss bushes. He could see the purple lake with huge patches of ice floating on it. On the other side, the waterfall was like a great torrent because of the melting snow.

Leo had seen Toby disappear behind the moss. He headed down toward the lake as well. He wasn't tired. He could feel his whole body focused on one goal: destroying the person who had betrayed him, whose family had made an alliance with the Grass people.

Leo was going to avenge his father, who had been murdered by the Grass people. And now that he knew what united Toby and Elisha, his anger had turned to rage. Toby was a dead man.

Leo let out a great cry that echoed around the cliffs. The echo came back to him, spinning like his boomerangs. A frightened moon hid behind an ashen cloud. In a few strides, Leo had reached the middle of the slope. He could no longer see Toby. He turned on the spot, hands on his weapons.

Swift as the wind, Toby jumped on top of Leo. Locking his arms around his adversary, he kicked him in the back of the knees. Both bodies crumpled, and they set off rolling toward the lake.

Just above, a young woman was watching this terrifying struggle.

It was Lila Asseldor. Her clothes were in tatters, and she had chilblains on both hands. She had no strength left to make any kind of gesture or to call out. But witnessing such a violent confrontation, all she knew for certain was that one of the fighters wouldn't get out alive.

The heat from the fire had numbed Elisha's body, but she recognized her mother's hand stroking her hair. Elisha must have fallen asleep with her head on Isha's knees. It was a special gesture, forgotten, and each movement of that hand felt like the first.

Elisha understood that this was a serious moment. The two boys were sleeping. A pink light was rising outside. Elisha felt a warm breath by her ear.

"I've never spoken to you about your father," Isha whispered.

Elisha didn't answer.

Her mother started to tell her the whole story. She talked about life in the Grass, about the arrival of Butterfly, and she talked about their escape. . . .

Elisha listened. It was as if now, in her own body, she could feel the swaying of that long journey she'd made across the Tree, in her mother's womb. Once more, her father's laughter came back to her. She knew she'd heard that laugh before. She knew she hadn't dreamed it.

"Your father had another life before us. He wanted to take us back to it. He had lost his wife two years earlier. He spoke so little about it. . . ."

Elisha listened to these words, her eyes closed, her breathing a little calmer. Something was unknotting itself inside her. It was as if the shutters on her life were being flung wide open. Everything was becoming light inside her.

Hearing the story of her father's death as he reached the Branches of the Tree, Elisha started crying. But she could feel a tender quality to her sadness. A dead father is still a father. She could love him, admire him. And, at last, she could cry for him.

"He fought back," said Isha. "The arrows were raining down on him, but he didn't give up. I never found out where those arrows came from."

Elisha snuggled closer to her mother.

"What kind of person keeps on attacking a man already shot through with arrows? He begged me to run away. I obeyed him because of you, Elisha. You're the one who saved me. Because I was carrying you inside me."

Elisha opened her eyes. Her mother was holding a small oval object in her hand. "I'll show you his face."

Isha's hand opened to reveal the portrait of Butterfly.

Elisha looked at it and felt a wave of fresh air wash over her. The face was almost alive. Butterfly wasn't exactly smiling, but he looked happy.

Behind that fine layer of lacquer, he was looking at Elisha.

Often there's little more separating the living and the dead than this fragile window, misty with grief.

There was a roar, and a crazed hand rose up from behind the two women to grab the portrait.

24
The Mute Man
Speaks

Plok was lying at the back of the house of colors, clutching the portrait of Elisha's father.

And he was talking.

Elisha listened to his mysterious muttering.

Plok was speaking.

Not in sentences, but at least some syllables were recognizable. Mostly, it was his tone of voice that was clear. He sounded as if he was defending himself, and he clenched his fists as he stammered.

After their initial shock, Elisha and her mother had gone to him. Mo, who had woken with a jolt when he heard the cries, was talking to Plok: "Calm down . . . Plok, listen to me. . . ."

Whenever a hand was held out to him, Plok kept repeating two words that sounded like, "Menotkill . . . Menotkill . . . Menotkillll . . ."

Elisha signaled to Mo to leave her alone with Plok.

"Menotkill . . ." Plok repeated.

She tried to translate. "You . . . didn't . . . kill?"

"Me not kill," Plok replied, nodding feverishly.

"Who didn't you kill?"

"Not kill *him*!"

And he waved his hands, which were still clutching the portrait.

"You didn't kill him?" asked Elisha.

"Me not kill," said Plok, shaking his head.

"I believe you. I believe you, Plok. I know you didn't kill him."

Isha and Mo were listening and watching Elisha, who had managed to put her fingers on Plok's wrist.

"Plok didn't kill," she said gently.

And Plok started breathing more easily.

"Plok didn't kill," Elisha repeated. "Plok didn't kill."

Then in the same reassuring tone, she asked, "Did Plok see?"

Immediately, he turned his eyes toward Elisha and conceded, "Plok see."

Isha shuddered.

Plok started up again, "Me not kill . . . Me not kill . . ."

Elisha fell silent for a while. Plok knew. Plok had seen. Plok had been a witness to Butterfly's death. This violence that had turned Plok's life upside down, that had robbed him of the power of speech, was perhaps the same violence that had shattered the lives of Elisha and her mother.

"Who killed him?" she asked.

But Plok huddled up even more and hid his face in his arms. "Me not kill . . ." he whimpered.

"Plok didn't kill," Elisha repeated. "I know Plok didn't kill. But who *did* kill?"

He shook his head. He didn't want to answer, and Elisha didn't want to push it. She left him in his corner and went to rejoin Isha and Mo. But she'd only taken one step before she stopped. Plok was whispering something.

Elisha turned back, all ears. He kept saying two words that were hard to make out; they sounded like paper being crumpled. She bent over very close to him and heard: "Joe Mitch."

She froze, dumbstruck.

He kept repeating these words until they gave way to gentle snoring. Plok had fallen asleep.

Joe Mitch was the murderer of Elisha's father.

Gently, Elisha opened Plok's hands. She rescued the little portrait, its frame now broken. The protective layer of transparent resin was now a fine powder that trickled between her fingers. All that remained was the thinnest sheet of paper, which Elisha took in her hand.

She stared at the portrait of her father for a long time before turning it over. On the back there was an inscription in capital letters, which had been obscured up until now by the frame. Elisha's lips mouthed the words: PORTRAIT OF EL BLUE, BY NINO ALAMALA

Elisha turned to face her mother.

"Who chose my name?" she asked.

"It was your father. He wanted you to be called Elisha."

Elisha.

El-Isha.

El and Isha.

Daylight slid under the door as far as Elisha's feet. She stood up. Isha was staring at her daughter, who looked so pale despite the shadow.

The door was suddenly pushed roughly open by a body that collapsed with exhaustion in the middle of the room.

It took several seconds for Mo, who was dazzled by the brightness of the morning light, to recognize his sister Lila. Even before he'd had a chance to take her in his arms, she got out the words, "Toby and Leo . . . By the big lake . . . They . . . They're going to kill each other. . . ."

Elisha leaped over the fire, out the door and disappeared into the light. She ran toward the lake. She couldn't even feel her legs under her.

She just kept running toward the lake.

El Blue. Her father was named El Blue.

As she sprinted, she could feel her tears drawing a horizontal line from the corner of her eyes all the way to her hair. Toby and Leo. Those two names clashed together inside her.

When she came out above the lake, she saw them. They were floating on an ice floe, in the middle of the water.

They were still fighting.

Elisha called out their names, but they didn't hear her. Their piece of ice was heading for the waterfall. Elisha started running along the cliff top.

The torrents of water drowned out her voice. Toby and Leo had fallen onto the ice again. She could see their bodies rolling around on it, leaving a trail of bloodstains. Elisha shouted out again, "Toby! Leo!"

Elisha was still up on high, at the top of the cliff, running toward the waterfall. As soon as she made it there, exhausted and hoarse, she started wading through water, getting nearer to the place where it gushed over the edge. She was battling against the current in her bid to see the two adversaries, as the edge loomed closer and closer.

No sound came from her mouth. She could see the bodies of the two boys far below, directly underneath the waterfall. Bodies that were hardly moving on the white lake.

She headed back up the current for three or four steps and then flung herself off, jumping into the water.

Her tiny body could be seen rotating in slow motion in the waterfall, tumbling inexorably toward the lake.

Down below, one of the boys had stood up and was looking at the other one. He bent over to scoop up an enormous block of jagged ice.

Elisha's body plunged into the water without a sound, a stone's throw from the ice floe, and disappeared into the violet shadows of the lake.

Toby was holding the block of ice above Leo Blue,

who writhed around, arms crossed, his face covered in snow and blood.

Flashing before Toby's eyes were all the times in his past that would be wiped out with this one gesture. He saw Leo as a small boy again, as someone he'd shared so much with. He remembered a friendship in which they had even combined their names. They were known as Tobyleo. They were inseparable.

Toby's nose was bleeding. He wiped his cheek on his shoulder, since his arms were taken up with the murderous block. He knew he had to go through with it.

Leo had no strength left to move.

"Once," said Leo, "I saved your life. . . ."

Toby felt his arms growing tired.

"Once," Leo went on, "a very long time ago, I was with those hunters in the night. I knew you were there, in that hole, and I blew out my torch, Toby. I saved your life. Do you remember? I . . . I'm not asking anything of you. . . . Just that you remember that. . . ."

Yes, Toby could remember that day, but he wasn't giving anything away. The blood was trickling down his neck. He had to bring this block of ice crashing down on Leo. He had to find the strength to hurl this block of ice.

A head popped up in the cold water close by, but neither of the opponents noticed it. Elisha took a few more strokes to get even closer to the ice floe. She grabbed hold of the ledge of ice and hauled herself up, body trembling, lips muttering inaudible words. She paused for a moment before crawling over the ice. Toby had his back to her, and Leo was blinded by blood.

Toby raised his arms even higher to ensure maximum impact. Leo closed his eyes.

Elisha tucked her arms around Toby's ankles and pulled with all her might. He toppled and felt the block of ice escaping his hands.

Toby's body slumped. The ice had exploded just a finger's width away from Leo's face. Elisha managed to clamber to her knees in her soaking-wet clothes. She looked at Toby. The cold was clawing under her skin now.

"Elisha . . ."

Toby had just sat up.

"Elisha . . ." Toby said again.

She was there.

She was there in front of him.

Elisha gathered all her strength to speak. She took a deep breath and collapsed on the ice.

Toby dragged himself toward her. Their ice floe had just washed up on the shores of the lake.

"Elisha . . . Elisha . . ."

He took her in his arms. The young woman's body was no longer moving. Toby held her more tightly.

"Elisha . . ."

His voice was weak. It was impossible to hear what he was saying. He spoke for a long time, close to her face, as if he'd never spoken before. From time to time, the odd word was decipherable on his lips, words such as "never" and "always" and "forever." The only other word that could be heard was "please."

But Elisha looked at peace, and her body no longer trembled at all. Just the scent of her hovered above, tickling Toby's nostrils with a hint of pollen or spice. It was a perfume that was still very much alive, a smell that brought tears to his eyes.

Choking with emotion, Toby fell quiet and put his cheek to Elisha's.

Elisha opened her eyes and let out a scream.

She rolled over with Toby as the boomerang embedded itself right next to them.

Leo had stood up and was holding the second weapon in his right hand.

Over on the beach, Arbayan had just appeared.

When Leo lowered his gaze to look at Elisha, he saw the blue glow under her feet.

A Grass girl. Elisha was a Grass girl!

"You're one of the murderers?"

"The Grass people never killed anyone."

"Be quiet —"

"Listen to me, Leo Blue. Listen to me," sobbed Elisha. "Your father —"

"Don't you dare talk to me about my father —"

"Your father was killed by Joe Mitch."

"Liar!"

A voice rose up immediately behind Leo. "Listen to her. . . ."

It was Minos Arbayan, and he had heard Elisha's words.

This time, the boomerang nearly took off.

"Stop!" roared Arbayan.

And then, adopting a flat tone of voice for his boss, he began to explain, "I was the one who sent El Blue to the Prairie. People had told me about a field of flowers, a paradise for butterflies, far away from here. I was frightened of going there. Your father, Leo Blue . . . Your father offered to undertake the adventure on my behalf. I entrusted him with my equipment. He set off alone. I never saw him alive again."

Toby and Elisha were still on the ice.

"What does that prove?" muttered Leo.

"I remember his body was found by a young Border Guard who was starting to breed weevils," Arbayan continued. "You know him. His name was Joe Mitch."

"You're a liar too!"

Arbayan seemed overwhelmed.

"Your father was a friend of the Grass people," said Elisha. "Your father was a friend of the Grass people!"

Elisha was talking and sobbing at the same time. "When he died, El Blue was accompanied by a woman who came from the Grass. He loved her!"

Leo brandished his boomerang again.

"Don't dirty the name of my father!"

"Let me speak. You can kill us afterward, if you still want to."

She caught her breath again and said, "When El Blue crossed the Great Border, he wasn't alone. There was a Grass woman with him."

"Be quiet, Elisha!"

"That woman was my mother. She was expecting me."

This time, Leo fell to his knees. Slowly, his head sank toward the ice. He put his forehead to the ground.

Arbayan hadn't moved. He was looking at Elisha.

So she was El Blue's daughter. Leo's half-sister.

Elisha closed her eyes.

Toby picked her up in his arms and carried her away. They walked along the beach and disappeared into a moss forest.

Arbayan put his hand on Leo's shoulder.

"Come."

Leo was stunned by Arbayan's loyalty. He turned toward him. "I want to ask you one final favor."

"Tell me what you'd like me to do."

"Yesterday I sent two men toward the Grass. They're already on their way. I'm begging you to find them and stop them from doing what I asked them to do."

Arbayan never took his blue eyes off Leo.

"What did you ask of them?"

Once again, Leo lowered his forehead into the mix of water and snow. "They're going to set fire to the Prairie."

Toby turned around to get a good look at the lake. He didn't dare wake Elisha; he could barely feel her weight in his arms. He saw Leo. From up there, he looked like a small cross on the beach. The water from the lake washed the blood from the ice and stroked his hair. Arbayan had disappeared.

Leo was alone.

Toby turned his back to him. He didn't even look down at Elisha, who had her head pressed against his heart. He just kept going toward the house of colors.

Had she been conscious, Elisha would never have let herself be carried like a child in his arms. She was too proud. Toby knew this and smiled at the liberty he was taking.

During the short journey between the lake and the house, he didn't think about the battles he still had to fight. He was looking beyond all that, to a horizon that was further away. He was contemplating the life that was lying in wait for him once the fight was over. . . . A life he wanted to spend seeing the sun journeying across the sky, watching bread rise, a life as a couple or a family of three walking together, holding hands.

A quiet life, where the biggest adventure is to set out in the middle of the night to free a gnat caught in a web. A neighbor wakes you up. The web is surrounded by lamps. And when the gnat finally flies off, everyone shouts, "Hurray!" Neighbors invite each other to celebrate with a drink, and households are woken up.

A quiet life would do for Toby from now on. A life with its fair share of good news and minor misfortunes. *A branch fell on the west side. . . . Nini's had triplets, you know. . . . The cicadas are late. . . . It's not going to snow tonight. . . .*

Toby realized that during this long struggle over so many years, this was all he'd craved. These little nothings.

And today, with Elisha in his arms, he'd never felt so hopeful of victory. He'd never before been so sure about this being the first morning of a new world.

25
Spring Uprising

Nils Amen had placed his head on the log.

Big Solken was gripping the ax, and his woodcutter's jacket was soaked through with sweat.

"You're about to kill an innocent man," said Nils, whose hands were tied behind his back.

Solken had agreed to execute the traitor. He'd brought Nils here at dusk, deep in the heart of a lichen copse. They were far from the clearings where children were playing in their pajamas, far from the houses teeming with life, where sheets were being tucked in for the night.

Solken was attempting to banish his fear.

He had to kill Nils Amen, the young prince of woodcutters, Norz and Lili's son. He was trying not to tremble, but his hand was clammy on the ax.

Solken was one of the wise elders, but his terrifying duty had come back to haunt him.

Shaine and Torquo, the Flying Woodcutters, had managed to postpone the punishment. They had talked about a young woman in love, who was supposed to return with evidence. But the girl hadn't reappeared. She was probably on the side of the traitors too. They couldn't wait any longer.

Solken took the ax in both hands.

A few strides away, Norz Amen was going berserk.

He was running and shouting at the same time, "Solken! Solken! Stop!"

But he couldn't find Solken.

Toby Lolness had just arrived. Nils was innocent.

"Solken!" groaned Norz as he cut a path through the moss. "Where are you? Answer me!"

Solken was trying to gather his strength. He heard Norz's voice calling in the distance. Nils's father must be going out of his mind with despair. He had to finish off the job before Norz found them. He didn't want to inflict this spectacle on a father.

Solken raised the ax above Nils's neck, but the young man didn't seem afraid.

"Lila . . ." Nils uttered her name as the shiny blade hovered above him.

Just then, a cry ripped the air apart, and Norz burst onto the scene.

"Stop!" he roared.

But the ax was already swooping down. Despite all

Solken's best efforts to stop it, the blade didn't deviate. Solken closed his eyes.

"He didn't do anything," implored Norz. "I've got the proof, Solken!"

Solken couldn't bear to open his eyes.

"I told you," whispered a voice at his feet. "I'm innocent."

Startled by his father's outcry, Nils had managed to slide his head to the side at the last moment. He had felt the breeze from the blade in his hair. The ax had just split the wooden log in two.

Nils was alive.

In the space of just a few days, the Tree looked completely different.

The first leaves had a gently crumpled skin, like the skin of newborn babies or old people. The buds started bursting open, one by one. Spring was painting the Branches green again. Once more, the Tree had stood up against the onslaught of winter and was shaking off the last remaining snow.

But this time, a little hope glistened with the spring. The most spectacular hatching of all was that taking place in the minds of the people from the Branches. Toby's return, the proof that the Grass people and the Lolness

family were innocent, Leo Blue's complete turnaround—
all this news swept across the Tree at a gallop. People were
up in arms about Joe Mitch's terrible plot.

This revolution, which they called the Spring
Uprising, began by winning over the woodcutters.

Norz Amen was broken by the shame of having unjustly
accused his son: when he tried to take him in his arms,
Nils stepped away. Still holding out his arms, Norz looked
at Nils. Then he let his oversize hands drop to his sides.

His son was refusing to forgive him, and Norz knew
that what he'd done was unforgivable.

"I understand," said the father. "I can understand, my
son. . . ." He walked backward, clumsily hiding his emotions, and headed off into the woods.

Near a plateau of climbing lichen, he passed a young
woman. He recognized her and turned his head away, so
she wouldn't see his red eyes.

The young woman looked at him. It was Lila
Asseldor. Norz knew that she had saved his son's life.

"He'll need some time," she said. "But he'll come
back to you."

"Thank you, miss . . ." said Norz, half turning around.

"Be patient. Woodcutters are known for their
patience."

"Yes, we are," Norz conceded without moving. And
he added into his beard, "But I'm old. . . ."

Hearing this, Lila went over to give Norz Amen a peck

on the cheek. He just had enough strength left to say, "I'm the traitor, because I didn't trust my own son. . . ."

The lumbering woodcutter headed off.

Nils and Lila stood for a long time facing each other, on either side of the clearing.

Staring into each other's eyes, they made the most of the distance between them, because they knew that as soon as their hands touched, nothing, ever, would separate them again.

Joe Mitch's intuition was as good as a bluebottle's. He could sense the trouble coming from whole branches away. Intuition is sometimes worth more than lots of brain cells and a healthy heart.

When hundreds of woodcutters surrounded and then invaded the Crater, they were angry to discover that Mitch had left the previous day.

Toby rushed toward the ravine where the elderly scholars had been kept. All the prisoners had disappeared. There was only one guard left in the Crater. Toby gave orders to keep on looking.

He heard his name being called.

It was Mo and Milo Asseldor, who were climbing up from the bottom of the ravine.

"Toby! They're locked up down here. We've got to break down the door. We can hear voices inside."

Toby ran as far as the dormitory and stood in front of the door. Big Solken was next to him, with Torquo, Shaine, and a few other Flying Woodcutters. Jalam was there too, along with a dozen Grass people who had found their pea-shooters again and refused to be separated from Little Tree. Only Elisha had left, to go and find her mother.

Toby took the ax from Solken's hands. He looked at the door. Could it be that this thin barrier was all that separated him from his parents? He raised the ax and brought it crashing into the wood. The plank split down the middle, like a theater curtain.

There, just behind the door, motionless, were the prisoners. Their expressions were serious as they looked at Toby and his friends. There was neither joy nor relief on their faces. Lou Tann, the old shoemaker, was wrapped in a blanket.

Zef Clarac and Vigo Tornett stepped out from the rows of prisoners. "We didn't know if anyone would come."

"They're alive!" Torquo shouted to the other wood-cutters, who were just arriving.

But Zef Clarac shook his head.

"No. We're not all alive."

The crowd of prisoners parted, clearing a pathway down the middle.

On the last mattress, right at the back, Toby saw a spotless piece of white cloth draped over a prostrate body.

Toby relaxed his grip on the ax and it fell, sticking into the wooden floor. He advanced between the long, gray faces as Mo followed him with a torch. He could feel the strong energy uniting the prisoners, the sort of

indestructible friendships that flourish in the darkness of labor camps.

Toby went over to the bed. He turned back for another glance at those faces, with Mo's torch flickering over them.

Toby gently lifted the sheet.

It was Councillor Rolden.

"He died in the night," gasped Lou Tann. "He was my friend."

"I know," said Toby.

"He wanted to see his branch again."

"I know."

A small man was propping up Lou Tann, and all eyes were fixed on Toby.

Vigo Tornett ran his hand over his beard.

"Mitch took your parents, little one. We have to find that piece of filth."

Toby had been expecting words to this effect from

Tornett. He knew that Joe Mitch wouldn't have released Sim and Maya Lolness.

"I'm coming with you," said Vigo Tornett. "I owe at least that to my old friend Rolden."

"Me too," called out another voice, behind Zef.

"And me!" shouted another.

"And me!"

A war cry rose up in the small dormitory. A rallying cry that the woodcutters took up and the Grass people prolonged in mysterious tones. The Tree shivered.

Only Lou Tann stayed behind, kneeling at the foot of Rolden's bed, whispering, "Old branch, my old branch . . ."

Before leaving the Crater, Toby ran his eye over the giant wound that looked like a dragon's lair. He wondered if the Tree would ever recover from this harm. A gust of wind made a cluster of leaves sing above them. The soothing lullaby reassured Toby.

The dragon had left. And not only was the Tree still standing— it was even singing.

Just then, Toby noticed two small figures on the other side, above the ravine. One of them was standing precariously facing the huge hole. The other, a child, was crouched down just behind.

Toby recognized Ilaya and Moon Boy.

Moon Boy had found his sister in a hole in the wall, chilled to the bone.

He saw Toby and gave a reassuring signal. He was looking after her.

For a split second, Toby's eyes met Ilaya's. Then he looked down and set off with his troops.

Moon Boy stayed behind his sister for hours. Her shoulders heavy with remorse, Ilaya stood there contemplating the chasm below. She leaned forward, playing with her balance. She wanted to die and felt that she was to blame for all the misfortune in the world.

Moon Boy began by talking to her gently, slowly getting closer to her. Then he hummed some songs. Finally, he stopped making any kind of noise whatsoever.

The night wind caused Ilaya's body to sway. The Crater had been completely deserted for some time now. The two of them were all alone, on the edge of the hole. Darkness filled it like a lake.

When Ilaya collapsed with exhaustion, there was a second when her body wavered on the edge of the Crater. But she stayed up there, on the side of life.

Moon Boy pulled her toward him and they slept, propped against each other.

During this time, the Spring Uprising was gaining ground in the Treetop. The numbers of those joining Toby's column kept growing. The people of the Tree were finding hope again. Men and women emerged from their homes, like owls blinking in the light, to join the general movement.

Joe Mitch was on the run. People had to pinch themselves to believe it.

"I told you! Good news passes nobody by," crowed a short man who was struggling to fit into a handsome suit from his youth.

"It's wonderful!" echoed his wife, sniffing. "It's wonderful. . . ."

Others came out into the night carrying torches. At last, children could be seen playing all over the branches again.

People were inspecting the Tree seriously. Their eyes had been opened.

"Is it too late?" some of them asked as they pondered the scarcity of buds in the Treetop.

But their neighbors rebuked them. "Roll up your sleeves, you load of misery-guts! It's never too late."

These people, who had dug their own unhappiness, were waking up to an extraordinary task that forced them to stand up and take notice. They started by filling in the tunnels and scratching the moss off the buds. Lovers even stopped carving their names into the bark.

Good news passes nobody by.

The Treetop dwellers, who had arrived as reinforcements, informed Toby that Joe Mitch was on the run. According to some witnesses, he was traveling on the last surviving weevil, with a few men at his side. They were still detaining two prisoners. . . .

Joe Mitch had been abandoned along the way by his supporters, some of whom were no doubt hiding in the crowd that now followed Toby Lolness.

But Toby knew that Mitch wasn't fleeing at random. He had a plan. Mitch had the most precious exchange currency between his hands: a scientist in a beret and his wife.

Vigo Tornett stuck to Toby's side. He had been overjoyed to learn that his nephew Plok had gotten away and that he was now safe in a house in the Low Branches. Vigo was rediscovering his youth, the green of his first springs.

One morning, at the base of a small branch, Toby noticed two old ladies watching them pass by. Two bony women, leaning on their walking sticks. Vigo told Toby that he would go and question them.

Toby kept an eye on brave Tornett from a distance. His friend could have passed for a bandit, but he greeted the two old women with dignity. Then, suddenly, Toby saw him shove his elbow into the spine of the first lady and crush her ribs with his knee. Tornett grabbed the second little old lady, shook her vigorously, and sent his fist smashing into her teeth. He threw her on top of the first one and stamped on the pair of them, dancing from foot to foot.

Toby hadn't budged.

Several woodcutters rushed over to tackle Vigo. The victims were groaning on the ground.

Toby got closer. He recognized them.

On the bark, half hidden by scarves and big granny dresses, Razor and Torn were whimpering. Mitch's ghastly stooges had deserted their boss and disguised themselves in the hope they'd be forgotten about.

It wasn't that the violence brought Tornett any relief, but he was thinking of Rolden, who had died in captivity before his eyes. Neither forgiveness nor revenge would bring his friend back.

Back on his way again, Tornett chucked a handful of the men's teeth, which had landed in his pocket, in their direction.

Weeks later, and very close to the Treetop, Toby set up camp on a smooth branch surrounded by young leaves covered in downy fluff.

Toby was worried. Followed by tens of dozens of men,

he had tracked Joe Mitch as far as these Heights. But Mitch's trail disappeared here. Toby no longer had any indication of which way to go. So he had decided to head down the following day, toward the North Branches.

The camp was asleep. Small fires were scattered over the thin layer of bark. A few Grass people could be heard singing melodies from their homeland.

Toby was trying to sleep, but he couldn't stop thinking about his parents. Their voices never left him. Those same voices that used to coax him out of his nightmares as a child. Back then, it was enough for them to say, "It's over now," as they kissed him on the forehead, for Toby to come back to reality.

Now he was imagining the stars above him. It had been a long time since he'd last headed up toward the Treetop.

It was a moonless night, just like that first night of his new life as a fugitive. *When there's no moon, the stars dance more brightly.* He was breathing in the dry air of the Heights, the air of the big sky that had cradled his childhood.

"It's beautiful."

Toby felt his heart leap. He rolled over onto his side and found himself face-to-face with Elisha.

"What are you doing here?"

Elisha didn't even bother answering a question like that.

"I told you to stay in the Low Branches," Toby insisted lamely.

She nudged him with her shoulder and stayed lying next to him. Their arms were touching, from their shoulders all the way down to their fingertips.

"I didn't want to wait anymore," she said after a long silence.

They could hear the fire crackling. Elisha was giddy with the purity of the air. Her mouth and eyes were open, and she could feel her fingers against Toby's. There was something tender about their skin not being the same temperature. They could feel their hearts beating against each other.

Toby didn't dare move. He wondered if he could become used to this. One note from Elisha's voice was enough to make his head spin; one movement from her wrist turned him topsy-turvy.

"Me too," he said, just in case.

And then he said it again, more intensely this time. "Me too."

They fell quiet for a moment. Not even the air weighed down on them anymore. As they lay there absolutely still, they noticed the stars between the leaves.

"It's crazy," said Elisha.

There was no other word for this tenderness.

Much later in the night, she held something out to him.

"Here you go."

Toby nudged his hand toward hers.

"We found it on our path."

She gave him a round, floppy object that Toby immediately recognized, despite the darkness. It was Sim
Lolness's beret.

"He must have lost it along the way," said Elisha.

Toby started laughing gently.

"Lose this? My father? He'd rather lose his head."

Scrunching up the beret, Toby went over to the fire.
He had removed a rolled-up square of paper from the
seam, which he unfolded by the light of a torch.

Heading for the Treetop. We're well . . . We . . .

Toby's fist closed over the piece of paper. Sim hadn't been
able to finish writing the message.

Elisha was looking at Toby. He was already somewhere else.

He stood up in the darkness, and with a single word
that rang out from fire to fire, he woke the entire camp.

26
On the Wire

Joe Mitch had entrenched himself in the South Egg.

The rest of the Nest looked abandoned. Toby and his friends chased away a huge spider that had settled in there, and in a matter of seconds they had the Egg surrounded.

According to the men who arrived first, there were just four people left in the shell. So Joe Mitch only had one man still loyal to him, who was guarding Sim and Maya.

Toby, on the other hand, had countless followers, but he knew that a knife against his mother's throat was all it would take to cede all power to the enemy.

Tiger was the first to appear, above the footbridge. He was clutching Maya as a human shield.

Toby watched his mother. Standing very upright, with a calm expression, she surveyed the crowd around her. When her eyes met Toby's, she raised her chin, her spirits buoyed by joy and pride.

This image of Maya at the mercy of barbarians affected Toby so profoundly that he found it hard to return her smile. He would have liked for Elisha to have been close to him. Where had she gone?

Toby took a step forward and waited for Tiger to speak. Clouds began to gather in the sky.

"We'll kill both of them!" shouted Tiger. "We'll kill them at the first move made against us!"

Toby shuddered.

"What do you want?" called out Vigo Tornett.

"Joe Mitch will tell you shortly."

Tiger pushed Maya inside the Egg. They disappeared.

Elisha was lost in the crowd. From far off, she had heard Tiger's threats. She was struck by how beautiful Maya Lolness was.

Suddenly, she felt a hand on her shoulder. Elisha barely recognized the hollow-eyed man who greeted her.

"Clot?"

Clot started trying to bow, but Elisha was quick to pull him back up again and hug him.

When he wasn't hiccupping, he managed to say, "I goth outh, dithn't I?"

"Yes, Clot."

He was too intimidated to hug Elisha back, so he kept holding his arms out wide as if she was sticky to touch. Elisha had put her head on Clot's shoulder.

Then she saw something that instantly blocked out Clot's stream of explanations. Elisha scrunched up her eyes. She had seen something sparkling gently in the overcast sky. Like a flash.

She waited for a few seconds before seeing that little glint of sunshine again. She hadn't dreamed it.

"I'll be back," she told Clot.

Elisha pushed him gently aside and made her way through the crowd to go find Toby. He listened to her and quickly glanced at the sky. His face lit up.

The next thing she knew, Elisha was watching Toby head off. Had she done the right thing, by giving him this idea?

A few minutes later, she saw Toby appear at the top of the Egg behind the crowd. He got up, stood there for a moment, and took a deep breath. Apart from Elisha, nobody had noticed him.

He opened his arms and took a step into the void. Elisha closed her eyes for a moment. When she opened them again, Toby was walking in the sky.

Slowly, step by step, arms outstretched, he was walking toward the South Egg. The wind had dropped. A small cloud passed by in slow motion behind him, filling in the last scrap of blue sky.

A spider had spun its invisible thread between the Eggs, and a glint of sunshine had revealed it to Elisha: a long thread that linked the tops of the two towers. This was the only way of taking the hostage-holders by surprise.

Down below, all eyes were on the entrance to the Egg as everyone waited for Joe Mitch's demand. Nobody saw the tightrope walker moving across the sky.

Little by little, Toby was making progress. His foot kept mysteriously finding the right position on the thread. It didn't occur to him that he was all but walking on thin air. He felt as if he was following someone.

When the crowd became agitated, Elisha thought that Toby had been spotted.

But it was Joe Mitch. What had just emerged from the Egg bore no resemblance to a baby bird peeking out of its shell. More than ever, he looked like a grinning lump.

Mitch was gripping Professor Lolness by the collar, and he held a huge crossbow with four arrows in the other hand. He relished the sight of the gathered crowd. The fact that everybody here was at his mercy provided him with a kind of desperate pleasure.

For one last time, he could do something utterly evil, and Mitch fully intended to surpass himself. He had vowed he wouldn't botch the atrocious crime he was about to commit. It would be his masterpiece, even better than building his empire on the murder of El Blue. At the time, it had been enough to accuse the Grass people and then present himself as the defender of the Tree against the threat they posed. Now he intended to top that.

Just as he was about to begin the blackmailing process, someone stepped forward from the first row of the crowd.

Joe Mitch grunted and raised one of his heavy eyelids. Who dared . . . ?

Elisha was on tiptoes, trying to understand what was going on. A man was heading toward Mitch.

The crowd clamored as it recognized Leo Blue. He was walking calmly toward his father's murderer.

He didn't look crazed. Nor did he look like he wanted to die. For the first time, a spark of joy was visible on his face. From now on, he would no longer have to fight against ghosts. His only enemy was directly in front of him.

After a few more steps, the carnage began. Joe Mitch loaded his crossbow. He aimed blurrily. An arrow landed in Leo's thigh. But the young Blue didn't stop; he just continued to push forward.

A second arrow pierced the top of his arm.

Elisha started shouting, but the roar of the crowd drowned out her voice. She was struggling to get through the front row.

Leo Blue didn't slow his pace. He took the third arrow in his right side.

Joe Mitch was starting to puff up with fury. Drops of sweat, as big as beetle eggs, were dripping down his back.

Tiger appeared at the door to the Egg, and he was shouting, "Leo Blue! Throw down your weapons!"

Leo obeyed. He reached slowly for his boomerangs, which were secured on his back, and tossed them to either side of him.

"Halt!" roared Tiger.

But Leo had started walking again.

Mitch let go of Sim Lolness, who fell to the ground. He took a step forward and fired his last arrow.

This time Leo Blue paused briefly, winded. His left leg buckled. It looked as if he would fall in the middle of the footbridge, but it wasn't a fall. It was a step. Another step toward the man who had destroyed his life, toward the person who had made a monster of him.

Joe Mitch threw away the crossbow. His hands were empty. He started retreating.

Suddenly, his cigarette butt reappeared in the corner of his mouth.

He was smiling.

Mitch had remembered that he still had one weapon left, a final weapon to stop Leo Blue: the ultimate weapon. He went over to Sim Lolness, who was writhing on the ground, and put his foot on his skull. He grinned like a snail—it was a slobbery smile that made him look soft in the head. His cigarette butt slid down his chin.

Leo Blue froze on the spot.

The slightest movement from him and Mitch would make the professor's head explode.

Elisha had stopped trying to push forward. She was

watching, just like everyone else. The rain began to fall. There was an eerie silence in the Nest.

And then the silence was interrupted by a spinning, whistling sound.

It all happened in a thousandth of a second.

The boomerangs that Leo had carelessly thrown to either side of him were both heading back at the same time, on the left and right. Having just completed a tour of the Egg, they now embedded themselves soundlessly in Joe Mitch's skull.

His eyes rolled in their sockets a few times. His mouth started to twist. He subsided onto the footbridge, like a puddle of mud, next to Sim.

Leo fell too, with a smile on his lips.

Terrified, Tiger hid in the Egg. He grabbed Maya, holding her tightly against him. He waved his harpoon. They were alone in the middle of the shell when Sim appeared at the door and shouted, "Maya!"

The wife called out her husband's name, but the spikes of the harpoon threatened to slit her throat.

Sim didn't dare advance any farther.

A cry.

A shadow falling out of the sky.

There was a sound like a piece of fruit going splat in the Egg.

Maya felt the spiked weapon slide against her skin; Tiger stiffened and then fell to the ground.

Toby had just leaped through the narrow opening at the top of the Egg. He had landed on his mother's attacker, crushing his ribs. Tiger wasn't breathing anymore.

Trembling, Maya rushed toward her son. Toby's head had smashed against the ground. Sim ran to join them.

Together, Sim and Maya leaned over Toby. He wasn't moving.

Maya spoke into his ear. Toby opened his eyes.

He looked at his parents. His lips moved. "You're wonderful."

Sim was too overwhelmed to say anything but his son's name: "Toby."

As he lay there on the ground, Toby opened his arms, and Sim and Maya snuggled up to him.

Elisha stayed for a long while, holding Leo Blue's head in the rain. He was still conscious and had just enough strength left to smile.

"It's over," he was trying to say. "It's over."

Elisha shushed him.

"We're going to take care of you. My mother knows how to cure everything. You're going to live, Leo. Your father wanted you to live. Life starts now, Leo. Life is only just beginning. . . ."

Leo's eyes clouded over; he couldn't feel his wounds anymore. Perhaps something was beginning. The rain soaked through his clothes.

Elisha ran her fingers through Leo's hair.

"My little sister," he said.

As they carried Leo off to be attended to, it was time at last for Elisha to be reunited with Toby. She walked inside the Egg, her hair and face soaking wet, and saw him together with his parents.

Maya recognized her instantly and called her over, holding out her hands to Elisha. It wasn't a reunion, because this was the first time they had met.

Sim and Maya left Toby and Elisha in the Egg, to the sound of the rain beating down.

Just as they were leaving, Sim glanced for the last time at Tiger's lifeless body. They walked through the doorway.

"Life has some strange twists," Sim remarked to Maya as he sheltered her under a black cloak. "Leo Blue has gotten rid of Joe Mitch, who killed his father. . . ."

Maya took him by the arm, finishing off his sentence, "And Toby has killed Tiger, the murderer of Nino Alamala."

She suddenly recalled that far-off night when Sim

had brought Toby to her as a little baby, wrapped in blue swaddling clothes.

"His father has just been killed in prison," Sim had explained, holding out the child to Maya. "He hasn't got anybody left. . . ."

Maya had pressed him to her heart. She had stroked the child's hair.

"What's his name?"

"It used to be Toby Alamala," Sim had said. "But we can't use that anymore."

"Well, then," Maya had whispered, "we'll have to call him Toby Lolness."

27
The Other One

A summer and a winter went by. That was year 1.
Everything had started again.

The Treetop Nest was forgotten about. An owl had
moved in there the following spring. At dusk, its hooting
could be heard as far down as the Low Branches.

The owl had laid five eggs and brought up its little ones.

The years went by. More owls nested there.

One day, one of the birds saw a man in a beret suddenly appear. The owl didn't move. It was protecting its
babies, who were sleeping beneath it. Sometimes a little
ruffled head would appear between its feathers, but the
owl would tuck it back under, never taking its eyes off
the visitor.

Not that the visitor looked dangerous. He could barely
climb up the steep branch that overhung the Nest.

"Piece of cake!" he said as he reached the top, exhausted. He greeted the owl with a nod and took off his beret.

A young man joined him. It was Toby. They sat down next to each other, on a twig.

"We're disturbing them," said Sim, indicating the enormous owl below them.

But Toby was looking somewhere else. His eyes were on the horizon, picturing the Prairie beyond.

"They say he's down there. . . ." said Sim.

"Yes, Isha Lee is looking after him. Like a son."

"She knows all the medical cures the Grass has to offer."

"She's brought him back from the brink."

"Poor Leo." Sim sighed.

"He's getting better. People also say that there's a girl with him, someone I know. . . ."

Sim smiled. A girl . . . That was still the best medicine in the world. He put his beret back on.

"Her name's Ilaya," said Toby.

Sim turned toward his son. He looked at him for a long time and wanted to talk, but gave up on the idea. . . .

"Were you going to say something, Father?" Toby prompted.

Sim was trying to come up with a sentence to replace the one he'd originally intended.

"No . . . Er . . . The butterfly hunter has stayed down there too?"

Toby confirmed this.

Arbayan . . . For months, he had pursued the two fire-raisers sent by Leo to burn down the Prairie. And so he had followed the route down the Trunk, through the roots and Grass, which was the very journey he hadn't dared make years before, the great expedition that had cost the life of his friend El Blue.

His mission accomplished, Arbayan had stayed in the Prairie, not far from Isha.

"And what about that crazy old poet, the one you told your life story to, my son?"

"Pol Colleen?" asked Toby, smiling. "He's started writing again. He's nearly finished."

"He's got such a talent for hearing everything. When we were young, I used to call Colleen the Grasshopper!"

It was the professor who had discovered, a long time ago, that grasshoppers hid their ears in their front legs.

Toby slid onto the branch below and ran down it.

Sim stayed on alone. He lifted his beret to scratch his head. Once again, he'd failed to tell Toby what he wanted to.

He sighed. The owl wasn't paying him any attention now. A gentle breeze stirred in the Treetop.

Toby reappeared.

He was holding the hand of a fragile and elegant woman. Sim Lolness got up and helped her to sit down.

"You shouldn't have climbed, Maya."

She patted his hand. "Don't pretend you're such a young man yourself, professor."

She was surveying the beautiful landscape.

"The Tree is doing better," she said.

And the Tree was indeed coming back to life. The lichen forests were slowly retreating. The Amens and Asseldors worked on them together.

The Crater was just an old scar that the bark was gradually covering over. Life had healed it.

Nobody knew that the Tree Stone lay there, six cubits under the bark. Toby had left it at the bottom of the Crater, and the new wood was burying it, year after year, far from the greed of people.

"The Tree is alive," said Sim. "They believed me in the end. It's been a long time now since anyone asked me for Balina's Secret. . . ."

And now he came to think of it, Sim wondered what had happened to the articulated toy that had started all the fuss.

"Tell me, Toby. . . ."

Sim turned around. Toby had disappeared again.

Maya and Sim contemplated the Treetop, in the horizontal evening light. The tips of the branches formed an endless plateau that made you want to stride over it.

The moon was rising and the sun hadn't yet gone to bed, giving a strange light.

"Did you talk to him?" asked Maya.

"No."

"You've been wanting to tell him for years." She smiled.

"I don't know," said Sim. "I'm not sure how to. . . ."

"He's bound to know the story of Nino and Tess Alamala. You just have to talk to him. He has a right to know the names of his parents. . . ."

Toby was listening, just behind them. He hadn't intended to surprise them, but as he climbed slowly back up in silence, he had heard everything.

Someone on his back, with her arm around his neck, whispered to him, "So now you know, my Toby. It's what you always wanted. . . ."

Two memories from the past rose up violently inside him: the winter spent in the cave by the lake and the way painting had mysteriously helped him to survive; and then walking on the thread, between the Eggs, the day that Joe Mitch had died. Walking on a thread . . . He remembered what it had felt like. That feeling of following somebody.

The painter and the tightrope walker. Nino and Tess.

His parents.

They had never left him.

When a red-eyed Toby turned to Sim and Maya a few moments later, he was still carrying a young woman on his back.

Let's not say she was pretty. She was better than pretty. Her hair was in two long braids. Sim and Maya made room for her.

"Piece of cake!" Toby said, laughing, even though he was out of breath.

"She can't be that heavy," said Maya.

"She's not heavy at all," Toby said. "It's the other one. . . ."

Elisha held a tiny baby in her arms.

Pol Colleen
The Low Branches, Christmas, Year 6